HEARTS

ACES UNDERGROUND FOUR

HELEN HARDT

This book is an original publication of Helen Hardt.

Cover Design: Shepard Originals
Edited by Eric J. McConnell

Paperback ISBN: 978-1-952841-46-0

HEARTS

ACES UNDERGROUND FOUR

Helen Hardt

PRAISE FOR HELEN HARDT

Wow! Mind just blown! A complete mindf**k...
~**GoddessWithanAttitude** on *Spades*

"Literally perfection."
~**Read with Aimee** on *My Heart Still Beats*

"Helen Hardt is a master at making you fall for the bad boy."
~**Words We Love By** on *Savage Sin*

"Hardt spins erotic gold..."
~***Publishers Weekly*** on *Follow Me Darkly*

"22 Best Erotic Novels to Read"
~***Marie Claire* Magazine** on *Follow Me Darkly*

"Intensely erotic and wildly emotional..."
~***New York Times* bestselling author Lisa Renee Jones** on *Follow Me Darkly*

"Christian, Gideon, and now...Braden Black."

~**Books, Wine, and Besties** on *Follow Me Darkly*

"This red-hot tale will have readers fanning themselves."

~**Publishers Weekly** on *Blush*

"Scintillating..."

~**Publishers Weekly** on *Bloom*

"Helen's intelligent writing style and skills have made this story a must-read."

~**FireSerene Reads** on *Bloom*

"It's hot, it's intense, and the plot starts off thick and had me completely spellbound from page one."

~**The Sassy Nerd Blog** on *Rebel*

"This book was fantastic! It was steamy, funny, romantic, and just about any other emotion you can think of..."

~**Steamy Book Mama** on *Lily and the Duke*

"*Craving* is the jaw-dropping book you *need* to read!"

~***New York Times* bestselling author Lisa Renee Jones** on *Craving*

"Completely raw and addictive."

~**#1 *New York Times* bestselling author Meredith Wild** on *Craving*

"Helen Hardt has some kind of skill I don't have the words to describe. Her writing is addictive. She sucked in my mind and I just don't want to read anything but her right now!"

~OMGReads Blog

"Helen Hardt...is a master story teller."

~Small Town Book Nerd

"Well, I don't want any to-day*, at any rate."*

"You couldn't have it if you did *want it," the Queen said. "The rule is, jam to-morrow and jam yesterday—but never jam to-day."*

"It must *come sometimes to 'jam to-day,'" Alice objected.*

"No, it can't," said the Queen. "It's jam every other *day: to-day isn't any* other *day, you know."*

"I don't understand you," said Alice. "It's dreadfully confusing!"

"That's the effect of living backwards," the Queen said kindly.

Lewis Carroll, *Through the Looking-Glass*

PROLOGUE

BIANCA

ROUGE SAVED ME WHEN I HIT ROCK BOTTOM.

But that doesn't excuse what she's done.

And I won't allow her to get away with this.

"Bianca!"

A harsh whisper from behind me nearly makes me jump out of my skin as I enter my dressing room. I turn with a start.

It's Harrison.

"Oh, thank God. You scared me."

"Sorry." He exhales. "I just saw you slip in here and wanted to talk to you. I think I might know where we'll find this writing raven."

I widen my eyes. "Really? Where?"

"The women's restroom."

I raise an eyebrow. "Why there?"

"I don't know for sure. But it's the only place I haven't looked yet, besides the places I'm not allowed to go." I pace back and forth. "But it makes sense for a place to hide something, right? Easy access from the secret entrance and all."

I scratch the side of my head. "Okay..."

He holds up a hand. "You're not convinced. Neither am I. But it's the only place I haven't looked. Obviously I can't go in and look without a woman going in first to make sure the coast is clear."

I'm about to tell him that what he's saying makes no sense, but then I feel the familiar twitch above my eyebrow. It could just be nerves—this is a high-stakes situation, after all —but it hasn't led me astray yet.

Maybe Harrison is right. There *could* be something in the ladies' restroom hiding in plain sight.

"Let's try it out." I check my phone. "I have fifteen minutes until my next set. Rouge sometimes comes in and checks on me during my breaks, but there are a lot of extra people here for the holiday. They should keep her busy."

He nods. "Great. Thanks for trying this out for me, babe."

I get on my tiptoes and kiss his cheek. "I have a feeling you might be right about this." I open my dressing room door and peek through. Rouge is all the way across in Spades, and no one seems to be paying much attention to the area surrounding the ladies' restroom. I gesture Harrison to follow behind me.

We cross quickly toward the restroom. I go inside first, and the coast is clear. The three stalls are empty, and there's no one sitting on the fainting couch at the entrance or adjusting their makeup in the mirror.

I open the door. "It's empty. Come in."

He enters, and together we push the fainting couch against the door to keep people from coming inside while we look around.

"Let's be quick," I say. "You never know when my sister might have to heed nature's call."

Harrison chuckles. "I didn't think Rouge would ever be caught doing something so human as taking a shit."

I let out a short laugh. It's a funny thing to say. Unfortunately, I *have* seen the human side of Rouge, and it might be even *more* terrifying than her Queen side.

"Let's look around. See if anything looks out of place."

He nods.

I check the mirror behind the sink—since mirrors seem to be important to this section of the club—but find nothing. No secret cabinet or anything. I run my hands along the upholstery of the fainting couch. It's all original stitching.

"That's weird," Harrison mutters from the stalls.

"What's weird?" I walk over to him.

"The stalls in this bathroom. They have writing on the locks. Like in an airplane bathroom. When you switch the lock"—he demonstrates—"it goes from 'vacant' to 'occupied.'"

I purse my lips. "So? That's not exactly uncommon."

He shakes his head. "I was in the men's room before I met you in the dressing room. I looked up and down the doors of those toilet stalls, seeing if there was a picture of a raven or something, and they don't have that feature."

"So? There probably isn't a fainting couch either. Sometimes ladies' restrooms are a little fancier than men's." But then I gasp. "My God! It's *writing*!"

"Yeah. As in the *writing raven*."

"I thought it meant that the raven was doing the act of writing. Not the writing itself."

He nods. "I was thinking about this earlier. The *river of tears* in the riddle wasn't referring to an actual river, or actual tears. So we have to think outside the box on the other half of the riddle as well."

"Okay. So what could *raven* mean?"

"I was thinking it could be *raven* as in raven hair. Like the color black." He gestures to the stall doors. "But the writing on all these locks is pink, just like everything else in this bathroom."

"Right." I grab my phone. "Let's see if there are other definitions of the word." I pull up Google and search for the definition of "raven." Several results pull up, and I pull up a dictionary website. "Well, the first definition is the bird, obviously. Then there's the adjective, like 'raven black hair.' And then..." I widen my eyes.

"Then what?"

"It's a verb, too. 'To raven' means 'to devour voraciously.' It must be where the word 'ravenous' comes from."

He taps at his chin "So we're looking for writing that is... eating something?"

"We might be at a dead end." I sigh and pocket my phone.

"Not necessarily." Harrison examines the lock of the first stall, turning it to 'occupied' and back. He then looks at the second one for a few seconds before moving on to the third.

There's a knock on the door. A woman's voice I don't recognize. "Hello? Is the bathroom closed?"

I swallow. "Just a minute. There was an incident. We're doing some cleaning."

"Is that Bianca in there?"

"N-No." I lower my voice. "But how sweet of you to think I sound like her. It's...Hilda, the custodian. I'm cleaning up. Someone got sick in here."

"Oh, heavens. How long will it be?"

"At least ten minutes," I say. "Maybe you could use the men's restroom."

"Not on your life. I'll go ask Rouge if I can use her restroom in her office."

"No! No! Don't do that!" I think quickly. "If you can just wait a few minutes, we'll be open momentarily."

"Okay… I guess I'll wait."

"Great. Thank you." I turn to Harrison. "Can you hurry it up?"

"I think I might have found something." Harrison exits the leftmost stall, the one against the wall. "Look here."

I cross. "Make it quick. We've got someone waiting."

"I heard. But look." He turns the lock on the stall to 'occupied' and points. "See here? Could these be little teeth?"

I point. On the right side of the 'occupied' end of the lock, there are a few tiny triangles. Hardly noticeable unless you're looking for it.

"And these aren't on the other two stalls?"

"Correct. If the word 'occupied' has these little teeth, then it kind of looks like it's eating the word 'vacant' when you turn the lock."

I blink. "The writing is…ravening."

"Indeed." He grins.

"Oh, my God. Did we actually figure it out?"

"I don't know, but we should check this stall out from top to bottom."

"And quickly"—I glance toward the bathroom door—"before Ms. Whoever outside decides to call Rouge for help."

"Right." He gets on his knees and looks around the toilet. "Anything odd?"

"No," I sigh. "It looks like a regular toilet to me." I look it up and down, from the bottom of the toilet to its bowl to its tank on top. I even remove the top to check the flushing mechanism on the inside, but everything looks like it should.

"Maybe we were seeing things with those little teeth." I rub at the back of my neck. "It seems like every time we get some momentum, we end up right where we started. Maybe this *is* all a wild—"

I stop as I examine the lever in front of the tank. I've never noticed before, but in tiny cursive writing it has the words "Flush Me" on it. I check the other toilets. They don't have the writing on the lever.

I walk in and flush the toilet, expecting something crazy to happen.

And the toilet simply flushes.

Damn it. Just like I said. Every time we...

But of course the nothing would be revealed if you flushed the toilet the regular way, by pressing the lever down. Then every single woman who came here and did her business would open some secret door revealing all of Rouge's deepest secrets.

I squeeze my eyes shut and think.

And the cool voice of my sister floats through my brain.

Here at Aces Underground, we pride ourselves on the weird and wonderful. Here we believe that turning the known upside down reveals the hidden.

My God. It's not just a motto. It's a clue.

An ordinary person would push the lever down to initiate the flushing mechanism. But an *extraordinary* person, who, as my sister would say, would thrive in this environment, would flush by pushing the lever up.

I do so, and a second later a groan echoes from the wall behind the toilet.

"Holy shit!" Harrison exclaims. "I think we figured it out!"

The walls give way to reveal a hidden crawlspace above the toilet, small enough for one person to go inside.

My heart pounds, matching the rhythm of the twitch of my eyebrow.

What we find in this crawlspace is going to change everything.

Just like the lever on the toilet, everything will be turned upside down.

I'm terrified...and excited.

"Looks like there's only room enough for one person to check it out," Harrison says. "You figured out how to open the door, so why don't you do the honors?"

I swallow down my nerves. "All right." I turn on the flashlight of my phone just as there's another knock on the door.

"Will the bathroom be open soon?" The same woman as before.

"Yes!" I call back. "Just five more minutes."

"All right! Thank you."

"Better make this quick." I hoist myself onto the top of the toilet and Harrison helps me up into the crawlspace.

It's dark, so I shine my flashlight around. The crawlspace leads to a small room, maybe five feet by five feet. Concrete walls, and the only object in the room is a small table. I look it over. It's a regular folding table, the cheap kind that would stick out like a sore thumb in the delicately furnished environment of Aces Underground.

But then my breath catches in my throat as I notice a few small drops on the table's surface. Dark brown.

The color of dried blood.

I look under the table as my heart thumps in my ears. Underneath is a small cooler, light pink in color.

"Anything in there, babe?" Harrison asks.

"Yeah. A tiny cooler under a table. I think there's drops of dried blood on the table."

"Damn. What's in the cooler?"

"I'm going to check now."

"Okay. Just be safe."

I get down on my hands and knees and remove the lid from the cooler. I shine my flashlight and view its contents.

And…

Oh, my God.

It can't be.

It's… It's…

I gag, but nothing comes out.

What's inside this cooler… It explains everything. It connects all the disappearances from Rouge's clubs, the payments she's received in red diamonds, the cruel deaths and dismemberments of her employees.

"Babe?" Harrison calls. "What's in it? What's in the cooler?"

I open my mouth to answer, but the words catch.

I can't answer.

Because once I tell Harrison what I just found, we won't be able to turn back.

And this… What's inside this cooler…

It's a hand not even the Ace of Clubs will be able to trump.

1

BIANCA

HEARTS.

Inside the cooler are *hearts*.

As in the organ.

The human organ.

Three human hearts lie inside.

"Bianca?" Harrison calls again from the restroom. "What is it?"

The words escape me again.

My mouth isn't functioning, but my brain is. The puzzle pieces are coming together.

God, I'm going to be sick.

The people who disappear from Aces are being killed. Their organs are harvested, sold on the black market to people wanting to delay their inevitable deaths, even for just a few years.

After their corpses have been disemboweled, their heads are removed, buried in a separate location, to keep people from identifying them. There isn't anything valuable in the head anyway. You can't transplant a brain.

Rouge sits on the board of Harrison's hospital. That's her in. She must sell the organs to St. Charles. They pay her in the red diamonds Alissa and Maddox found in her safe. No need to launder money when it's in the form of precious stones.

But organs can't last that long before they're transplanted. I don't know the exact science, but it can't be more than a few hours.

Which means...

My blood runs cold.

These hearts were harvested recently.

And someone will come to collect them soon.

We have to get out of here.

A pound on the door again. The muffled voice of the female patron waiting outside rings all the way into this crawlspace. "Hello? Are you almost done cleaning up?"

No time to think.

I can't take these hearts with me. They're evidence. Stone-cold evidence of my sister's wrongdoing. If I take them, Rouge will find out. She'll see security footage of Harrison and me entering the ladies' restroom. It won't be hard to put two and two together after that.

She's my sister, but I'm sure she'd have no trouble finding a new home for my hearts, lungs, and eyes. The thought nauseates me.

The woman at the door pounds again. "I swear to God, let me in now!"

I close the cooler, place it back under the folding table, and exit the crawlspace. I pull the flush lever up again to close the opening.

Harrison's eyes are wide. "Babe, what was in there?"

I swallow, take a shaky breath in. "No time now. We just need to get out of here."

He grabs my shoulders. "What is it? Are you in danger?"

I shake my head. "I'll be fine. But you need to get the hell out of here. Now." I depress the club-shaped button on the wall that opens the wall up to the staircase of the waitstaff entrance. "I'll meet you back at your place."

"But we took your car here," he says.

"Take a cab home. I'll cover the fare. Just go."

"I'm not worried about the fare," he replies. "What the hell was in there?"

"There's no time." I check my watch. "My next set is up soon. If I'm late, Rouge will know that I found out what's in the crawlspace."

"And *what* exactly is in the crawlspace?"

I shake my head. "You wouldn't believe me if I told you." I grab his shoulders, lead him to the staircase, and press the button again to close the secret door in the wall.

Harrison turns around to defy me again, but the walls close over his stunned face before he can get another word out.

I turn and move the chaise out of the door's way, finally opening the door to reveal the identity of the female patron.

"Mrs. Roth." I bow my head.

She drops her jaw. "Bianca! I thought you were the custodian."

Right. I said I was Hilda. We don't employ anyone named Hilda. We don't even have custodial staff. The cards clean up the club after it closes every night. It was just the first name that came to mind.

I blink. "Yes. Well, I was...embarrassed. My own bathroom is out of order, and I've been experiencing some"—I lean in—"*feminine* troubles this evening. And things came in a bit stronger this month than usual."

Mrs. Roth grimaces. "My God, Bianca. Be a little more discreet."

"Apologies." I cross my arms. "I didn't want anyone else to come in, so I blocked the door. I didn't think I'd be in here as long as I was. I'm so sorry for keeping you, ma'am."

Mrs. Roth rolls her eyes and huffs past me into a stall. I breathe a sigh of relief. She didn't choose the one that leads to the secret crawlspace.

I leave the bathroom and make a beeline toward my dressing room. When I get there, I finally allow the weight of my discovery to fall on me, if only for a moment. The tears starts flowing, and I scream into a lacey makeup towel while trying not to lose whatever is left in my stomach.

I allow myself three minutes.

That's all the time I have.

When you're an actress, you learn to leave your personal life at the door when you walk on the stage for a performance.

Even the discovery of the cooler of hearts, as horrific as it is, can be compartmentalized. It has to be. I have no choice.

I take a deep breath in. Another. A third.

Harrison is safe. Rouge didn't find him in the club tonight.

If she had...

God, I can't think about *his* heart sitting in that cooler.

He's okay.

That's what matters right now.

Everything else can wait.

I wipe my eyes, retouch my makeup where it's been blurred by my tears.

I swallow down the feelings and exit my dressing room, head to the stage.

Showtime.

2

HARRISON

WHAT THE FUCK WAS IN THAT CRAWLSPACE?

Bianca wanted me out of here as quickly as possible.

I lean against the red door that leads to the women's restroom. The stifled hustle and bustle of female patrons using the facilities buzzes through.

I can't go back inside. They'd scream, and then Rouge would find me.

But I'm wearing next to nothing. I came here in a trench coat, but Bianca threw that in her dressing room once we got to Aces.

More importantly, I don't have my phone or my wallet.

I can't call an Uber. Can't even pay for a cab.

All I have on me is this extremely tight, extremely small pair of black shorts.

It's March. Mid-March.

The seventeenth of March. St. Patrick's Day.

Happy fucking birthday to me.

It's not too cold outside, but it's not exactly balmy either.

We took Bianca's car. She has a reserved spot in the Aces parking garage, and my Cadillac is a little too conspicuous for us to have brought it. I'm sure Chet and Rouge know everything about me, and they'd be able to figure out something was up if they saw my vehicle parked in Bianca's spot.

Bianca's face was sheet white when she emerged from the crawlspace.

Whatever she found back there has her fucking haunted. And she wanted me to get out of Aces as quickly as humanly possible.

Will she be okay?

I want nothing more than to go back through to Aces and make sure she's all right. I can't even text her without my phone.

Fuck fuck *fuck*.

But I can't go back through the waitstaff entrance. And I certainly won't get past Chet in the patron entrance.

That's not what Bianca wants anyway. She clearly thinks I'm in danger if I stay here.

The best thing I can do is figure out how the hell I'm getting home and then contact her from there. We'll regroup and she can finally tell me what exactly she found in that hidden area above the ladies' toilets.

Now it's time to think.

I'm nearly naked. No phone, no wallet, no keys.

What's my next move?

I'm not too far from St. Charles. It's a brisk walk from here.

Particularly brisk since I'm essentially in my underwear.

I open the door that leads to the alleyway off the main one we normally take into Aces. I'm barefoot, of fucking course. So I have to avoid the small stones and broken shards of glass that litter the alleyway. Once I'm on the actual streets, it's a little smoother.

But now people are staring at me.

I pay them no mind. I keep my eyes forward and head toward the hospital.

This is Chicago. I'm not the first weirdo who's wandered the streets in next to nothing. At least the good bits are covered up. I won't be arrested for public indecency.

God willing no one who sees me will recognize me.

The last thing I need is this getting back to the higher-ups at the hospital. If they received word that one of their doctors was spotted wandering the city wearing nothing but a tiny pair of booty shorts, I'd be looking for another job. They'd think I was drunk or strung out.

But it doesn't matter if someone *does* see me. I'd give up my whole career and all the perks that come with it to help Bianca.

Once we bring this to light, Rouge will go to prison for a long, long time. Whatever Bianca found was clearly evidence of something terrible.

I don't take the main entrance of the hospital, of course. I'd be recognized there. It's one thing for a guy to wander the streets in his underwear. It's a whole other thing for him to enter a hospital.

The staff entrance in the back is more private, and a code is required to get inside. I walk over and punch in the numbers. One-eight-seven-one.

Thank God, no one is around. I steal into a medical supplies closet around the corner and throw on a set of scrubs, a medical coat, and a pair of slipper socks. There aren't any shoes in here, but no one will be paying that much attention to my feet. I hope not, anyway.

I take the elevator to my ward and make my way to the nurses' station, praying that Dinah is on the clock tonight. I'd hate to have to explain this night to anyone else.

She is. Another stroke of luck.

Her eyes widen as I approach. "Doctor! What are you doing here?"

I lean in, lower my voice. "Can you walk with me toward where we're keeping our...special guests? It's been a hell of a night."

She blinks. "Of course."

As we walk, I fill her in on the events of the evening. My disguise as a waitstaff member, my exploration of the club. I leave out the part where a male patron—Mr. Rose—fondled me in the middle of the Clubs section. It's not relevant, and not a memory I'd like to revisit anyway. I tell her about how we discovered a hidden crawlspace, and how Bianca went in and then rushed me out once she discovered what was in there.

"But you didn't learn what she saw?"

I shake my head. "All the color had drained from her face. She insisted I leave that very second. She thought I was in danger if I stayed at Aces even another moment."

"My God." Dinah swallows. "I can't even imagine what could be so awful. It couldn't be more horrifying than that poor girl's head Alissa and Maddox found in the nature reserve out west."

"I have no idea. Knowing Rouge Montrose, it *could* be worse." I take a deep breath in. "Speaking of Maddox and Alissa, how are they doing?"

She offers a small smile. "They're okay. Responding to the IV's well. Maddox is still only conscious for a few minutes at a time, but all his vitals are improving. I checked on them both an hour ago, and they were both sleeping. I think it's best not to disturb them, let them rest."

"Agreed. I'll swing by and check on them in the morning."

"They'd love that," Dinah says. "With luck, Maddox will be awake by then. He asked about you the last time he was conscious. I told him you were the one who rescued him."

"It wasn't just me. I had you and Bianca with me."

"Yes, well. You drove." She grins. "I'm guessing, since you're without a phone and wallet, that you need me to order you an Uber home."

"If you don't mind. I'll pay you back for it, I swear."

She rolls her eyes. "Doctor, this one's on me. You've had a hell of a night."

THE UBER DROPS me off in front of my house. Never have the words "there's no place like home" rung so true.

I don't have my keys, but I keep a spare in a fake rock in the garden behind the house. I walk over to my backyard, find it and open it, and enter through the back door. I quickly disable the security system. Everything is as we left it. No one's been here.

I let out a sigh of relief as I spot my phone and wallet right where I left them on the kitchen counter. I quickly text Bianca.

Made it home safe. Let me know how you are.

She doesn't respond immediately, but she's probably in

the middle of her set. She keeps her phone in her dressing room.

I remove the doctor's coat and scrubs and change into a pair of sweats and a T-shirt. I sit down on my couch, turn on the TV. I'm not watching, but it's good to have a little white noise to keep me from freaking out about Bianca's safety.

I have a headache.

Of course I do. It's been a hell of a night. I can't remember the last time I drank any water.

I go to the fridge to grab a Gatorade. That'll help replenish some electrolytes.

But I'm out. Damn.

I keep some in my trunk. We gave one to Alissa after we found her and Maddox at the Caterpillar Hotel.

I grab my keys—also untouched on the counter—and walk out to my garage, pop the trunk.

I grab a red Gatorade. That one always seems to help the most with headaches. Probably just in my head. I'm about to close the trunk when I notice something.

A colorful gift bag.

I spotted it the other night when I was in here grabbing a crowbar to break the door into Alissa's room—her prison cell, really—at the Caterpillar Hotel. But of course I haven't given it a second thought after everything that's gone down.

Maybe Bianca left it for me as a birthday gift?

But she didn't even know today was my birthday until after we found Maddox and Alissa. I'm pretty tightlipped about it anyway. It's connected to the greenest day of the year, St. Patrick's Day, and I can't see anything green without thinking about the highlights in Ray Sinclair's hair that evening at the Dimpsey house. The darkest night of my life.

Until tonight, maybe.

I pull out the gift bag. It's on the heavy side.

I bring it back into my house and set it on the kitchen table with a *thunk*. I dig through the tissue paper and pull out an ornately decorated object.

I widen my eyes, set it gingerly on the table.

What the hell?

3

BIANCA

I finish my set. It wasn't my best singing, but I'm going to forgive myself given the gruesome discovery I made not forty-five minutes ago.

Hearts.

Hearts.

Who did they belong to?

Someone who certainly didn't consent to their organs being removed from their body.

Rouge is running an organ harvesting ring.

The patrons and servers who disappeared from Aces, from the Jade Sanctum, from Second Star and the rest of my sister's clubs...

These are their organs.

And I bet they end up inside of Rouge's friends. The club patrons who hold influence. Cale Calloway, the man who died on top of me a week ago, was in his late nineties. Most people that age are confined to their homes. They're certainly not going out every weekend and bedding lots of young women. I'll bet he's been through a few of those hearts.

Hell, he probably died with the heart of a woman he's fucked inside of him.

The Seven of Spades. May, her real name was. The girl whose head Alissa and Maddox found buried in that Forest Park reserve.

It could have been her heart. Calloway liked her.

Or perhaps it was Timothy Mann, the friend of Aus Waverly's at the Jade Sanctum who went missing. Aus told us he lost everything in pursuit of a woman who didn't love him back. And now he's literally lost his heart.

She's on the board of Harrison's hospital. She could easily use that position to sell the organs she harvests to them. I'm not sure how organ donation works, but there must be a connection there.

I retreat to my dressing room and splash cold water on my face. It'll mess up my makeup, but fuck it. I have much more to worry about right now than maintaining a perfect smoky eye.

I glance at my phone. I haven't checked it since I went back onstage for my last set.

A text from Harrison.

Thank God. He made it home.

He left his phone there, so the fact that he's texting means he's okay.

And... Wait. Oh my God.

He didn't have his phone on him when I threw him out of the ladies' restroom. He didn't have his wallet either. The shorts the male waitstaff wear have no pockets in them.

But he somehow made it home. Maybe he walked over to the hospital, had Dinah get him a ride home.

I unlock my phone and read the text.

Made it home safe. Let me know how you are.

A sigh of relief escapes me.

Harrison's okay. His heart is still beating in his chest.

Same can't be said for countless other innocents, thanks to my sister.

But he's all right.

For now.

I quickly text him back. Better keep things vague in case anyone is tapping into our messages.

I'm okay. Will be leaving Aces soon.

I feel terrible, throwing him out on the street wearing next to nothing. But I still think he was safer out there than he was in here.

I've never felt unsafe at Aces.

In many ways it's been my sanctuary.

I've never been head over heels in love with my position here, but it's better than working a nine to five. I'm getting paid a living wage to sing, to perform. It wasn't exactly what I envisioned when I first got off that plane in NYC all those years ago, but it's a hell of a lot closer to the dream than a lot of people get.

I've worked here nearly five years. The *Reflections* callback was in early summer, and I started at Aces soon after that.

I've seen so many people come and go. I've made very few friends here—the one time I tried to do so, it failed catastrophically—because of how impermanent everything is. Once a server fulfills their contract, they go off into the world.

Or so I thought.

Just like the waitstaff at Rouge's other clubs, we never see them again.

And now I know why.

A cooler of human hearts hidden away is damning evidence,

but I have no hard proof that they're connected to the disappearances. It could be circumstantial. They could have been planted.

But how the fuck is a cooler full of hearts circumstantial?

Ugh. But how can I know for sure?

I almost slap myself in the face when I realize how simple it is.

Harrison works in a hospital. The same hospital Rouge sits on the board of.

He can look into this. See if any unexpected organ donations made their way to him. Alissa mentioned an older couple who got organs that were perfect matches out of the blue. They had signed a form indicating they'd refuse treatment if a match wasn't found in a month. Then, miraculously, a heart and a pair of lungs showed up.

As soon as I finish up here tonight, I'll go to Harrison's and we'll figure out how he can investigate this further. He's an attending physician in the hospital, so he must have access to records my sister would rather keep private.

Now I just have to keep my head—

A knock at the door.

Oh, God. Please be an old creep wanting to fuck me.

Anyone but—

"Bianca!"

Damn it.

It's her. My sister. It's like she's clairvoyant. She always shows up at the worst possible moment.

I take a deep breath in. *She doesn't know that I know. She doesn't know that I know.*

The mantra does nothing to ease my nerves.

I paste on a smile and open the door. "Good evening, Rouge."

She bustles into the room, brushing past me. She takes a seat at my vanity and crosses her legs. "I just had the most fascinating conversation with Mona."

I raise an eyebrow. "Mona?"

"Mona Roth. One of our patrons."

Right. Mrs. Roth. The woman who was trying to get into the bathroom.

Time to think on my feet.

I crinkle my eyes in a way that I hope looks like innocence. "Of course. What did you two talk about?"

Rouge cocks her head. "She said you locked yourself in the ladies' restroom. That you blocked off the entrance, kept her waiting on the outside for several minutes."

I force a laugh. "It was all a big misunderstanding."

"I told her as much," Rouge counters. "I asked her why you would possibly be using the ladies' restroom when you have your own private toilet here in your dressing room."

"There's a logical explanation, as I told her."

Rouge curls her lips. "You told her your bathroom was out of order, and you were experiencing a particularly turbulent menstrual cycle."

"Well, I was a bit more discreet than that—"

"Even though"—Rouge's eyes shine with amusement—"you and I both know you're not due to bleed for another week or so."

I widen my eyes. "You and I both? Have you been tracking my period?"

She sniffs. "Don't act all surprised. I keep track of the cycles of all my female employees, especially those who sell their services to the gentlemen of Aces in the private suites. I need to know when one of my workers will be out of commission for a few days, unless of course the patron in question prefers it that way."

I almost gag at her words, but I swallow it down. "Fine. If you *must* know, I ate something that didn't agree with me. I was experiencing some...gastrointestinal distress."

"Then why not wallow in your own private toilet? Why take it public? I know as well as you that your bathroom is not out of order."

I think fast. "It was on my break. You know that sometimes the musicians hang out in my dressing room during the break. I was afraid it would be noisy. I didn't want them to make fun of me. And the feeling hit out of nowhere, so I panicked. Ran into the ladies' room. It was empty, and I didn't want anyone else walking in, so I pushed the chaise against the door."

She clasps her hands across her lap. "That's an awfully big chaise for a petite woman like you to handle all by yourself."

"I scooted it. It's not that heavy. I'm stronger than I look."

Rouge narrows her eyes. Then she gets to her feet and glides to my dressing room door, glancing dismissively over her shoulder. "I hope you feel better, Bianca."

I blink. "I already am. Thank you, Rouge."

She opens the door slowly, keeping her eyes on me until she's finally departed.

I lock the door and lean against it.

She didn't buy it.

I gave her an answer to every question, but she's my sister. She knows when I'm lying.

But what she doesn't know yet is *why* I was lying.

There are lots of reasons I could have gone into the restroom and not wanted anyone in there with me. Maybe I took a lover in there and hooked up with him. I couldn't have used my dressing room because the musicians were in there.

Maybe I was shooting up some illicit substance. I wouldn't be the first Aces patron to do something like that in the bathrooms. We've dealt with a lot of overdoses.

The least likely explanation is that I was uncovering my sister's organ harvesting ring.

At least that's what I'm hoping she'll think.

Rouge is smart. Smarter than I am. I'll be the first to admit it.

But she underestimates my intelligence. She couldn't possibly think I'd uncover her deepest, darkest secret.

God willing that's the case.

I look at my watch.

Thirty minutes until closing.

One more set and I'm home free.

4

HARRISON

"Every time Harry doesn't come home from school, the first place I check is the ravine behind our neighborhood."

My mom's said that countless times. And it's true.

This is my place to hang out by myself. It's a half mile or so away from my parents' trailer park. The school bus drops me off nearby, and I'll usually hang out here for an hour or two before finally going home.

There's not a whole lot there waiting for me after school lets out anyway. Mom and Dad both work at least until five, sometimes later if they need overtime. My older brothers Harold, Harrow, Harvey, and Harker usually hang with their own friends. My one younger sibling, Harlan, thinks he's my best friend and will glom onto me the second I get home. He's two years younger than I am, just started first grade. He's having a hard time adjusting and I'm like a security blanket to him.

My time in the ravine is the only time I have to myself. The only time I'm not in school or packed with my family like a bunch of sardines in our tiny mobile home.

Sometimes I'll catch bugs while I'm down here—one time I got a praying mantis—and sometimes I'll throw rocks into the little creek. Sometimes I can make one skip across the water. Harold is really good at it, but he's good at most things.

But mostly what I just do here is think. I think about a lot of things. What I want to be when I grow up. What kind of girl I'm going to marry. What kind of house I'd like to build.

One thing is for sure. I'm going to get out of this part of Des Plaines. I want to live in downtown Chicago. Maybe I'll be a doctor at a big hospital or something.

I get off the bus and head down to the ravine. But today, for the first time, another boy is there. He looks about my age, and he's dressed in a fancy striped sweater with a white dress-shirt collar sticking out. Pressed khaki pants and fancy-looking brown shoes—the kind Dad saves for special occasions, like Nana O'Rourke's funeral.

This kid's going to mess up his fancy shoes. It can get muddy in the ravine.

I approach him. "Be careful. Those clothes look expensive."

He looks up at me. His eyes and hair are both dark. He looks a lot like me, come to think of it, except cleaner. More put together.

He rolls his eyes. "I don't care if I mess up my clothes. I don't care about anything."

"You don't? Not even your mom and dad?"

He huffs. "Especially not them. My dad only cares about one thing. His job. And Mom just cares about her ladies' clubs and stuff." He kicks at a nearby pebble. "They don't care about me at all."

"That can't be true." I take a few steps toward him. "Moms and dads care a lot about their kids. Maybe they're just super busy with life."

My mom and dad aren't perfect, but they do love all six of their children with their whole hearts. They give us everything they can. It's just not a lot.

The boy shakes his head. "My parents could *care. They just choose not to." He sits on the edge of the ravine, stares into the rushing water. We had a big rainstorm last night, so it's flowing faster than usual.*

I sit down next to him. "Well, that sucks. I'm sorry about that." I extend a hand. "My name is Harrison. Harry for short. What's yours?"

He looks me up and down and gives me a small smile. "Maddox."

"Nice to meet you, Maddox."

He looks around. "Do you live around here?"

"Yep. My family and I live in the trailer park just a few blocks from here."

"A trailer park?" He wrinkles his forehead. "I'm sorry."

I cock my head. "What's there to be sorry about?"

He swallows, blinks a few times. "Sorry. I mean... I'm sorry that I said I was sorry."

I chuckle. "You're not from this area, are you?"

He bites his lip. "Not exactly. My family's driver picked me up from school on the way to the airport. He's picking up Dad from a business trip. I... I pretended I was going to be sick, made him pull over as he was getting off the highway. And then I just...ran."

I drop my jaw. "You ran away?"

He smirks. "I guess so."

"Where are you going to live?"

He shrugs. "I'll figure it out."

I decide to change the subject. "What do you like to do for fun?"

"Dad's trying to get me into fencing. Water polo. Horse racing. It's not really my thing."

"What is your thing?"

He shrugs. "I don't know. I had this uncle—he died about a year ago—who ran this men's clothing store in Chicago. I always thought it would be cool to run a store like that."

Men's clothes. There's a subject I know nothing about.

"What else?"

He shrugs. "I don't know."

"What's your favorite food?"

"Cake." He laughs. "You?"

"Spaghetti. But I also love cake. Favorite drink?"

He frowns. "Okay... Don't make fun of me, but I really like tea."

I jump to my feet. "Really? Me too!"

He narrows his eyes. "You're kidding."

"I'm not. I freaking love tea. I brew a pot almost every night."

"What kind?"

I shrug. "The Lipton kind?"

He stands, pats my shoulder. "There's so many more kinds than that. You ever try Earl Grey?"

"Who the heck is he?"

He laughs. "It's like black tea with an orangey flavor. And that's just the beginning. There's all kinds of—"

Maddox's eyes widen as he steps toward me and slips in a patch of mud. He falls backwards, right into the rushing water.

My heart pounds as the roaring stream carries him away.

"Hey!" I call out. "Try to get your footing!"

But I don't think he can hear me. He's not used to this waterway. I am, though. I've fallen in countless times. I know how to get out. But Maddox needs help.

I quickly take my shoes off and jump in after him. I swim down to him and wrap an arm around his waist. Once I get a tight grip around him, I reach up and grab a tree branch and pull us to safety.

I lay Maddox across the bank. His eyes are closed. I place an ear against his mouth and nose. I don't think he's breathing.

I've seen CPR on TV. I've never tried it before. But there's always a first time.

I push down on his chest a bunch of times and then plug his nose and perform a rescue breath. A couple of more compressions and his eyes shoot open. He spits out a bunch of water.

I slap his back a few times. "You're okay, Maddox."

He finally gets his breath under him before looking over at me, his eyes wide. "You saved me, Harry."

Tea.

That was the first thing Maddox and I ever bonded over. The one thing that we had in common, despite coming from different worlds. Right before I pulled him out of the ravine and saved his life.

Eventually, a teapot became a symbol of our friendship. It became our go-to gift for birthdays and Christmases. Often we'd give the same teapot back that we'd just received. It was a fun little tradition that laid a base for a lifelong friendship.

And now, I'm holding a small, elaborately decorated teapot. Hand painted with tiny blue leaves and vines across its surface. Too small to be an actual teapot. There's a windup key on the side. I slowly turn it and let it go.

A tune tinkles out of its spout.

It's a music box.

Huh?

But no one else knows what the teapot means to us. Maybe Maddox shared that information with Alissa, but it's always been an inside joke between the two of us. Dinah certainly wouldn't know about it, so this can't be a gift from her as I previously thought.

No. This has some deeper meaning.

The tune has stopped, so I wind the key up again and listen to it in full.

It starts off with four disjunct notes and then plays an unrelated tune. It's a lilting waltz in a minor key that sounds like something out of a Tim Burton movie. Something must be wrong with the cylinder inside the music box, though, because there's a weird pause toward the beginning of the waltz, and then it keeps playing notes that sound like they don't belong with the tune. Halfway through, a note plays that sounds too long. Pretty soon it starts over with the same weird four notes.

Very strange.

Who the hell left this in my car?

It's not from Bianca. I'm pretty sure it's not from Dinah. It's certainly not from Maddox or Alissa. No one else has had access to my car the last few days.

Except...

The valet driver at Bianca's apartment!

Of course, that's a nonstarter. I have no idea what he looks like. His face was entirely obscured by a large scarf, a high collar, and a large pair of sunglasses.

Maybe he was disguised on purpose.

A different guy was on duty when we left Bianca's apartment. He seemed confused when I told him someone else had taken my car. We told him it was a guy who was bundled up, and he said it was probably some guy named Chad.

But maybe it was somebody else entirely. Someone who dressed up as a valet driver to get access to my car, plant this mysterious gift in my trunk.

It must be a message, but I have no idea what on earth it could be.

Some of the notes sound like they're wrong, but I have no idea where to start since I don't know the actual tune that's playing.

Maybe the move is to go back to Bianca's apartment, see if there's security footage of this valet driver, try to identify him.

That might help. It's late, but I can hop in my car and go to Bianca's apartment right now and—

My phone buzzes.

It's a text.

Two texts, actually. The first one came in a few minutes ago, but I didn't notice it because I was looking at the teapot.

They're both from Bianca.

The first just says, *Made it home safe. Let me know how you are.*

The second?

On my way to you now. Don't move.

5

BIANCA

I DIDN'T GIVE MY SISTER ANY TIME TO WAYLAY ME AFTER MY last set. I flew into my dressing room, grabbed my things, and went straight to the Aces parking garage.

Part of me wanted to leave right after that awkward conversation with her. If she suspects the worst, then the clock is ticking.

But an early departure would have really tipped her off, so I decided to stay. Keep things routine so as not to arouse any suspicion.

No matter what, our time is limited. It will only be so long before Rouge visits the Caterpillar Hotel. She'll see that Maddox and Alissa's rooms have both been broken into, and then she'll follow our tracks and figure out what we know.

She checks the Caterpillar weekly. She won't be there for a few more days.

As luck would have it, I'm not due back at Aces until Friday. This is Tuesday, a night that the club is normally closed, but Rouge opened it specially for St. Patrick's Day. I have the next few days off, and hopefully that will be long enough for Harrison and me to pinpoint our next maneuver.

Just in case Rouge visits the Caterpillar earlier than we anticipate, though, it's best that I lie low. I don't think returning to my apartment is a good idea, which is why I'm on my way to Harrison's now. Rouge has no way of connecting this to *him,* so he'll have to let me hunker down with him for a few days.

I have a feeling he will. He's as big a fan of sleeping with me as I am with him.

Of course, it might be safer if we figure out some third location to stay together. Book a hotel under an assumed name or something.

We'll figure it out.

I pull into Harrison's driveway, park my car, and get out. I trudge up to his front door and knock.

He opens it almost immediately—it's like he was standing right there—and throws his arms around me. "Thank God you're okay," he breathes.

I squeeze him. "Same for you. I was so worried after... After..."

The words catch in my throat.

I haven't told him yet.

All I want to do right now is crush my lips to his, tangle our bodies together, and let his thick cock pound me into oblivion, take me to a place where my sister can never touch us.

But it's not the time.

He breaks the embrace. "So what the hell did you find in there?"

I swallow. "You'll want to sit down for this."

He frowns. "Will I want a drink?"

I exhale sharply. "Possibly. But you might want your wits about you, too."

He leads me to his couch.

I close my eyes, take a slow breath in. "When I went into the crawlspace... I found a small cooler under a folding table."

He nods slowly. "Uh-huh."

"Inside the cooler...were three human hearts."

He drops his jaw. "*What?*"

"Hearts. As in the organ. I think Rouge is killing her waitstaff at the end of their five-year terms and then selling their organs on the black market, primarily to her older patrons."

Harrison blinks for several seconds and then rubs at his forehead, his eyes squeezed shut. "Fuck."

"You're probably rethinking that drink right about now."

"No fucking kidding." He stands, paces the living room. "It does all connect to the disappearances. But what about the red diamonds Alissa and Maddox found in Rouge's office?"

"I think they're payment. A lot more discreet than cash."

"Diamonds are hardly discreet."

"But they're not trackable. You don't have to launder them like you'd have to with money."

He swallows. "But your sister is covered in head to toe in those damned diamonds. To have that many, she'd have to have sold..."

"Hundreds of organs, yes. Possibly even thousands."

He breathes heavily. "Sweet fucking Jesus." He pinches the bridge of his nose as creases form across his forehead. "And you're sure what you found was legit? Not some, I don't know...realistic Halloween decoration or something?"

I shake my head. "These were real, Harrison. We could go back and you can see for yourself."

"Abso-fucking-lutely not." He stops pacing, crosses his arms. "There's no way either of us is setting foot back in Aces until your sister is behind bars...or six feet under."

I stand and face him. "I agree. We should approach this delicately, but we also don't have much time before Rouge figures out what we know."

"Right. Right." Harrison gazes out his front window. "Holy shit, Bianca."

"Holy shit doesn't begin to cover it." I walk up behind him, rub his shoulders. They're tensed. No amount of massage is going to loosen them. "Do you have any idea where we should go from here?"

He turns. "I was about to ask you the same question." He widens his eyes. "Wait. This might be something." He crosses over to his kitchen counter and brings a tiny teapot into the room.

I narrow my eyes. "What the hell is that?"

"It's a music box. I found it in my car trunk when I got home. It was placed there before we rescued Alissa and Maddox. I noticed the gift bag in my trunk that night, but obviously with everything else going on, I didn't give it much thought past that." He places the music box on a side table by the couch and winds it up. "The tune is disjointed. It's some kind of code."

"Code?"

"Yeah. Remember what Alissa told us? Maddox found a riddle that led them to that poor girl's head in the nature reserve out by O'Hare."

I lean down and examine the small teapot. "How did someone even get this in your trunk?"

"Remember when we left your apartment and picked up my car? The valet driver didn't recognize me because I'd left my car with someone else?"

I widen my eyes. "Right. You were freaked out someone had stolen your car."

He nods. "I think some guy disguised himself as a valet so he could take my car and plant this music box inside it."

"But who would have done that?"

"I'm not sure." He sits down with a sigh. "He didn't speak, and his face was completely hidden by his outfit."

"Are you even sure it was a *he* at all?"

"I'm pretty sure. He was super tall. Most women aren't as tall as this guy was."

I widen my eyes. "How tall was he?"

He bites his lip. "Pretty freaking tall. He made me feel short, which isn't something I'm used to. At least six-six, maybe six-seven." He shrugs. "This could be a nonstarter, though. The valet said it could have been some guy named Chad."

I shake my head. "Chad has parked my car before. He does wear a lot of scarves, but he's average height."

He shifts his gaze. "Oh, shit."

"Yeah." I sit down on the couch next to him. "Come to think of it, I've never seen a valet driver at my complex that tall, and I've been there a few years now. And why would a person of that height take a job where he'd have to be cramped inside tiny cars all day? Doesn't make a lot of sense." I tap at my chin. "You don't see men who are considerably taller than *you* every day. It's not impossible, but it's uncommon. In fact, the only person I know who's that tall is..." I clamp a hand over my mouth.

He leans in. "Who, babe?"

I blink several times. "The only man I've met in Chicago who is as tall as this valet driver you describe…is *Chet.*"

6

HARRISON

ALARM BELLS GO OFF IN MY BRAIN.

At Bianca's words, I want to open my window and chuck this little teapot as far as I can from my house.

Chet? *Chet?*

Alissa told me under no uncertain terms that Chet was not to be trusted. He gave them the riddle that led to them finding May's head, but then he turned around and betrayed them when they were ransacking Rouge's office. He's the reason they starved for a month at the Caterpillar Hotel.

Still... he's not the only unusually tall person in the city of Chicago.

Anyone could have planted the music box. It might not even be the valet driver at all.

Mr. Night seems to be on our side. He recognized me when I was masquerading as the Ace of Clubs and didn't reveal me.

"It might not have been Chet, though," I say. "It could be another Aces employee. Someone who's trying to get even with Rouge. Mr. Night, perhaps. Maybe one of Rouge's Kings, too. They're all big and tall."

She scoffs. "I'd trust Chet before I trust one of the Kings. They're all devoted to Rouge. I've heard there's a rigorous process through which she tests their loyalty." She scratches her chin. "Mr. Night could be a clue, though. But he's not tall."

"Like I said, it might not have been the valet at all. He could just be a red herring."

She sighs. "The music box itself could be a red herring. A dead end. It might just have been a gift to you."

I shake my head. "I don't think so. Like I said, the tune is a little funky. There's some kind of message, but I have no idea how to figure it out. Besides, the fact that it's a *teapot* has some meaning as well."

"It does?"

"Yeah. A teapot… It's a symbol of my friendship with Maddox. The very first thing we ever bonded over was our mutual love of tea. We came from different backgrounds, but we found some common ground there."

"Interesting. And does anyone besides the two of you know about that?"

I frown. "I don't think so. Maddox might have mentioned it to some other people. It's not like it was this dark secret."

"Not like keeping human hearts in a cooler behind a toilet," she murmurs.

I exhale sharply. "Exactly."

She bites her lip. "I guess you're right. It might not necessarily be Chet. It could be someone we don't even know, someone lurking in the shadows, clearing a path for us to figure out how to bring my sister to justice."

"Or it's a trap," I add weakly.

"Yes, but if this music box is our only lead, we need to follow it. If there's any chance it will save lives, it's our moral duty to see this through."

I swallow. "Agreed. But again, I have no idea where to start. The tune sounds like some of the notes are wrong, and there's a weird pause toward the beginning that's out of time. A long note in the middle, too. And four notes at the beginning that are completely separate from the rest of it."

"Can you play it for me?" she asks.

I wind up the teapot again, let the macabre waltz play again.

She listens. "It does sound disjointed. But I don't know the actual song. I don't know which notes are wrong and which ones belong." Her eyes light up. "But you know who might recognize the tune?"

"Who?"

"Didn't Dinah mention that Alissa has two degrees in music?"

I slap my palm across my forehead. "Shit. You're right."

Bianca smiles. "She might know. Do you think she'll be feeling well enough to give this a listen?"

I nod. "I think so. Even if she's tired, she'll want to help. But not tonight."

"Why?"

"I was just at the hospital. That's how I was able to get a ride home after I left Aces. Dinah called me an Uber."

"Right." Her gaze falls. "Sorry I threw you out on the street with no clothes, by the way."

I wave the concern away. "Now that I know what you discovered, it makes total sense. But Dinah told me they were both resting. We should give them the night. Start fresh in the morning."

"That sounds good to me. Speaking of which." She grabs my hand. "Do you mind if I crash here tonight? I feel like I'd be a sitting duck if I went back to my own apartment."

I squeeze her hand gently. "There's no one I'd rather have in my bed than you."

I PEEL off the Clubs shorts and slip into a fresh pair of boxer briefs. Bianca's in my bathroom, wiping off her makeup. She emerges wearing an oversized T-shirt I loaned her.

It's the first time I've seen her not dressed to the nines.

And my God. She looks ravishing.

She walks over to my bed, a frown on her pretty little face. "I'm afraid I might have stained the hand towel in your bathroom removing my makeup. I should have used a black one. I'm sorry."

I grab her by the arm and take her into an embrace. "Bianca. I couldn't give less of a fuck about that damned towel." I lower my head to hers and kiss her.

She wraps her arms around me and squeezes my bare chest. We keep kissing, and it deepens. It's not too long before her tongue is probing the seam of my lips. I'm happy to let her in.

She runs it over my teeth before tangling it with my own.

But then she breaks the kiss, her cheeks flushed.

"What is it?" I ask. "Bad breath?"

"No, of course not." She swallows. "It's just... I shouldn't kiss you like that. Not... Not after what I saw tonight."

I reel her back in, kiss her forehead. "Maybe it's precisely because of what you saw tonight that you should kiss me like that."

She looks up at me, her mouth open. "I… I…"

"Yes?"

She narrows her eyes. "I…can't argue with that logic." She gets on her tiptoes and kisses me again, this time with the desperation of a woman who's seen the unimaginable, who needs to be taken away, if only for a moment.

I'll gladly be her guide.

Our kiss crescendos in intensity, and soon she jumps up and wraps her legs around me. I squeeze her sweet ass.

Eventually I bring us both down onto the bed and lie back. She peppers kisses over my chest, over both of my nipples, down my abdomen until she arrives at my boxer briefs. She runs a hand over the outline of my dick, sending a shiver through me.

But she doesn't remove my undies. Not yet. Little tease.

She keeps kissing down my legs. Down my thigh, my calf. She lands on my feet, planting a delicate kiss on each of my toes. It tickles in the best way.

I sit back up and meet her again in another kiss, our mouths clashing. It's a mess of lips, teeth, and tongues, but within the mess is perfect harmony.

Disjointed, but perfect. Like the tune in the music box.

I grab her tits through the T-shirt, squeeze them both. She moans into my mouth. I pull at the bottom of the shirt and she takes the hint, bringing it over herself and exposing her beautiful milky body.

Fuck. She wasn't wearing any underwear under the shirt. She's completely naked.

Completely. She's not even wearing makeup. She wiped it off in my bathroom.

And she's the most beautiful woman I've ever seen.

The tip of my tongue itches with the instinct to utter those three little words.

But I swallow them down. Don't want to ruin the moment. That's not what this is about.

I take her left breast into my mouth, swish my tongue around her nipple. She cries out as I bite down gently. I give her right breast the same treatment, and then I reach down and dip a finger into her pussy.

She lets out another moan and straddles me, kissing me again as I continue to finger her. I drill into her, again, again, again...

She shatters.

And we kiss again.

Again, again, again...

This is the most we've kissed in a lovemaking session. It's the home base we return to after every new action is initiated.

That's what I want to be for Bianca.

Home.

7

BIANCA

HE'S SO BEAUTIFUL.

Never has there been a more beautiful man than Harrison O'Rourke.

And he thinks I'm just as beautiful.

We complete each other.

This time is different. We're not pawing at each other like wild animals. There's a caress to every move, a gentleness lining the firmness.

His finger in me felt like heaven. I can't wait to get his cock.

But before that, I want to treat him like the man he is.

I move down his body, slowly pull down his boxer briefs, unsheathe his cock.

I've seen it several times at this point, but I'm still stunned at its length and girth.

Magnificent doesn't do it justice.

His cock is superhuman.

I run my tongue up his shaft, making him shake. Finally,

once I've teased him enough, I bring the tip into my mouth and lick his soft head.

"Fuck, Bianca..."

So easy to please this man. So easy to *want* to please this man.

I cup his balls as I move my mouth up and down his length. He's long, so I can't get all of him down my throat. But I can sure as hell try.

I'm moving fast. Up and down, up and down.

His balls start to scrunch up in my hand. He's getting close.

But he's not coming in my mouth.

I'd gladly swallow every drop, but I want him inside me.

I release his cock, and he quickly gets to his feet.

"Lie back on the bed," he commands.

I'm happy to obey.

He stands over me, raking his gaze over my body. "Damn it, Bianca."

"What's wrong?"

"Nothing. Nothing's wrong at all. You're just so...fucking... beautiful."

I smile. "Thank you."

He gives his cock a few pumps and then enters me, filling me to the brim. He moves slowly at first, leaning down to kiss me again as he drives himself into me.

His kisses grow deeper. More tongue, more collisions between our teeth.

He's plowing me, going faster and faster. His eyes roll back in his head as he reaches the brink. A millisecond before he does, I reach the peak myself.

I feel his warm come spill into me, his pulses syncing with

mine in an earthshaking orgasm. He stays inside me for a few endless minutes.

Then we sleep.

I WAKE TO BIRDSONG. Harrison must have cracked a window during the night.

I never missed the suburbs during my time in New York and then downtown Chicago, but now that I'm waking to such serenity, I wonder if I should consider a move to this part of town. Being in the middle of everything is convenient, but it's also loud and unyielding.

Harrison's home in Oak Park is a haven away from all that.

I crack a small smile. This is the first time Harrison and I have ever slept together.

In the literal sense, that is. We've had sex several times, but this was the first night I spent in his arms.

And there's no place I'd rather be.

I sit up, rub my eyes. Harrison is still asleep next to me, snoring softly.

He's instinctively placed himself on the side of the bed closest to the door. I read somewhere that when a man does that, he's subconsciously being protective of his mate. Any intruder would have to go through him first to get to me.

It's a small gesture, but despite everything that's gone on the last few days, despite the ticking time bomb that could go off at any minute, I've never felt more safe and secure.

Harrison wakes up an hour or so later. I've gotten up and prepared a light breakfast of scrambled eggs and sausage patties. He walks into the room in a robe and looks absolutely luscious with his exposed chest hair and bedhead.

"You made breakfast?" he asks.

"Surprised?"

He smirks. "Of course not. It was just nice of you to do."

"I should thank you for having such an organized kitchen." I grin. "Very intuitive. Everything was where I expected it to be."

He shrugs. "Guess I'm full of surprises."

We sit down and enjoy the breakfast, washing it down with two glasses of fresh-squeezed orange juice. I have a change of clothes in my car—workout clothes I haven't used in forever. I change into them after breakfast and then we head to the hospital to meet up with Alissa and Maddox, our music box in tow.

The hospital isn't too busy, and we're able to walk in discreetly, heading to the empty wing where Alissa and Maddox are being kept. When we get there, Dinah is just closing the door to Alissa's ICU room. She smiles as we approach.

"Dr. O'Rourke. Bianca. I'm so glad you're both okay."

"You and me both, Dinah," Harrison replies. "How are our special guests?"

"Better and better. They're both such troupers. Maddox is still a little out of it, but Alissa is pretty alert."

I swallow. "How alert? Can she stomach some...troubling news?"

Dinah widens her eyes. "Oh, God. What is it now?"

"We'll tell you," Harrison says. "But answer Bianca's question. Is she stable enough that some shocking news won't sent her into a panic?"

Dinah bites her lip. "I think so. You'll have to see for yourself, Doctor."

We walk into Alissa's room, and she waves as we enter. "Good morning! Thank heavens you two are okay. I've been worried all night."

"You don't need to worry about us," I tell Alissa. "How are you feeling?"

"Not too shabby," Alissa replies. "I've been better, of course. But I'm feeling stronger. Dinah suggested we call in a physical therapist later today to start getting my body moving. I just had some scrambled eggs, and those stayed down. They're going to try something more substantial for lunch."

"That's great," I say. "I'm so happy you're feeling better."

"You and me both." She looks us both over. "How about you two?"

Harrison inhales deeply and sighs it out. "There's been...a development."

Alissa widens her eyes. "What?"

I sit at her bedside, squeeze her hand. "Are you sure you can handle it? You won't freak out?"

She rolls her eyes. "I'm a lot sturdier than people seem to think. Need I remind you I was the one who discovered May's severed head in that hatbox?"

I sigh. "This is about the same level of gruesomeness."

"I can handle it," she says. "Tell me what you found."

Harrison and I recount our evening at Aces. How we disguised Harrison as the Ace of Clubs, complete with the branded shoulders and tight shorts, how we figured out the meaning of the "writing raven" in the locks on the ladies' room stalls, and how we revealed the secret compartment. And finally…what I found in the cooler.

She drops her jaw. "No. It can't be."

I pat her arm. "Are you okay? I don't want this to upset you."

"Who *wouldn't* be upset about this?" Alissa asks, the color draining from her face. "But if you're worried I'm going to go into some sort of catatonic shock, I can take it." She closes her eyes, steadies her breathing. "It does make a certain sort of sense. That's why they removed May's head. They'd have no need for it, since the brain can't be—" She gasps. "My God! Lou and Carol!"

Harrison nods. "I'm afraid what you're thinking might be right. Their donations might have come from May."

"And if not from May, then some other poor innocent that Rouge killed in cold blood." Alissa buries her head in her hands. "I might be sick."

I quickly grab a nearby bedpan and give it to Alissa, but she waves it away.

"No. I'm just starting on solid foods. I'm not going backwards. I'll keep it down." She raises her head, wipes a tear from her cheek. "How are we going to stop this?"

"*We* aren't doing anything," Harrison says. "You need your rest, Alissa. You and Maddox both. You can leave this to me and Bianca."

"But how?" she asks. "Do you have any leads from here? It's not as if you can tell the police what you saw. They'd never believe you in a million years. And knowing Rouge, she'd sock away the evidence the moment she got any whiff of cops on Aces property."

"You're right. Which is why we have to be careful." Harrison reaches into a small tote bag and produces the teapot-shaped music box. "This might be a clue. Since you're our resident music expert, we thought you might be able to interpret the message in this music box."

"Message? What message?" she asks.

"I'm not sure. But you might be able to figure it out." Harrison winds up the key and places the music box in Alissa's trembling hands.

The first four notes—the discordant ones that don't match the rest of the tune—ping out of the little teapot.

And Alissa's jaw drops.

8

HARRISON

"What is it?" I ask.

"Those first four notes. They're a code Shostakovich used in some of his most famous works," Alissa says.

"Shosta-who-vich?" I ask.

She smiles. "One of my favorite composers. Dmitri Shostakovich. He wrote music in the mid-nineteenth century in the Soviet Union."

"And those first four notes are a code?" Bianca asks. "What do they mean?"

"They're more of an autograph than a code, I suppose. The notes are D, E-flat, C, and B. In German musical notation, they spell out D-S-C-H. His first initial, and then the first three letters of the German spelling of his last name. He used it every so often in his compositions, most notably his tenth symphony, his first violin concerto, and his eighth string quartet."

That's odd. The music box is in the shape of a teapot—a symbol of my friendship with Maddox. And the first four notes of it refer to Alissa's favorite composer?

Whoever gave us this clue knows both of those facts. No way it's a coincidence.

Bianca wrinkles her forehead. "So whoever gave this to us is telling us that Shostakovich has the answer?"

Alissa shakes her head. "I'm not sure. Wind the box back up. Let's listen to some more."

Alissa holds the teapot to her ear. She listens to the whole thing, her eyes glazing over from focus. "The piece is a messed-up version of the second waltz from Shostakovich's suite for variety orchestra, often erroneously referred to as his jazz suites."

I raise an eyebrow. "That sounds nothing like jazz. It sounds like a song from a Tim Burton movie."

"Exactly why it ought not be referred to as such," Alissa says. "Let me listen to it again." She winds the music box back up and listens to the whole thing through a second time. "Yes, several notes are wrong. And there's an extra rest—a musical pause—in the second measure. Then, right in the middle, one of the notes is held three beats too long. It's a waltz—in three-quarter time—so a measure cannot mathematically have four beats."

"Do you think this might be a code?" I ask.

"I believe so. I think the use of the DSCH motif at the beginning—easily recognizable to anyone familiar with the composer's work—indicates that a code is to follow. The wrong notes in the waltz itself must spell out a message." She frowns. "I don't have perfect pitch, unfortunately, so I can't identify the notes by myself. If I had a piano, I could plunk them out and see what the incorrect notes spell out."

"There's a music room in the children's wing of the hospital," I say. "There's probably a keyboard in there. Would that help?"

"Yes," Alissa says, winding the music box for a third time.

Before Dmitri What's-His-Name's special code rings out again, I'm already out the door, headed to the children's ward.

9

BIANCA

The door slams behind Harrison, making Alissa jolt in her bed. Her heartrate spikes on the machine.

I grab her hand, squeeze it gently. "You okay?"

She nods slowly. "The sound of the door jarred me a little." She sits up. "But tell me about these other clubs you frequented. I'm sure it was an intense evening."

"It was." I sit on the edge of Alissa's bed. "The clubs themselves were marvelous. My sister doesn't half-ass anything, that's for sure. Whether it's decoration or organ harvesting, she puts her all into it."

Alissa chuckles lightly but then covers her mouth. "Sorry. I shouldn't laugh at that."

"Better to laugh than to cry." I pat her hand. "Besides, Harrison and I will see this through. We're going to make sure Rouge finally sees justice for what she's done."

"I hope so." She bites her lip. "So...the clubs?"

"Right. The first place we went to was the Noir Parlor, and it was outfitted like a mid-century TV studio. Everything in black and white. Even the servers."

She cocks her head. "How'd they manage that?"

"Makeup. Most of the people they hire at Noir are actors, so they have a decent idea of how to handle makeup anyway. They must put gray pancake all over their face and hands and then cover the rest of their bodies with clothes in shades of black, white, and gray."

"Fascinating." Alissa sighs. "Your sister is so creative. If only she used that creativity for good."

"Agreed."

"And Noir Parlor had missing waitstaff as well?"

I nod. "The head, Lucille, told us she never heard back from anyone who worked there except for one. Mr. Night?"

Alissa furrows her brow. "Mr. Who?"

"You probably don't know him. He works in the Clubs section, which you probably didn't check out too much since neither you nor Maddox are smokers. Very old man."

She shrugs. "I might have seen him. To tell the truth, those first few days at Aces, I had eyes only for Maddox."

I smile. "You're in love with him, aren't you?"

She blushes. "I am. I was afraid to say it out loud at first. Everything happened so fast, I couldn't help wondering if it was just all the trauma that had made me develop feelings for him. But once I accepted that I was truly, deeply in love with him, I realized we could get through anything together. Even that horrible hotel, the two of us starving, we would talk through the wall, tell each other how much we loved one another. I think that kept us going, if I'm being honest."

"I'm so happy for you."

She grins. "You feel the same way for Dr. O'Rourke, don't you?"

I widen my eyes. "Oh... I mean... I definitely like him, if that's what you mean."

She laughs out loud. "It's not just *like.* It's not as if he's your chum."

"But it's too soon," I sputter. "I'm sure that in some time I'll know for sure."

She shakes her head. "You know for sure now. I can see it in your eyes. The way you look at him when he enters the room." She grabs my hand. "When I was in that hotel, it forced everything in my life into perspective. My whole life, I tried to keep everything neat and pretty. Straight lines, never bending. But there really *isn't* such a thing as a straight line, is there? Our planet is round. So even the most level street isn't actually a straight line, though it may feel that way to us. It curves with the shape of the earth."

I swallow. "I never thought about it that way."

"I had a lot of time to ponder life's deepest thoughts in that bloody hotel," Alissa says. "There are no guarantees. The world is a confusing place, filled with both great good and great evil. Things don't make sense...until they do." She gazes into my eyes. "You and Harrison... Maddox and I... Through all the nonsense the four of us have been through, the love we have for one another has been our only source of stability."

I brush a tear from my cheek. "My God, Alissa. I think you're right."

She chuckles. "I *know* I'm right. But I didn't mean to get all philosophical on you. You were telling me about the clubs."

I blink. "Right. Yes. So after Noir, we went to MINOS. Same thing, the guy who runs the club, Zeb, told us he'd never heard back from the waitstaff who left once their contracts were up. And he also told us about this woman, Dishari, who got into a public argument with Rouge. A few days later, a venomous snake escapes from the zoo and bites her, killing her in her sleep."

She gasps.

"Then we went to Second Star. Again, a waitress named Tina vanished into thin air. Same with the Jade Sanctum. Aus Waverly—the guy who runs it—told us he had a friend named Timothy Mann who was working at the club and disappeared one day."

She crosses her arms, shivering. "This is clearly a lot bigger than Maddox and I initially thought. We thought we were dealing with two needless deaths. But if Rouge has been killing off people in her clubs since she started taking over…"

"Exactly. It could run into the hundreds. Rouge started taking the reins from my father when she turned eighteen. That was over two decades ago. Our father died right after I returned to Chicago, which was when she *officially* became the head of all our family's enterprises, but she could have been organizing this organ harvesting deal for the better part of two decades." A chill runs through me.

Alissa's face twists. "It's difficult to think about all those poor people." She scratches her chin. "You know, Maddox didn't just find red diamonds in that safe in Rouge's office. There was also a manifest. When we were there, we saw the last two names were May and Svetlana, the last two women to disappear. I bet that manifest lists every single person they've done away with. Not just at Aces, but everywhere else, too."

I widen my eyes. "So if we get hold of that manifest…"

"That in tandem with the cooler of organs you found might just be enough to put Rouge away. She's got power and influence, but no one can fight the court of public opinion once all the evidence has been revealed to the world."

"I agree. The chief of police is in her pocket, but even he

won't be able to look the other way at this." I frown. "Speaking of which, why do you suppose you and Maddox weren't killed and harvested as well? Obviously, I'm glad you weren't, but still..."

"I've thought that over as well. Maddox comes from a long line of politically powerful people. I think Rouge wanted to keep him around, break him in the Caterpillar Hotel, and then use his influence to add to her power."

"Then why keep you around?"

"I would have been leverage. He'd have to do as she said or she'd have me killed."

I swallow. "Thank God it didn't come to that."

She frowns. "The only thing that doesn't gel with that theory is the fact that Rouge left us for dead. Maddox was already passed out when you arrived. Harrison himself said he wasn't sure he would make it." Her lip trembles, but she steadies it.

I shrug. "Honestly, I have no idea how Rouge's mind works."

"But she's your sister. Surely you have some idea—"

I hold up a hand. "I've never been able to figure her out."

I LOVE PLAYING with my dollies.

In their world, I'm in charge. I choose what they wear, who they have tea parties with, what they do.

Mommy gives me a new doll almost every week. I have so many now that they take up almost all the space in my playroom.

Honestly, the dollies are the only attention I get from Mommy. She and Daddy spend all their energy oohing and aahing over

Rougey. Daddy used to pay me lots of attention when I was littler, but now he's focused only on my sister.

She's six years older than I am. Just turned thirteen. She's great in school, and she's immediately good at everything she tries. Piano, art, archery, softball, fencing.

I'm okay at stuff. But Mommy tells me that I'm best at being pretty and playing with my dollies.

So here I am.

A sudden wave of frost shivers through me. It's a feeling I'm used to. It comes every time Rougey is near. I look up and sure enough, she's standing in the doorway.

She walks in, sneering at the dollies. "Playing dolls again, Bianca?"

I swallow. "Yeah. Mommy says it's what I do best."

She rolls her eyes. "You realize that's not a compliment, right? Mom thinks you're dim in the head, that you're never going to amount to anything." She tosses her long red hair. "Not like me. She thinks I can be anything I want to be. Daddy's already talking about giving me his clubs when I'm old enough."

Daddy runs clubs downtown. I don't know a whole lot about them. I know they're different from like chess club at school. It sounds like they're a place where grown-ups go to dance with each other. Seems silly. You can dance at home, and you can do it in your jammies there.

"That's great, Rougey." I don't know what else to say.

She squats down, frowning. "You know, if you want to make something of yourself like I will, there are different games you can play. More grown-up games than tea party with your dollies."

"But I like tea parties with my—"

Rougey holds up a hand. "No, you don't. You just think you do. Mom doesn't see your potential." Something changes in her eyes. "Not the way I do. Isn't there anything else you like to do?"

I scratch my head. "I guess I like to sing. It would be fun to do plays like the ones we see downtown."

"There you go. Keep thinking in that direction." She picks up one of my favorite dolls, a Malibu Barbie. "In the meantime, you'll have to stop playing with dollies if you want to get there."

"But Rougey—"

She snaps my Barbie's head right off.

I gasp and start to cry. "Mommy! Rougey broke my—"

But Rouge is behind me in a flash, covering my mouth. "Mommy isn't here right now, Bianca. And our nanny is on the other side of the mansion. Neither of them can hear you. So crying isn't going to do you any good." She uncovers my mouth.

I wipe my eyes and sniff a few times. "Why did you break my Barbie?"

She grins. "Because you're so much more than Barbie. You're Bianca."

I get up and grab a tissue to blow my nose and wipe the rest of my tears away. "Then what kind of games should *I play? What are the grown-up games?"*

She extends her hand. "Come with me down to the basement. I'll show you."

I get to my feet and follow Rougey, but as I do my left eyebrow twitches.

That's weird. I've never felt that before.

Mommy sometimes has a twitch like that in her eyebrow. I asked her about it once. She said she just had too much coffee that day, but she looked a little scared when she told me.

She then got a phone call and learned that Daddy had been in a car accident. He was in the hospital, so she scooped me up and took me along. I never got to ask about her twitch again.

My eyebrow twitches a second time.

It's probably nothing.

I'll ignore it.

10

HARRISON

I KNOCK ON THE DOOR TO ALISSA'S ROOM. JUST AS I THOUGHT, there was a small electric piano in the kids' music room, which I promptly unplugged and dragged back up to my ward. It's lightweight, so I didn't need any help.

"Come in," Bianca says.

I open the door and enter. Bianca is seated at the side of Alissa's bed, right where I left her. She has a distant look in her eyes, but when she sees me she smiles.

"You found a piano!"

I take the piano to the other side of the bed and set it up on its flimsy stand. "It's not exactly a Steinway, but it should help you decipher the code in the music box." I plug it in and the keyboard lights up.

Alissa plays a few notes, her lips twisting at the tinny sound that comes out. "Not much, but you're right. It'll do. Can you hand me the music box?"

Bianca hands it to her, along with a piece of scratch paper and a pen.

She winds up the key and listens through the tune once

more. She jots some notes down. She listens to it a few more times, each time writing a few more notes down. After five listens total, she shows us what she's written, her lips pursed.

A-C F B-E-A-D-B-Eb

She sighs. "I'm afraid it's nonsense. Maybe it's just a broken music box. The cylinder is off-kilter or something."

"Hold up," I say. "That first word could be 'ace,' couldn't it? Maybe it's referring to me?"

"I don't think so," Alissa says. "The word 'ace' can be easily written in regular notation, since E is a musical note. It would be more obvious."

I rub at my forehead. "Right. And this music box was in my car before I dressed as the Ace of Clubs, anyway. So it can't be referring to that."

"How are you sure some of the wrong notes are connected?" Bianca asks. "I see you put hyphens between some of them."

"There is a measure of correct music between each set of wrong notes," Alissa says. "If it is indeed a message—which, based on this, seems like a lost cause—it denotes three separate words."

I stroke my chin. "Okay, but that composer you like. Shosta-heiney."

Alissa chuckles. "Shosta*kovich*."

"You said he used the *German* system to spell out his initials, right? The notes he uses in that code are D, S, C, and H. But S and H aren't notes on the musical scale."

"Not in our system, no." She strokes her chin. "In the German system, the note we call B is H, and the note we call

E-flat is Es, because the flat is an S in German instead of the little symbol we have that resembles a lower-case B."

"Okay, so what if the first four notes at the beginning of the tune, the ones that indicate the Shosta-whatsit motif, mean that we're supposed to use *that* system?"

"Worth a try," Alissa says. She rewrites the notes again, this time replacing the B's with H's and the E-flat with an S.

A-C F H-E-A-D-H-S

She shakes her head. "Still nothing."

Bianca wrinkles her nose. "Well, he had the word 'head' followed by 'HS.'"

"Head... High School?" I suggest. "Like a principal?"

"Still doesn't explain what on earth the first few words could mean." Alissa bites her lip. "And does a high-school principal have anything to do with what we're doing? Have you met anybody who matches that description?"

"No." I pace a few steps. "Damn it. Maybe this is a dead end."

"Hold on." Bianca touches her finger to her eyebrow. "I think we're on to something. We just have to think harder." She closes her eyes. "Whoever planted this in your trunk probably thought we were close to figuring out what Rouge is up to."

I nod. "The cooler of hearts." Then a lightbulb. "Wait! The last word. Could it be 'hearts?'"

Alissa widens her eyes. "Oh my God. The tenth symphony. How could I be so stupid?"

"What about the tenth symphony?" I ask.

"It's the same symphony that Shostakovich uses his

DSCH motif in. There's another musical code in the third movement. A code honoring a fellow composer, Elmira Nazirova, with whom he had a lifelong friendship. He likely had a romantic interest in her. The theme he wrote around her name and the DSCH motif tangle with each other throughout the movement."

Bianca blinks. "But that name can't be spelled out with musical notes, either."

"Precisely. Shostakovich combined German and *Italian* notation to write her name out. The notes as we know them spell out E-A-E-D-A. But the Italians don't use letters for notes. They use the solfège syllables, like in *The Sound of Music*." She sings the scale. "*Do, Re, Mi, Fa, So, La, Ti, Do.* C is Do, D is Re, and so on. Combining the Italian and German notation, the musical theme spells out E-La-Mi-Re-A, which is much closer to Elmira's name."

"And this woman has to do with our code because...?" I ask.

"Because we can replace the D and the second H—formerly a B—in the last word of the puzzle with an R for Re and a T for Ti, spelling out the word 'hearts.'" She erases the letters and presents us with the newest version of our code.

A-C F H-E-A-R-T-S

"All right!" Bianca says. "We have the last word."

"I think we do," Alissa says. "Unfortunately, the first two words are still nonsense, I'm afraid."

I pace the room. "Do you think this was trying to tell us about the hearts we were going to find? An extra push in the right direction? If so, it's a little late. We already found them on our own."

Bianca sighs. "That could be the case... But it still doesn't explain the first few words. I don't see how they could be twisted around to say something like 'find the hearts in the ladies' restroom.'"

I scratch at the side of my head and glance back toward Alissa. "But you mentioned that there were a few other bits of the tune in the music box that were wonky. But they weren't wrong notes."

Alissa raises her eyebrows. "Right. I was so hyper focused on listening for the wrong notes, I forgot about the other elements." She winds the teapot once more and listens through. "Okay, right. The first thing that's off is the extra beat of nothing, even before the first wrong note is played. There's an awkward one-beat pause that throws off the waltz rhythm."

"And there was something else," I say. "A note that was too long."

"Right. A four-beat note in waltz time. Shouldn't be possible. A whole note. And that occurs before the F." She erases her notes and then writes everything down, including a few new symbols I recognize as the quarter rest and the whole note in music notation. "This... This might be something."

𝄽-A-C 𝅝-F H-E-A-R-T-S

"The...Zac of Hearts?" I wrinkle my nose.

"That can't be it," Alissa says. "The quarter rest looks more like a J than a Z to me."

Bianca's jaw drops. "The *Jack of Hearts.*"

11

BIANCA

Three bucks, two bags, one me.

The girl whose dreams were too big for her has landed back in Chicago. She took the job her big sister dangled under her nose right after she hit rock bottom in her attempt to climb to the top. A leading role in a Broadway show was in her grasp, and then she put her own body on the line to clinch the contract.

But it wasn't enough.

So here I am, tail between my legs, officially giving up. Falling back on my family's wealth and businesses in the Windy City.

It feels particularly windy today. There's a bite in the air as chilly gusts burst from Lake Michigan. It's early summer, but dark clouds hang in the air blocking the sun, so the air is unusually icy for June.

Perfect weather for a girl to hang up her dreams and call it a freaking day.

It's my first night working at Rouge's club, Aces Underground. I follow her directions to the letter, to the alleyway off Randolph and State, to the discreet black door adorned with the four playing-card symbols, and into the foyer where I'm greeted by fur-lined couches and the strangest-looking man I've ever met in my life.

His snow-white eyebrows rise as I walk in. "Miss Bianca. We've been expecting you."

"H-Hi." I cross my arms, running my hands up and down them. "Yes. I'm the new singer. And you are?"

"Chester Tabbitt, Miss Bianca. But you can call me Chet."

"And you're...what? The bouncer?"

He grins. "Something like that. I'm new to this post myself. Still learning the ropes." He checks the watch on his wrist. It's misshapen like the clocks in that Salvator Dalí painting. "We have fifteen minutes before opening. Come. I'll show you around."

Chet takes out a ring of keys and opens another door that leads to a staircase lined with mirrors. For a second I'm concerned that my sister has sold me into sex slavery—it wouldn't be the worst thing she's done to me—but then Chet flicks on a light switch, illuminating the way down.

He gestures to an emerald door at the bottom of the stairs. "This is the Green Door."

"Thank you. I was able to tell that for myself, actually."

His eyelids twitch. "I see you're a regular comedienne, Miss Bianca." He runs his yellowed fingernails up and down the wood of the door. "There are many entrances to and from Aces Underground. This one is Green. Another is Red. Find the third and you're already dead." He lets out a wheezy laugh.

What the fuck?

He opens the door and leads me into the main area of Aces. It's gorgeous. Different colors illuminate each section—one for Spades, Diamonds, Clubs, and my domain, Hearts. The floor is a checkerboard floor in black and white. The waitstaff dart about, making preparations for the evening. The women are in bikinis and the men are shirtless with tight shorts. Both uniforms, if you can call them that, are speckled with the symbols of their respective section.

"And this, Miss Bianca, is your stage," Chet says, gesturing to a glittering pink stage in the center of the Hearts section. There's a standing mic right at the center and a pink baby grand to the side along with chairs for the other musicians.

I've practiced with them already. They're nice guys. Rouge booked us space at the Fine Arts Building downtown. I'm not sure why we couldn't practice here, but then again, I've never been able to wrap my head around my sister's mind.

"Your dressing room is through that pink door," Chet says, pointing. "There's a private bathroom, as well as a bed."

I cock my head. "A bed? Why on earth would I need a bed in my dressing room?"

Chet's eyes shine. "In case you'd like to...lie down, I suppose." He lets out that wheezy laugh again before turning his gaze back to me. "I'll leave you to it. Your sister will be starting out at one of her other clubs this evening, but she assured me you will be exquisite."

"I'm sure I will be." I extend my hand toward Chet. "Thank you, Chet."

He stares at my hand a minute and then wraps his long fingers around my thumb—only my thumb—before scampering back through the door to the mirrored staircase.

What a weird little fucker.

Not so little. He's at least six-seven.

Certainly not a guy I'd want taking care of my kids, if I had any.

I have a book of sheet music for the band, which I told them I'd lay out on their music stands before they got here. I guess I'll do that now. I open my notebook, and—

Shit!

The rings popped open. Looseleaf paper flies everywhere. I get down on my knees to gather the music as best as I can, but it's strewn all over the dance floor. I look up just as one of the waiters approaches. He's wearing the same outfit as the other men—tiny shorts and a bare chest. On the black shorts are little hearts, and on his right shoulder is the letter J.

I grin. "The Jack of Hearts, I presume?"

He nods, his eyes bright.

I extend a hand. "I'm Bianca. The new singer."

Again he nods as he shakes my hand.

I narrow my eyes. "Are you not supposed to speak?"

He shakes his head, pantomiming locking a key against the corner of his mouth.

"Why?"

He shrugs.

"Well... Nice to meet you."

The more I get to know this club's culture, the less I like. Chet's a freaking weirdo, and now the waitstaff can't speak.

The pianist might have mentioned that when we rehearsed the other day, come to think of it. I wasn't listening much. I think my musicians aren't allowed to speak either. Maybe that's why we had to rehearse offsite.

Jack—I guess that's what I'm supposed to call him—kneels and helps me collect the rest of the sheet music. He points to the title of one of the pieces—"I Put a Spell on You"—and pats his heart.

"You like that one? I'd only ever heard of it because of Bette Midler singing it in Hocus Pocus*."*

He drops his jaw into an open-mouthed smile and pats at his heart again.

"You like that movie?"

He nods vigorously.

"Well, maybe we can hang out sometime. Have a movie night." I smirk. "I realize it's June, but you don't need to wait until October to watch Hocus Pocus. *Or we can watch something else. I don't have any local friends. Maybe tonight?"*

He nods again.

"Perfect." I rip off a corner from one of the pieces of sheet music and jot down my address. "This is my apartment. It's not too far from here. Walkable."

He frowns for a moment, but then takes the paper and gives me a thumbs-up.

It's a date.

Well, that wasn't a complete disaster. I sang through my set half a dozen times this evening, and I received a warm ovation from the Aces patrons. My voice is tired, but I'll steam when I get home tonight.

Except I invited Jack over. Right.

He seems nice enough. Hopefully he isn't a complete weirdo. I probably should have determined that before inviting him to my place.

I'm walking out, purposefully avoiding eye contact with Chet, when Jack waylays me in the alleyway. He's changed into a tight T-shirt and a pair of athletic shorts.

"How'd you get here? Were you behind me?"

He shakes his head. "Waitstaff entrance. Around the corner."

He speaks with a heavy accent. Russian, I think. Makes sense. Rouge told me a lot of the Aces waitstaff are immigrants from Eastern Europe or South Asia.

"Okay."

He cocks his head. "I can still come? Movie night?"

I smile. "Of course, Jack. Or... I suppose that isn't your real name."

He shrugs. "Jack is fine."

On our walk, I get to know Jack a little better. He is indeed from Russia and has worked at Aces for a few months. He started toward the end of March, and so far he likes it, says that the tips are great. He's gay, which is a relief. I'm not exactly hurting to get hit on anytime soon after the fiasco that was my Reflections *callback. He came from a poor village in rural Russia, so he's excited to live in a country where his sexual orientation will be more accepted, where he can live the American Dream.*

I don't have the heart to tell him I tried to take my slice of the American Dream for the better part of a decade in New York City and failed miserably. Maybe things will work out better for him.

We get back to my apartment. Unfortunately, I don't have a copy of Hocus Pocus *on DVD, and I can't seem to find it on the few streaming channels I subscribe to. We finally settle on watching* The Devil Wears Prada. *Jack's English is limited, so I'm not sure how much he's getting out of it. We spend most of the film chatting, anyway.*

"Meryl Streep. I love," he says.

"Yes, she's great." I lean back on the couch. "So tell me, Jack. What are your hobbies?"

"Hobbies?" he asks. It must be a new word for him.

"Sorry. What do you like to do for fun?"

"Fun? Oh, yes. I love to bake."

"Oh really? What do you bake?"

"Lots. Cakes and cookies. Pirozhki, vatrushka."

"What are those?"

"Very tasty. I make for you."

"That's very kind." I smile. I like Jack a lot. It's nice to have a friend. "Do you have a specialty? Something you make that is the best?"

"Oh, yes. Cherry tart." He rubs his belly. "Delicious."

"Really? You know, that's one of Rouge's favorites."

He widens his eyes. "Rouge likes cherry tart? Perhaps I make for her?"

I laugh at that. "I'm sure she'd appreciate the offer, but I doubt Rouge would ever eat anything she didn't make herself."

JACK.

I hate how things ended between the two of us. We were such good friends those first couple of months when I worked at Aces, but then we had a falling out a year or so after we met. I can't imagine how much fun we would have had if we'd stayed friends for the nearly five years I've worked—

Wait.

Five years.

Jack started just a few months before me. In March of that year.

"Oh, my God." I spring to my feet, pace around Alissa's bed.

"What is it, babe?" Harrison asks.

"The Jack of Hearts. He's an employee at Aces. In the Hearts section. And his five-year contract is about to end."

Alissa's eyebrows shoot up. "So you think..."

I nod gravely. "He's the next one on my sister's list. The next person she'll kill."

"Then this music box is telling us to keep an eye on him," Harrison says. "Maybe we're supposed to follow him after he finishes up his last day. See if we can save him."

I bite my lip. "There's only one problem with that plan."

"What?" Alissa asks.

"The Jack of Hearts... He kind of hates my fucking guts."

12

HARRISON

The day after I pulled Maddox Hathaway out of the ravine and saved his life, someone knocks on the door of our mobile home.

I open it to see the face of a man I've seen plastered on billboards and TV commercials. He's the guy running for mayor. Henry Something.

I widen my eyes. "Yes?"

He offers me a toothy grin—the kind as fake as the Easter Bunny. "Little boy, is your mommy or daddy home?"

"Um, my mom is." I call toward the kitchen. "Ma!"

She lumbers toward the front door. Ma is a big woman, and the entire mobile home shakes every time she takes a step. She drops her jaw as she recognizes the man at our door. "Mr. Hathaway!"

He bows his head. "Ma'am."

"What brings you to our humble home?" Ma looks back into the house. Dirty dishes and socks litter the floor. "I apologize for the mess. I would have tidied up if I knew the man who is running for mayor was going to visit us today."

"No problem at all, ma'am." He looks down at me. "Is this little Harry?"

"It is." Ma clasps my shoulders. "But how do you know his name?"

"This young man saved my son's life yesterday. He got separated from our driver. Wandered into an area not too far from here. A little ravine. He apparently slipped and fell in, and your son pulled him out and saved his life."

Ma looks at me in shock. "You did?"

I nod. "I guess so. He fell in. I've fallen in lots of times. I knew how to get him out safely."

"You've fallen into that ravine lots of times?" Ma asks. She grins sheepishly at Mr. Hathaway. "I guess I don't know enough about my own son, sir."

Mr. Hathaway grins. "I empathize. Raising kids is the hardest job anybody can ever have, isn't it? Doesn't matter what part of town you come from, it's always a challenge."

I hold back a scoff. Maddox probably grew up with a bunch of nannies. He mentioned yesterday that his parents don't pay him any attention. But it would be rude to bring that up in front of his dad right now. Especially now that I know his dad is one of the most famous people in Chicago.

Ma grabs me into a hug. "My brave little leprechaun! Wait until I tell your father. He's going to be so proud of you, Harry!"

"Who is it, Ma?" a voice from behind me grunts.

It's my older brother Harold. He and I are the only two of my brothers home right now.

Ma beams at Harold. "Your little brother saved the son of Henry Hathaway!"

Harold raises an eyebrow. "Huh. Good for him."

"If I may," Mr. Hathaway interjects, "I'd love to invite Harry

over for a playdate. I think it would be good for Maddox to socialize with someone who lives in a...different part of town."

"Of course, Mr. Mayor." Ma blushes. "Or rather, Mr. Soon-to-Be Mayor. You certainly would have my vote if we lived in Chicago proper." She glances toward the kitchen. "Can I get you a drink or something? It's a long drive from downtown Chicago. You must be parched."

Mr. Hathaway gazes inside the house, his nose wrinkling. "That's very kind of you to offer, but I have some Perrier in the town car. Perhaps you could bring Harry to our Chicago residence after school tomorrow?" He hands her a card. "Here's the address."

"Of course. Harry will be there with bells on. Anything's better than that damned creek!"

"Wonderful. Thank you, ma'am. You and your husband are welcome to come as well. I can have our housekeeper prepare some light hors d'oeuvres. Perhaps we'll open a bottle of Champagne to celebrate your son's bravery."

"That would be lovely, sir. Thank you!"

"Thank you, Mrs. O'Rourke." Mr. Hathaway turns around and steps into a limo—yeah, a freaking limo*—parked outside our home.*

Ma claps her hands to her cheeks. "Harry! My sweet little boy. So brave! So wonderful!" She peppers kisses all over my cheeks. "We're going to have to buy you some new clothes. If you're going to be friends with a Hathaway, you'll have to dress the part." She walks toward her bedroom. "I'm going to call your father, see if we can't find a few extra bucks in our bank account to buy you a nice tie!"

"A tie, Ma? For a playdate?"

"Of course, sweetie. I'd rent you a full tuxedo if we could afford it." She goes into the bedroom where the phone is. We only have one.

Harold and I are still in the living room. He scoffs.

"What?" I ask.

"You realize what that was, don't you?"

I wrinkle my forehead. "No. What?"

He rolls his eyes. "Do you really think Henry Hathaway gives a flying fuck about you? About Ma and Dad? About any of us?"

I shrug. "I mean, I did save his son's life."

"Yeah, and I don't doubt he's grateful to you. But he's a politician, Harry. People like him see everything in terms of the news cycle. And this is a big win for him."

"What do you mean?"

"You know what they call the Hathaways, don't you? The Kennedys of Chicago?"

"I've heard that, yeah."

"Yeah. And with the Hathaway name comes the stink of elitism. They're rich beyond belief." He flops down on our worn-out couch. "You saw that limo. That's probably one of half a dozen they've got lying around in their garage. Imagine how people will look at him when they see him letting his son hang out with trailer trash like you."

"We're not trailer trash."

Harold chuckles. "Doesn't matter. To them, it's what we are. But when people see the photographs of Maddox Hathaway—and I'll bet you on Ma's life there'll be photographers there—slumming it up playing fucking choo-choo trains with a boy from the other side of the tracks, he might just secure the vote of a new demographic. He's just like us, *they'll think."*

My lip trembles. I thought I found a true friend yesterday. "So it's all a big political stunt?"

Harold grins. "Aw, buck up, bud. It's not all bad. Ma and Dad need money bad. Six kids in a mobile home... That's pretty fucking sad. We're already sleeping three to a bedroom. If you play your cards right, you might just be able to secure a nice little donation in exchange for your heroism from the Hathaways. If they're going to use us, we can use them right the hell back."

I SCRATCH MY HEAD. "He hates your guts?"

Bianca nods. "We were friends the first several months I worked at Aces. But then we had this big fight, and we haven't spoken since."

"How could you speak with him at all?" Alissa asks. "The waitstaff aren't allowed to speak."

"I mean *outside* of Aces. He'd hang out at my apartment sometimes after the evening was up. We'd watch old movies, hang out. He learned a lot of English that way, so it worked out nicely. And I was in desperate need of friends after coming back from New York."

"Okay..." I rub my temple. "Well, even if the two of you aren't exactly on the best of terms, I'm sure he doesn't want to be killed and then have his organs ripped out of him. So he might still be interested in our help."

Bianca bites her lip. "God, he's going to kill me."

"I'm sure whatever kind of row you had will be water under the bridge once we explain to him what's going on," Alissa adds.

"You don't understand. The reason we started fighting in the first place was because he suspected Rouge was up to something nefarious. And I didn't believe him. I took her side." She buries her face in her hands. "And now it's years later. Who knows how many countless lives could have been spared if I'd just listened to him then?"

I wrap my arm around her waist. "Babe, you can't think

that way. Hindsight is forever twenty-twenty. What matters is that we can help the Jack of Hearts *now.* And everyone else at Aces, and at Jade, Second Star, and the rest." I pace the room again. "I don't love that more people I care about are going to have to put their lives on the line to get this done. Who knows what we'll run into if we follow Jack back to the Caterpillar Hotel after his last night at Aces? Hell, this wasn't even *my* escapade to begin with. It was Maddox's. He was the one who dived down the rabbit hole in the first place with you, Alissa."

"He did so at my urging," Alissa admits. "It wasn't until he brought me to Aces, saw it through my eyes, that he began to see the cracks in the plaster."

"Even so..." I rub at the back of my neck. "I don't even know what I'm trying to say. It just... Sometimes I feel like this isn't my story."

Bianca looks up at me with those stormy dark-blue eyes. "It's *all* our story. Yours. Mine. Maddox and Alissa's. And we're going to finish it." She gestures to the music box. "Someone clearly wants us to do it."

"And what if the music box is a trap?" I ask. "It could have been Chet who planted it in my trunk. And we know we can't trust *him.*"

"But what we *do* know is that Jack's tenure *is* coming to an end," Bianca says. "No matter what, he's next on the docket. There is probably a patron who's already put down a request for his heart."

I squeeze my eyes shut, take a deep breath in. "I need... I need to check on Maddox."

"Do you want me to come with you?" Bianca asks.

I shake my head. "I'd love your company, but I need to talk to him in private if he's conscious."

"Of course." Bianca grabs my hand and squeezes it. "I'll

keep Alissa company. Once you get back, we'll plan our next move."

"Right." I kiss her on the lips, give Alissa a nod, and then cross over to Maddox's room. I check his vitals. They're all good. Dinah's been doing a great job nursing them back to health.

I shake his shoulder gently. "Hey…Maddox."

His eyelids flutter for a moment, and then he raises his head weakly when he sees me. "Harrison O'Rourke, as I live and breathe."

"It's thanks to me you're living and breathing at all. Me, Bianca, and Dinah, that is."

"And Alissa," he says. "Even back in that hotel, before I passed out, when I could feel myself starting to slip away…the thought of leaving her alone to fend for herself… It kept me here." He twists his lips into a small grin. "I love her, man."

I chuckle. "You knew her for all of two weeks when you walked through the gates of hell with her. I'd hope to God you at least liked her at the time."

He shakes his head. "I'm serious. She's the woman I'm going to marry. The woman who's going to carry my children. I knew it the moment she walked into my shop."

"How did you know?" I ask. "Because I think I might feel the same way about Bianca."

He grins. "Dinah told me you were getting along with her. I'm glad it's working out. She's gorgeous." He shifts his gaze. "But she's a Montrose. You sure she can be trusted?"

"She's nothing like her sister. But we're getting off track. How did you know about Alissa?"

He shrugs. "Probably the same way you know about Bianca. I just…*knew*. There was this sudden clarity the moment I met her. Like every failed relationship up to that point didn't work out for a reason. Because my heart was waiting for one woman and one woman alone. Her."

Damn. It's the same way with Bianca. She's perfect in every way—even in her imperfections.

I squeeze Maddox's shoulder. "We're going to make this right. We're going to bring Rouge to justice."

"I know you will." Maddox coughs a few times. "Because you're the best fucking guy I know, Harrison." He swallows. "But watch out for Rouge."

"Of course. We're not going to let her—"

Maddox silences me with a wave of his hand. "I'm serious, man. She's into some fucked-up shit. The things I've seen..." His heart machine starts to beat rapidly.

"Hey. Stay calm. It's all right. Deep breath in."

He squeezes his eyes shut, inhaling slowly through his nose and then exhaling through his mouth. The heart machine slows down.

"I'm not going to let Rouge hurt me. Or Bianca. Or you and Alissa. Or anyone fucking else. You have my word."

He nods. "I know... But you should know the kind of woman you're dealing with." He takes another deep breath in. "There was this time... She invited me into her office. I thought it was for a little fun. I had the hots for her when I first started coming to Aces."

I exhale sharply. Rouge *is* gorgeous, so I get it. But I've always seen her as attractive in an untouchable way. Like a majestic lioness who won't hesitate to rip your throat out with her teeth.

"What happened?"

"We *did* fuck. At least, as far as I remember. She made me take these magic mushrooms before we did it. I was tripping the fuck out. And after we—you know—did the deed, she gave me a goblet to drink from. And inside it was... blood."

I drop my jaw. "What the fuck?"

"Yeah. She offered it to me as if it were some kind of ritual."

Maddox doesn't know about the hearts we found. Only Alissa does.

I don't want to tell him about them now. He'll just get worked up again, and he needs more recovery time than Alissa.

But I imagine the goblet of blood she offered to Maddox is related to the hearts. Maybe Rouge drains the blood of her victims...and then consumes it.

What kind of Vlad-the-Impaler-ass banshee is she?

"We know what we're dealing with," I tell Maddox. "We're going to be careful. And then the four of us will live happily ever after. You can take that to the fucking bank."

"Thanks, Harrison. I had no idea how lucky I was that day I met you. When I fell into the ravine." He chuckles. "I bet you're wishing you'd have just let me drown right about now."

"Not in the slightest." I punch his shoulder. "And hey, I saved your life that day. It can't be that hard to do it again."

13

BIANCA

I've enjoyed hanging out with Jack. His English has gotten a lot better the last few months, and he credits our time together watching movies and playing board games when we're off from Aces for his quick progress.

He's really smart. Way too smart to be working at Aces, but he promised five years of service to Rouge in exchange for her bringing him over to the States and handling all his immigration documents. I guess it's a fair trade. He grew up in a small village in a very poor region of Russia and could barely read or write when he met Rouge. She explained to him—in perfect Russian, he tells me—what she could offer him in the States. He jumped at the opportunity.

Of course, he didn't know the grislier details—namely, that he would be expected to sell his body to club patrons on the side. The male waitstaff don't get nearly as much attention as the women, but he still ends up taking two or three clients to the private area behind the velvet curtains most weekends.

"It is entirely optional," he says. "Rouge made that very clear."

"Is it, though? Your regular wages can't be nearly enough to live off."

We're in the middle of a game of Settlers of Catan. It's been our game of choice the last month. I'm getting pretty good at it. Today, though, I'm not paying much attention.

"The extra money is nice. But we don't need *to do it," Jack counters. "We're not paying rent, after all. Our meals are comped as well. So this is just extra cash to sock away for when we go off on our own. By the way, I'm building another settlement."*

"Damn it!" I haven't been watching Jack, and he's gathered the necessary resources to bring him only a few points from winning the game. I hand him one of the orange-colored settlement tokens from the game box, which he sets up on a prime spot.

He grins. "Don't hate the player. Hate the game."

I roll my eyes. "I can hate you both." I look over my own resource cards, but they might as well be written in Swedish, because my brain isn't firing on all cylinders right now. "Sorry. I can't seem to focus tonight."

He eyes my half-full glass of Sauvignon Blanc. "Have you had a lot to drink?"

I chuckle. "Half a glass of white wine isn't enough to get me wasted. It's just..." I sigh, placing the cards back down on the table. "Rouge has been pressuring me to... *'entertain' as well."*

Jack cocks his head. "Really?"

I nod. "Some of the patrons have been offering three or four thousand bucks an hour."

His eyebrows nearly fly off his head. "You're joking. The most I've ever made is seven fifty."

I smirk. "You should raise your price then."

Indeed he should. Jack is gorgeous, with his wavy sandy-blond hair that covers his ears. He's got a slim build, but his pecs and biceps are magnificent, barely constrained by the tight black T-shirt he's wearing tonight. He's cleanshaven with a good jaw and enchanting hazel eyes. If he weren't exclusively into guys, I'd have asked him out myself by now.

He scratches his chin. "It sounds like you're thinking about it."

I scoff. "Of course I'm thinking about it. That kind of money is serious stuff." I glance around my modest two-bedroom apartment. "If I were taking a few clients every weekend at that rate, I could get a luxury apartment in a high-rise in the Loop. Be right in the middle of everything."

"Plus you could invite your best friend to hang out there," Jack says with a grin.

*I swallow. "But... I mean, you get this. Once you sell your body, you can't...*unsell *it."*

He exhales sharply. "Seller's remorse is definitely a thing you'll deal with."

I cross my arms. "Be honest. How bad is it?"

He shrugs gently. "I mean... It's not always pleasant. But you learn to... What's the word? When you remove yourself mentally from what you're doing physically?"

"Dissociate?"

"That's the one. I go into auto-pilot, letting out a moan every now and then to make the client feel like he's doing a good job. But every so often a patron I'm attracted to purchases me. That's always nice."

"But nine times out of ten it's going to be someone you'd rather not sleep with."

"Of course."

"Then how do you dissociate?"

He sighs. "I think about lying on a warm, sunny beach. Letting the waves tickle my toes. I listen for the sounds of seagulls and the distant blowing of ship horns. And here's a little industry secret." He lowers his voice, even though it's just the two of us in the room. "They pay for an hour, but most of the sessions are done within fifteen minutes or so."

I widen my eyes. "You're joking."

"Of course not. Most of these men are on the older side, and they've only got one shoot in them. Once they get there, they're usually done. The clarity kicks in and they realize what they've done. They silently gather their things and head out, leaving the cash on the nightstand. And then I have the rest of the hour to myself before Rouge expects me back on the floor."

"They don't ever want to...cuddle or anything?"

"Every now and then. But it's pretty uncommon. Most men want to get their rocks off and then get back to their drinks."

I take a deep breath in. It doesn't sound all that bad.

Like Jack said, not pleasant. But manageable.

If I got through that unending tryst with Mr. Shippe at my Reflections *callback, I can get through anything. And the reward for these sessions will be guaranteed. Shippe put me through the wringer and then proceeded to not even cast me in his show.*

In a way, I've already sold my body. I just got screwed over in the process.

The toothpaste is already out of the tube.

What's a few more times? Just enough to cover rent for a nice apartment in the good part of town?

It's just sex, right?

People enjoy sex.

Can it really be all that bad?

~

I'm not looking forward to this.

It's been a little over four years since I've spoken with Jack.

He works in my section, so seeing him is unavoidable.

Speaking with him, however, is entirely optional.

He's not allowed to speak while he's on Aces grounds anyway. When I do bump into him, I just course correct like a Roomba in a cluttered room, turn the other way and find something else to do.

The last time we spoke, he was screaming in my face before slamming my own door on me.

I moved out of that apartment the next day. I'd finally saved up enough money from sucking and fucking the Aces patrons to size up. I wasn't going to make the official move until a few days later, but after that last night with Jack, I couldn't bear living in a space I associated so much with him.

I never played Settlers of Catan or any of our other favorite games again, either. I donated my entire collection to Goodwill and threw myself into furnishing my new apartment.

Of course, knowing now what I know... Jack was right all along.

I don't look forward to that part of the conversation either.

I get into my car and make the drive out west to Forest Park and the Caterpillar Hotel.

Harrison wanted to come with me, but he's working today. He's been playing hooky enough as it is. But while he's at the hospital, he can also look into the St. Charles patients' organ donations, see if any evidence points to a connection to Rouge.

If he can find that connection, we can avoid tracking Jack to see if anyone is going to try to kill him at the end of his contract. But I know my sister. She'll have buried her involvement in this beneath several layers of scapegoats and red herrings. I doubt Harrison will uncover anything damning, but we have to attack this from all angles.

I told Harrison that, while Jack and I have some bad blood between us, he would never lay a finger on me. Harrison wasn't wholly convinced, but I promised him I'd be safe doing this on my own. Even so, he insisted I text him at every juncture on my outing today.

I pull out my phone. *Just parked*, I text him.

Good. Let me know when you're safely back at the car.

Will do. Thanks for looking out for me.

Of course, babe.

The Caterpillar Hotel parking lot is empty, so I parked a few blocks away to remain inconspicuous. Rouge isn't supposed to do her weekly check-in at the hotel for a few more days, but just in case she makes an unplanned visit, I don't want her to see my car in the lot. We did the same thing the night we rescued Maddox and Alissa, and we got away with it then.

Speaking of which, I check their rooms first. We broke down the doors to each room, but Dinah discreetly had a handyman who owed her a favor replace each of them after we got Maddox and Alissa to the hospital to cover our tracks. They don't quite match the rest of the doors of the hotel, but they're close enough to look the same from a distance.

The doors are unlocked, and I peer into each room. Everything is the same as how we left it. As far as I can tell, Rouge hasn't been here. Neither has Chet or any of her Kings.

I let out a sigh of relief and then head up to Jack's room on the fifth floor. I take a deep breath in and knock.

A moment later, the door opens. The chain is still on, so it only opens a few inches. I catch a fleeting glimpse of Jack's hazel eyes and wavy blond hair before he slams the door back shut.

I knock again. "Jack, please. It's important."

"I have nothing to say to you." From the other side.

"It's been four years, Jack."

Silence.

I knock a third time. "Hear me out. What you told me about Rouge... I... I think it's true."

No response for a few minutes. I'm about to knock again, beg him to answer, when he slowly opens the door. He's wearing a striped tank top and fleece pajama bottoms with bare feet. His gaze is narrowed. "I'm listening."

I swallow. "Can I come in?"

He peers out the door. "Did anyone follow you?"

"Not that I know of."

"Fine. Come in. You have five minutes."

I walk inside Jack's room, and he locks the door and resecures the chain in place.

All the months Jack and I hung out outside of Aces, he always came to my little apartment. This is my first time in his personal space. The Caterpillar Hotel isn't exactly a luxury resort, but he's kept the room clean and the linens pressed. A few knickknacks—mostly Chicago souvenir store finds—adorn his dresser, along with a few framed photos of him with some other Aces waitstaff. No pictures with me, of course.

He crosses his arms. "You were saying?"

I sit on the foot of the bed. I can't give Jack all the details. If he knows his head is on the chopping block, he might run for the hills. We need him to stay in place for this plan to work correctly, but he also needs to be aware of what we're doing.

"Rouge is…up to something."

He rolls his eyes. "No shit."

"We don't have all the specifics yet, but—"

He lifts a hand. "Spare me, Bianca. If this is you coming to apologize, you're off to a shitty start."

"I'm *not* here to apologize, Jack. I'm here to help you."

"I don't need your help." He gestures to his dresser. "I've got thousands saved up for when I finish up here. When I'm finally released from my contract, I'll be getting as far away as humanly possible from Aces fucking Underground."

"You don't understand. I don't think you're going to *have* that option."

He raises an eyebrow. "What do you mean?"

I run my hands through my hair as I try to articulate my thoughts in a digestible way for Jack. "What you think you saw that night—the night our friendship ended—I think it could happen to you."

He drops his jaw. "No. That can't be. I've been a fantastic server for five years. Rouge would never—"

"She *would*, Jack. You've known it for years. I imagine you've just denied what you saw as a bad trip."

"I *was* pretty hopped up that night." He bites his lip. "It's not like I could leave anyway. Rouge has had a stranglehold on me for nearly five years."

"We don't have a lot of evidence so far"—not technically a lie, but a cooler full of human hearts is pretty damned incriminating—"but my new boyfriend and I want to keep an eye on you as your contract draws to a close."

"Why would my contract ending be an issue? The girl I saw that night… She was barely through her first year. She broke the rules. I've kept my nose clean."

"Think of all the waitstaff who've kept their noses clean,"

I say. "The ones who finished out their contracts and went out into the world. Have you heard from any of them?"

He blinks several times. "What are you saying?"

"I'll take that as a no."

"I haven't. But I never got super close to any of them. After things fell apart between you and me, I decided to stick out the rest of my time at Aces as a lone wolf. It's always been discouraged for us to fraternize amongst each other anyway. Half the servers here don't speak a word of English besides 'vodka,' 'gin,' and 'tequila.' And the ones who do... Well, suffice to say we don't have a lot in common."

Of course. Jack said as much when we started hanging out all those years ago. He was a very specific personality type, highly intellectual. While some of the other waitstaff have been intelligent, they were never quite at Jack's level. The only person he considered his intellectual equal was me.

Which is hilarious, because I never thought I was that smart. Certainly not compared to my sister.

"The people who work at Aces do their time, and then they go out into the world. Why would they want to look back?" Jack scowls as he looks around his tiny room. "I certainly won't be."

"You *really* won't be looking back if you're dead, Jack." I sigh, pace the room. "I think what you saw that night is the fate of *all* the Aces waitstaff. The waitstaff for all of Rouge's clubs, and even some of the patrons. It doesn't matter if you stuck to the rules. I've been looking into it. There have been unexplained disappearances—and a few confirmed deaths—for years now."

Jack swallows. "If you're saying what I think you're saying...then all of the people I've worked with who have gone on..."

My lip trembles. "They're dead, Jack. All of them."

The color drains from his face. "And you think I'm next?"

I nod slowly. "After your last shift. Which I'm guessing is pretty soon."

"Oh, it's soon." He gulps. "My last shift is tomorrow."

14

HARRISON

Back to work.

I've taken the last few days off. And my God, so much has happened since I last clocked in to a shift at St. Charles.

I've been here several times, of course. Just two nights ago, I sneaked in the back way wearing barely anything. Before that, I was smuggling in Maddox and Alissa, both of whom were on the brink of death.

Now they're doing all right, and if I took another day off, it would have started to look suspicious.

Rouge is on the board of this hospital, after all. I'm sure she's kept an eye on me since I grifted my way into Aces the night I met Bianca.

I'm not going to be doing a lot of work today. I've delegated a lot of my regular duties to my interns and nurses, because the real reason I came in was to find out if we've been receiving black-market organs from Rouge.

The timing is undeniable. Carol and Lou got organs almost instantaneously after that poor girl's head was found in the nature reserve by O'Hare.

But we're still missing our smoking gun. We need to collect as much evidence as possible to get Rouge convicted of what she's doing. The cooler of human hearts was a start, but Rouge could simply deny having any knowledge of it. She'd throw one of her Kings or someone else under the bus, and because of her power and influence among the city elites, she'd get away with it.

No. We need to build a rock-solid case against her. That's the only way to ensure she'll see justice for what she's done.

I sit down in my office, out of the way from the day-to-day hustle and bustle of the hospital. I pull up a list of our most recent organ recipients. There have been a few since Carol and Lou, but they're still near the top of the list when I sort it by date. I try to track down where their organs came from, but that leads me to an error page.

The data must be in here somewhere. It's just encrypted, and I don't have access to it.

I pick up the phone and call the hospital's IT department.

"Yes, Dr. O'Rourke?"

It's Kit. She's one of the newer IT hires—only a year out of college—and normally gets saddled with the department's bitch work while her superiors get the more complex jobs. She's the one I call when I need to recover a patient's file that accidentally fell through cyberspace.

I was hoping she'd be the one to pick up. She's the youngest, the hungriest for approval.

"Hi, Kit. Can you swing up to my office? I have an unusual request."

"What is it?" Papers shuffle over the line.

"I'd rather discuss it in person. I'll buy you a coffee for your trouble."

She chuckles. "I'm more of a tea person, Doc."

I smile. I knew she'd see eye-to-eye with me. "Even better. I'll owe you a tea."

If she pulls this off, I'll buy her a first-class ticket to the UK to get her all the tea she wants.

Ten minutes later, she knocks on my door.

"Come in," I call out.

She opens the door. Kit is cute in that hot-librarian way. A messy bun of curly red hair on top of her head, horn-rimmed glasses, and bursts of freckles on her cheeks. She's wearing a fitted blue cardigan over a slightly wrinkled blouse, khaki pants, and sensible dark shoes.

She crosses over to my desk. "What can I help you with today, Doc?"

Kit is the only person who has ever called me "Doc." She's probably too young to have watched any Bugs Bunny cartoons, so I've written it off as a quirk. If she weren't so young, I'd have asked her out before I met Bianca.

"I'm having trouble tracing the identity of an organ donor."

She purses her lips. "Well, Doc, that's probably because you're not allowed access to that information."

Of course. Kit plays by the book. I was prepared for this.

"Normally I'd agree with you. But unfortunately one of our organ recipients is exhibiting symptoms of HIV. We did the standard testing when we received the heart, but it must have slipped through. I need to know the identity of the donor so that any other people who received the organs know they should get tested."

Flimsy reasoning, I'll admit. But Kit isn't a doctor. She might not know this explanation is bullshit.

She frowns. "I'm not sure if I'm allowed to pull up those files on that rationale. I may have to phone my supervisor."

I stand quickly. "Kit, let's not bother Barry with this. Time is of the essence when an issue like this pops up. I'll smooth it over with IT myself if anyone gets their panties in a twist."

She pauses. "You sure this is okay?"

"Of course. Come on, Kit." I offer a smile, hoping my good looks will be enough to charm her. "You've worked here a while now. Would I ever ask you to do something you're not supposed to do?"

Her face softens. "I suppose not."

"Thank you." I pull out my phone. "Where's your favorite tea place? I'll order a gift certificate for you."

"That's very kind." Kit's cheeks flush. "I love the Flamingo Tea Room just around the corner."

"Done and done." I gesture toward my desk chair. "Have at it. The patient who received the transplant is Lou Chambers. The surgery took place a little over a month ago."

Kit sits down at my computer and clacks away on the keyboard. After a few minutes, she's able to bypass the privacy server that keeps me from seeing where the organs come from. "Looks like the heart in question came from a Shinzo Life Center, a non-profit procurement organization. Their address isn't too far from the hospital, in fact. Makes sense, I suppose. Organs are only viable for a few hours after the death of the donor." She frowns. "That's funny."

"What?"

"There isn't a name listed for the organ donor. Just Shinzo Life."

That tracks, based on how Rouge operates. If the donors are waitstaff who have no identifying documents, their names wouldn't be included on the file. Rouge herself makes them identify only by their number and suit.

"That might be enough for me to go on, Kit. Thank you."

She furrows her brow. "You sure? I thought you wanted a name? To ensure that any other recipients get tested—"

"I'll take that up with Shinzo Life personally. They'll be able to point me in the right direction." I gesture to the door. "Thank you, Kit. I'll make sure that gift certificate is sent to your email."

She blinks a few times but then turns the doorknob and exits the office.

I sit back down at my desk. Finally, some progress.

I didn't like lying to Kit. I'll make sure she doesn't get in trouble for this. Hell, if we end up putting an end to Rouge's reign of terror, Kit will be partially responsible for saving countless lives.

I look up the Shinzo Life Center. Luckily, they're registered as a non-profit, so all their information is public by law. I pull up their tax records. Unfortunately, everything looks aboveboard.

But it would, wouldn't it? Rouge isn't stupid.

I leave the tax records for now and look up Shinzo's actual website, and the first shoe drops.

They're located in the same building as the Aces Underground foyer. Aces itself is—as its name implies—underground, utilizing vacant space that was going to house a subway station that never came to fruition. Rouge's grandfather, Ruskin Montrose, bought the space and used it to open a speakeasy during Prohibition. But the foyer, where Chet works, is on the ground level, sharing building spaces with several other entities, including this organ procurement center. The entrance to Shinzo is off Dearborn and Washington, the opposite corner from Randolph and State.

And I'd bet dollars to donuts it's connected to that secret crawlspace Bianca and I found.

I look through the rest of the website. Everything looks normal. No indication that the company is run by a madwoman masquerading as a nightclub owner. In fact, Rouge seems to have installed a puppet CEO named Romeo Sturgeon.

Weird-ass name. Imagine being named after a Shakespeare character and a fucking fish.

But as I look at the name, the other shoe drops.

Romeo Sturgeon isn't just a weird name. It's an anagram.

An anagram for "Rouge Montrose."

15

BIANCA

TOMORROW.

Jack's last day is *tomorrow*.

Damn it.

I thought Harrison and I would have more time to come up with a plan.

No time like the present, I suppose.

"Will you give me just a second?" I ask Jack. "I have to make a quick phone call."

Jack shrugs. "Be my guest."

I quickly dial Harrison's number and press the call button.

It rings a few times.

"Hey, babe. You okay?"

I run my free hand through my hair. "I'm fine. I'm at the Caterpillar Hotel. In Jack's room."

"Are you able to speak freely?"

"Yeah. I told him what he needs to know. How are things at the hospital?"

"They're good. I've been doing some digging. I think I

figured out the name of the organization that your sister is selling the organs to St. Charles under."

I widen my eyes. "Really?"

"Yeah. Shinzo Life Center. It's on the same city block as Aces, just on the opposite corner."

I nearly drop the phone. "I've passed the front of their business hundreds of times! I assumed it was a life coaching place or something." I frown. "Are you sure that's the place?"

"A hundred percent. And here's the kicker. The CEO's name is an anagram for 'Rouge Montrose.'"

I swallow. "That's it, then. She's behind all of this."

Not that there was much doubt at this point. I've known since I was seven years old that my sister was capable of doing terrible, evil things. But I pushed the memories away whenever they threatened to emerge, especially when she offered me help the day I got rejected from *Reflections*. She pulled me out of the ocean when I was at my lowest point, so I forgot and forgave.

No longer.

I've been looking the other way for far too long.

"Why don't you come over to my place tonight? We can figure out what our next move is."

I glance back toward Jack. "Actually, we should probably make the plan now. Jack's last night is Friday. As in tomorrow."

"You're kidding."

"I wish I were."

He sighs. "Damn it. I thought we'd have more time."

"So did I. But it's now or never. From what Alissa told me, Svetlana—the Nine of Diamonds—disappeared the same night she finished up her contract. If Jack is their next target, we'll have to act fast."

"Right... Right..." He pauses. "Obviously then, our move is to keep Jack in our sight at all times tomorrow evening."

"Agreed. You can disguise yourself as the Ace of Clubs again, and I'll be there as a singer. Jack works in my section, and Clubs is close by, so between the two of us, we'll be able to keep an eye on him."

"But that wouldn't make much of a difference. Even Rouge can't murder a man in front of a hundred witnesses."

"Right." I pace the room. "We'll have to follow Jack home. You'll get on the bus with him—you'll be dressed as a waiter, so you won't have any trouble getting aboard—and then I'll follow behind. We can join Jack in his room at the Caterpillar and make sure nothing happens to him."

"And what do we do if someone *does* come to collect?"

"We'll be ready. I doubt they'd do away with him at the actual hotel. But if they do, we'll have our phones. We can record everything. Maybe you could start an Instagram livestream or something. Make sure everything that happens is documented. Then we'll be practically invincible." I swallow. "Worst case, we call the cops."

"Worst case is we get killed too, Bianca."

I bite my lip. "If my death means countless other lives are saved, it'll be worth it."

A long pause in the conversation.

"Are you there, Harrison?"

"Yeah. I'm just thinking it over. Because no way in hell am I going to allow you to put your life on the line."

"You don't have a choice. It's *my* life."

Another long pause. "I would be devastated if something happened to you."

Warmth fills my heart at his words. "I would feel the same

way about you, but we're talking about the bigger picture here."

He sighs. "I'll do everything in my power to ensure that doesn't happen."

"I've never felt safer than when I've been with you."

"I'll do my damnedest to make sure you're okay." His voice darkens. "Even if it means laying my own life down."

"It won't come to that."

"It better not. I have a whole life ahead of me, and I want to spend it with you."

Again my heart soars. But it's not the time for us to be declaring our feelings for each other.

"Do you have a firearm?" I ask. "We should be armed."

"Yeah. I'll have that on me. Except... Shit. I won't. I'll be in my Ace of Clubs outfit. Those shorts don't even have pockets."

"Even if they did, someone would easily see you were packing."

Harrison's bulge is already conspicuous in those teeny shorts. A gun would be extremely obvious.

"I'll hand the gun off to you, then. Have you ever fired one before?"

I exhale. "No."

"Fuck. And we don't have enough time to get you to a shooting range to practice." He sighs. "Well, you'll learn quickly. Point and shoot, pretty simple. But I can only loan it to you on one condition."

"What's that?"

"Only use it if your life is in immediate danger. If there's no other choice."

"Of course."

"Good."

My heart thrums. I'm not getting cold feet, but I'm starting to get anxious. This is getting real. Harrison's talking about me actually shooting someone, ending another human life. Likely the life of one of Rouge's Kings.

But possibly the life of my sister herself.

She's evil incarnate, don't get me wrong. But she's still my sister.

My sister who knows where I live. Who knows everything about me.

"Harrison..."

"Yeah, babe?"

"If something goes wrong, I probably shouldn't go back to my own apartment. Rouge knows that's where I live. She's never visited me there, of course, but it's where my checks are addressed to."

"You're welcome to crash at my place."

"I'd love that, don't get me wrong, but I think it might be best if we got a hotel for the next couple of nights. It'll be harder to track us that way."

"Won't you be booking the hotel under your name?"

"No." I walk over to my purse, grab my wallet, and reach into a hidden pocket behind my driver's license window. "I never told you about my pickpocket ex-boyfriend, did I?"

"Your what ex-what?" His voice is tense.

"Calm down. It's ancient history, and we parted on decent terms. But he knew a guy who knew a guy who could make great fake ID's. They're practically indistinguishable from the real thing." I pull out the fake from the secret pocket in my wallet. "We'll book it under my pseudonym. Whitney Royale."

He lets out a short, humorless laugh. "Sounds like a cocktail."

"My ex said it sounded like a stripper name."

"That, too."

"Does Rouge know about your alter ego?"

"No. And she'd have no way of finding it out."

A pause. "Okay. You can book the hotel. Get somewhere near Aces."

"I will. I'll stop at my place and pack a few days' worth of clothes. You should do the same once you finish up with your shift at the hospital. Once I make the arrangements, I'll text you the details."

"Sounds good. See you in a few hours."

I smile. "I'll count the moments."

I DECIDED on the Gilded Rose, a historic hotel off Michigan Avenue that's within walking distance to Aces. I booked the room online and am now on my way there, lugging a small carry-on bag behind me.

Harrison is waiting in the ornate lobby when I get there with a small suitcase of his own at his side.

I widen my eyes. "I thought you were going to be working for a few more hours."

He shrugs. "I had already delegated most of my duties to my interns and nurses, so I took off early. I didn't like the idea of you at this hotel without me."

I wrap my arms around him, squeeze him tight. It feels like an eternity has passed since we were last together. "I wasn't too fond of the idea either. But are you sure your patients won't need you?"

He strokes my hair. "I have a fantastic staff covering for me. I won't be missed."

"I'd certainly miss you." I finally break the embrace, regard his handsome face. "I guess we'd better check in then."

He gestures to the marble slab to our right manned by people at small computers. We cross over.

A woman with curly blond hair and half-moon spectacles waves us over. "Good afternoon, and welcome to the Gilded Rose. Do you have a reservation?"

I place my fake ID on the counter. "Yes. For three nights. The name is Whitney Royale."

"Wonderful. Just one moment, Ms. Royale." She grabs my ID, looks it over, and then returns to her screen. "Yes, you're in our system. I'll just need a credit card for incidentals."

I widen my eyes. I don't have a credit card with Whitney Royale's name on it. I forgot about that.

Harrison clearly is thinking faster than I am, because he quickly grabs his wallet and takes out a card. "Those are on me. I'm treating my girlfriend to a weekend of pampering."

The receptionist smiles at Harrison. "Lucky lady." She grabs the credit card and runs it through her system. "Everything seems to be in order. One question, though. Would you be interested in upgrading to our luxury suite? It's almost always booked, but not this weekend. We offer a last-minute discount to guests."

"How much would it be?" Harrison asks.

She clacks on her keyboard. "It would be a little under five hundred dollars to upgrade for the whole weekend, sir."

Harrison grins. "Let's do it. Charge the extra money to my card."

I grab his arm. "You really don't have to do that."

He sears his gaze into mine. "I really think I do."

And in his eyes, I see what he means. We're about to put

our lives on the line to save Jack and the rest of the waitstaff at Aces Underground. We could be six feet under by this time tomorrow. We may as well live a little.

I turn back to the receptionist. "Okay, we'll take the upgrade."

"Excellent choice." The receptionist smiles. "The luxury suite is truly something special. You'll be quite comfortable. Will two keys be sufficient?"

"Yes," I reply.

"Perfect." She grabs two key cards, swipes them through another machine, and gives them to us in a small envelope. "You'll be on the seventh floor. Have a wonderful first night, and please don't hesitate to call the front desk if you encounter any issues."

"Thank you," I say weakly.

"Thank *you*, Ms. Royale. And welcome to the Gilded Rose."

We take the elevator—it's one of those old ones that's controlled by an operator sitting on a tall bench in the corner—up to the seventh floor and Harrison swipes his keycard, letting us into our suite.

We open to a living space that's lavishly decorated with nineteenth-century art adorning emerald-green wallpaper. Over the room's light-pink carpet, two cream wingback chairs stand across from a loveseat in the same color, both outfitted with soft leather. They surround a dark cherry oval-shaped coffee table holding a golden vase with a bouquet of red roses. In the corner stands an elegant wooden desk with assorted stationery.

"Damn, this is nice." Harrison plops down on the loveseat. "I should stay downtown more often."

It is nice, but it does nothing to quell the goosebumps

popping up over my arms. This may very well be the last place I ever sleep.

Harrison gets back to his feet. He walks over to me, brushes a finger over my cheek. "Everything's going to be okay. You know that, right?"

I swallow, look down at my feet. "I'll feel a lot better after tomorrow night."

"Of course. We both will." He tips my chin up and gives me a kiss.

It's sweet, chaste.

And that's the last thing I want right now.

I place a hand on either side of his head and kiss him back much harder.

His eyes pop open. "Babe?"

"It's okay, Harrison. I want this. Everything might go well tomorrow, but just in case it's our last night on earth—the end of the world—I want to... I want to make love to you."

He blinks several times.

I didn't say the three little words. But this is the closest I've come.

But the moment passes, and he crushes his lips to mine, prying them open with his tongue. I gladly let him in, and we stand there locked in each other's embrace for an unending moment. Eventually he leads me to the loveseat, and I lie back. He crawls on top of me.

He breaks the kiss for a minute and caresses my cheek. "Fuck, Bianca. You're so beautiful."

"So are you," I sigh.

He brings his mouth back down and unbuttons my blouse. Eventually I shimmy it off my shoulders, exposing my lavender bra. He fondles my breasts, still kissing me.

I squeeze his cock. Already he's so hard for me, ready to

fill me the way only he can. He moans as I tease him through his jeans.

He's working my bra off now, and in a few seconds my breasts are free. He pinches my right nipple and brings his mouth down on the left.

And it's heaven. Paradise.

He swishes his tongue over the areola and then wraps his lips around the nub, driving electricity directly between my legs. I unbutton his shirt and push it over his shoulders, exposing his hard chest. He groans against my sternum, sending vibrations through my entire body.

Now he's unbuttoning my jeans, and he slides them off in a single pull. He whips my panties off and dives tongue-first into my pussy.

Stars. Planets. Celestial bliss.

And before I realize it, I open my mouth and a stream of words pours out.

"God, I love you, Harrison!"

16

HARRISON

I FREEZE IN PLACE, MY TONGUE STILL DEEPLY EMBEDDED INSIDE Bianca.

Did she really say what I think she said?

I'm making things up. Or she didn't mean it.

It's too soon… Too…

But it's not.

Because I feel the same exact fucking way.

I slowly rise, bring my gaze to hers.

Her face is beet red. "I'm sorry. I didn't… I mean… I didn't want to say it like that."

I cock my head. "But you mean it?"

She bites her lip. "I mean… I wanted to say it in the right setting. Over a candlelit dinner, string quartet playing in the corner."

I chuckle—my first real laugh all day. "I don't need a goddamned string quartet. I just need *you*, Bianca. Because" —I swallow—"because I love you, too."

She widens her eyes. "You're not just saying that?"

"I would never just say that." I lean down, whisper

directly in her ear. "I love you more than I could ever express. I love your beautiful long hair, the way it almost glows, that's how light it is. I love your dark-blue eyes that are the color of the deepest sea, one I could happily get lost in forever. I love everything from your little button nose to your sweet, delicate toes. But more than anything, Bianca, I love your spirit. The way you lost yourself when you performed that song from *West Side Story* the night we met, and when I caught you singing in your apartment." I lift my head, meet her gaze. "Suffice to say, I love *you*, Bianca. More than I will ever love another person for as long as I live."

Her lips tremble, and a solitary tear runs down her cheek. "My God, Harrison."

"I mean every word of it, my angel." I brush the tear off her face and bring my lips back to hers.

The kiss is gentle at first. But then it deepens, and soon our lips, teeth, and tongues are clashing. It's not long before I'm heading back down to her beautiful pussy, licking her slit and playing with her delicate folds, doing everything in my power to pleasure the woman I love.

Soon she's thrashing, kicking her legs up in the air as I home in on her clit.

"Harrison... Harrison... *fuck!*"

I'm able to pull another climax out of her with ease. Then a third.

She whimpers as I leave her pussy and trail kisses up her beautiful body, stopping at each nipple on the way before I meet her gorgeous mouth once more. While we kiss, she unbuckles my belt and whips it off my waist.

"Bianca," I say. "I want you to suck my dick."

She giggles. "That was my next stop."

"No, but—" I eye the belt on the floor. "I want to give

myself to you fully. I want you... I want you to tie my hands behind my back with that belt."

She drops her jaw. "Really?"

"Yeah. I want to be restrained, give you free reign to place that beautiful mouth, your silky tongue, anywhere you want on my body."

She grins. "Twist my arm, why don't you?" She glances toward the suite's adjoining bedroom. "Might be a little comfier in the bedroom, though."

"Right." I help her to her feet and then lead her by the hand into the suite's bedroom. More of the same greens and pinks as the living room, with a king-sized bed topped with colorful throw pillows and an elegant down duvet. I toss the pillows off the bed and sit on the edge, turning my back toward Bianca and twisting my arms behind me.

She slowly wraps the belt around my wrists. I scoot over so my back is against the headboard. "Take my pants off," I command.

She unbuttons my jeans and slowly slips them down my legs. She peels each of my socks off but leaves my underwear.

"The undies, too," I say.

She smirks. "You seem to have forgotten who's in control right now."

Right. The whole point is letting her be in charge. It's harder to relinquish than I thought.

"Of course." I bow my head.

She tips my chin back up. "No. I want you to look at me. See everything I do to your beautiful body."

I chuckle darkly. "Have at it, my queen."

She blinks a few times at my chosen pet name—it's what the Kings call Rouge, so I probably could have chosen better—but as she breathes it in she seems to relish this new role.

My queen.

My beautiful queen.

She runs her arms up my legs, massaging them gently. It feels incredible, but my hard cock is aching behind my boxer briefs.

She descends to my feet, massages them as well. I can't remember the last time I had a foot massage, but damn! It feels fantastic.

But my feet aren't the part of me that wants her the most.

"Bianca... Please..."

She grins. "You want me to free that gorgeous cock of yours?"

"Yes. God, yes."

"Very well." She peppers kisses up my legs before reaching up the left leg hole of my boxer briefs, grazing my balls with her fingernails before wrapping her fingers around my dick. Her eyes widen. "You're so thick. I always forget how thick you are."

I grit my teeth. "It's all you, babe. You turn me on so much, make me so fucking hard."

She pulls my dick out through the leg hole and tenderly strokes it. It takes everything in me to not blow right now.

She finally pulls off my briefs.

I really have to strain when she finally wraps her lips around my head, licking it softly.

"Fuck, Bianca..."

She looks up, my dick still in her mouth, bouncing her eyebrows playfully. "We'll get there, love." She returns to my dick, running her lips up and down the shaft, driving me fucking nuts.

She accelerates and pretty soon I'm jackhammering into her skull. Normally I'd hold a woman's head while she sucks me, but mine are behind my back, so I have to put my hips into it. But it makes it feel ten times better than any other blow job I've gotten, even from Bianca.

She's sucking me up and down, up and down, up and down.

Finally I can't take it anymore. "Bianca, please... Sit on my dick."

She brushes a lock of hair from her face. "As my king commands." She straddles her legs over my body and then slowly sinks her pussy over my engorged cock.

And it's...everything.

She's just tight enough to hit every nerve ending in my dick. It's fucking phenomenal, and I'm quickly thrusting inside her, making her entire body bounce with my rhythm.

Her eyes roll back in her head as I hit her G-spot. "My God, Harrison. My God... My God... I'm going to... I'm going —" She throws her head back in orgasm number four.

The reverberations of her pussy clamp down on my dick, and with a few more shoves into her, I release.

It's volcanic, and her body twitches as I shoot inside her once, twice, three times. Filling the woman I love, taking her forever and never letting her go.

Without being asked, she unbuckles the belt and frees my wrists. I wrap my arms around her, kissing her warmly. We sink into a spooning position on the bed, and my heart thumps against hers.

As the post-sex haze falls over us, I pray we'll both be alive after this weekend has finished.

~

I'M AWAKE.

It feels early. The sun has barely begun to rise. I get up and pad to the living room to check my phone.

A little before seven a.m.

Good. We have the whole day.

I cross back into the bedroom, check on Bianca. She's still snoozing, her hair splayed across her head like a crown.

Even in the morning, she's beautiful.

And we finally confessed our true feelings for each other last night.

It's early in our relationship, but I couldn't give a rat's ass. When you know, you know.

And we know.

My stomach growls lightly. When was the last time we ate?

I grabbed a protein bar on my way to the hotel last night. We didn't eat dinner.

I'm hungry. I open the Google app on my phone and search for breakfast places nearby.

I don't want to go to a sit-down place. The less time we spend on the Chicago streets today, the better. But there's a bagel place just a few blocks away, one that claims to have bagels that rival New York's.

I'll let Bianca be the judge of that. She lived there for the better part of a decade.

I order a dozen assorted bagels along with some cream cheese and butter. The food delivery app says it will be ready in ten minutes. Perfect. Just enough time for me to put some clothes on and walk from the hotel. I scribble a quick note letting Bianca know what I'm up to and leave it on the bedside table.

I open my suitcase on the living area couch—it never made it to the bedroom—and pull out a clean pair of undies, socks, jeans, and a T-shirt. I slip them on and then put on my leather jacket. I call the elevator and the operator brings me to the ground floor.

I pull out the Maps app to figure out which direction to go after I exit the hotel. People always say it's easy to tell which way is which in Chicago, since Lake Michigan is due east. But it's hard to see which way the lake is when you're surrounded by buildings, so I've learned not to shame myself for using the tech at my disposal to figure out where the hell I am, even in a city that I'm familiar with.

I pull it up and am charting a route to the bagel place when I run into someone. I drop my phone, and I bend down to pick it up. "Sorry about that," I murmur.

"You should be. Watch where you're going." A man's voice.

I look up to tell him to watch his tone and my stomach flips. The man I ran into is wearing a charcoal suit with a navy tie pinned into place. Gray mustache and thinning silver hair.

I recognize him too late.

Mr. Rose, the patron at the club who tried to get in my pants Tuesday night.

The night we found the hearts.

The night everything fell into place.

And now he's here.

Fuck.

The hotel is called The Gilded *Rose*.

He's not the owner, is he?

I whip my head to the side, hoping he didn't see my face.

"Ace?" he asks quietly.

Too fucking late.

I blink a few times, return my gaze to his. "I'm afraid I don't know what you're talking about, sir."

Rose chuckles darkly. "Don't play coy with me, Ace. It didn't work Tuesday night, and it won't work now."

"Sir..."

He silences me with a finger to my mouth. "I thought you weren't supposed to talk."

Fuck. He's not going to think I'm someone else.

"When we're outside of the club, we can speak," I mutter.

He cocks his head. "And Rouge allows you to leave the club, wander the city unattended?"

"From time to time."

He presses his lips together. "But surely The Gilded Rose is a bit luxurious for a waiter's salary. I've run the place for years, and I've never seen a card here. Especially one who just started, who isn't yet taking"—he brushes a finger over my cheek—"*clients*."

"I came into a little money and treated my girlfriend to a weekend away," I say.

"But isn't Aces open on weekends?" Rose asks. "You'll be busy every evening while you're here."

Fuck.

I'm not thinking straight.

Time to nip this in the fucking bud.

"Can we speak in your office, Mr. Rose?" I ask. "I don't think Rouge would like to find out a patron of hers was speaking of the club so publicly."

He lifts his eyebrows. "I've known Rouge for years, Ace. I know far more about her than you."

Damn it.

Think fast, Harrison. Think fast.

I have one more ace to play—pun intended.

I steel myself and then run a finger over Rose's chest. "I really would prefer to meet somewhere *private*, Mr. Rose. If you get my drift."

He furrows his brow. "You're offering the services you denied me Tuesday night?"

"Think of it as an olive branch, sir." I bow my head, hoping Rose doesn't see how clenched my jaw is.

He glances toward the elevator. "And you're here with your girlfriend..."

"I swing both ways, sir."

"I'm not offering any money."

"Of course not. I want"—I grip his shoulders tightly—"I want *you*. No charge...this time."

Rose grins. "All right then. Right this way."

Into the lion's den I go.

I'm not going to have sex with Rose. But once I'm in his office, maybe I can talk my way out of this.

As Rose walks ahead, I grab my phone out of my pocket and start a voice memo. Maybe I can get Rose to say something I can use against him as leverage.

He opens the door. "After you, Ace."

"Right, sir." I walk inside.

Rose's office is decorated in the same colors as the suite Bianca and I are staying in. Green wallpaper, sparkling pink tiles on the floor. A dark wooden desk anchors the office's center, with two computer monitors, a large calendar, and a marble bust of a man I'm guessing is his father.

"I'm ready." He unbuttons his pants and displays his droopy dick and balls. "Get on your fucking knees and suck my cock."

Fuck. Why did I think this was a good idea?

I slink across the room, hoping inspiration will strike me before I find another man's penis in my mouth.

And then I see it on his desk.

A framed photo of Rose, a woman with a beehive hairdo, and three kids who all inherited his condescending smirk. Judging by the darker color of Rose's hair, this photo was taken fifteen years or so ago.

I pick up the photo. "This your family, Mr. Rose?"

"Never you mind who they are. Your business is here." He snaps his fingers and then points to his dick.

Thank God I chose to record this conversation.

I back up toward the door.

He cocks his head. "Where do you think you're going?"

I pull my phone out of my pocket, displaying the still-recording voice memo. "I think I now have what you might call leverage, Mr. Rose."

He widens his eyes. "You little bitch."

I point to the family photo. "I have a feeling *Mrs.* Rose might not be so happy to hear you've been cheating on her. With a man, no less."

"We didn't do anything, you prick."

"Yes, but you took your pants off and displayed your dick. I think that counts. Plus, I know you've slept with countless other men at Aces. The Jack of Hearts, for example."

It's a bluff, but I'm playing my odds.

Rose hastily rebuttons his pants, runs his fingers through his silver hair. "What do you want? I'll be happy to pay you off for your silence. I've got plenty of money. Name your price."

"No money. Just forget you saw me here. Don't mention it to Rouge or anyone else. My girlfriend and I are here on our own private business. It doesn't concern you." I tap on my phone. "But say anything and I'll make sure it does."

"Illinois is a two-party consent state, you know. You could get in trouble for releasing that recording."

"I'm sure I would, Mr. Rose. But as much trouble as I'd get in with the CPD, you'd be in twice as much with your wife." I glance around the room. "It's a nice hotel. I'm sure she'd love to get her hands on half of it in the divorce."

Rose squeezes his eyes shut, takes a deep breath in. "Fine. It's a deal. My silence for yours."

"Excellent." I open the door and exit the office. "Good-bye, Mr. Rose."

He doesn't respond as I close the door behind me and leave the lobby.

I'm proud of myself for thinking on my feet, worming my way out of that precarious situation. And all this early in the morning.

I played Rose like a fucking fiddle.

But as I walk through the revolving door onto Michigan Avenue, I can't help but wonder if I should have just killed the bastard.

17

BIANCA

I've lost track of how many nights I've performed at Aces.

I could pull out a calendar and count the nights. It's been several months at this point.

When I was trying to make it as an actress, I booked a few runs of shows at regional theaters. The longest run I had was twenty-two shows singing and dancing in the ensemble of White Christmas *with a dinner theater in Tennessee.*

Even with that long of a run, though, I remembered each individual show. I could tell you which moves I messed up on the twelfth show, which note I flubbed on the seventeenth, and how relieved I was to see the contract come to an end on the twenty-second.

But I've sung my set, largely unchanged since Rouge insists on sticking with the "tried and true" classics, far more than twenty-two times. I'm probably in the hundreds by now, and the performances are blending together.

Is this what I'm going to do forever?

I pack up my bag after my final set and exit through the

server's entrance out of the ladies' restroom. I'm in the same two-bedroom apartment I started renting when I moved back into town, but I'll be moving to a nicer one in a high-rise right in the middle of the Loop soon. Ever since I started taking clients into the private suites behind the velvet curtains at Aces, my income has quintupled. It's been nice returning to the lifestyle I grew up with. And at the low cost of throwing my dignity to the wind whenever a gentleman at Aces enlists my services.

But I abandoned that the day I slept with Mr. Shippe at the Reflections *callback. Once you pop, it's hard to stop.*

I walk up the three flights of stairs to my apartment. I won't miss the daily climb. My new place will have an elevator that opens right up to my apartment. Rent is steep, but I can afford it now.

I've barely closed the door and latched the chain behind me when a series of loud knocks reverberates from the other side.

I put my eye up to the peephole. It's Jack.

Shit. Did we have plans to hang tonight?

I completely forgot if we did.

I open the door, pasting on a smile. "Jack. I'm so sorry, were we supposed to do something tonight?"

He shakes his head. His eyes are wide, like he's seen a ghost. "No, we didn't. But can I come in?" He glances over his shoulder as if he's expecting someone to be following him. "There's something I need to talk to you about. Now."

"How'd you even get here?" I ask. "I usually give you a ride. And you guys aren't allowed to have phones, so it's not like you could have called an Uber."

"I hitchhiked."

I gasp. "Jack! That's so dangerous. Any weirdo could have picked you up and hacked you into pieces."

"Just goes to show how much I needed to talk to you." He walks into my apartment and slumps down on my couch. "Do you have any booze?"

"I'm afraid not. I usually only buy it when I'm expecting to have people over."

He runs his hands through his sandy hair. "It's okay. Probably best to say sober, anyway."

"Would you like a glass of water?"

He blinks a few times. "Sure."

I pop a few ice cubes out of the tray in my freezer and put three in one glass and a single one in another. According to Jack, Americans are obsessed with their drinks being cold. In Europe, ice is rarely included in water. I hold the two glasses under the tap and fill them up, bring them into my living room, and place them on two coasters on the coffee table.

Jack leans over and grabs his, brings it to his lips. "Thank you."

I sit down next to him. "What's going on?"

He closes his eyes, takes a deep breath in. "I guess I'd better start at the beginning."

I smirk. "A very good place to start."

We just watched The Sound of Music *the other night.*

Jack ignores my quip. "Rouge approached me yesterday after we closed up. Told me she wanted to talk with me about my 'career.' Said it was important, that she was considering me for a promotion."

"That's great news!"

"So you'd think. She told me she'd carve an hour out during tonight's service. Said she'd have the Two of Hearts cover for me so we could discuss what she had in mind."

"And?"

"So tonight, a few hours into service, I knocked on her office

door. And she welcomed me in, told me to take a seat. She told me how happy she was with my work ethic, with my loyalty to Aces since my contract started back in March, and that there was an opening for a new King of Hearts."

"Really?"

"Yeah. She told me I was allowed to speak, so I asked what it would entail. I mean, I know the Kings work security, but there always seemed to be more to the gig from what I could tell. So Rouge told me the Kings are her confidantes, and they also serve as her personal assistants. They do things like pick up her dry cleaning. Apparently the King of Hearts is the King she depends on the most, so it was a big deal to ask me. I guess the last guy didn't live up to her expectations."

I press my lips together. I remember the last King of Hearts. I didn't interact with him a whole lot, since he mostly stood in the corner of the Hearts section staring ahead stoically like a Buckingham Palace guard. I have no idea what he might have done to get fired.

"She went on, telling me I would no longer be expected to sell my body to the club patrons, that my compensation from just serving as a King would double the current amount I'm making."

"But don't the Kings... Don't they service Rouge herself? *Like... sexually?"*

"Yeah. She mentioned that. But she told me she was aware of my sexual orientation, that I wasn't into women. She said the other three Kings could take care of her in that way. She would just need me to be emotionally available, the way I am to you."

My eyebrows nearly fly off my forehead. "She's aware that we're friends?"

"I don't think there's anything that goes on at Aces that Rouge isn't aware of," he replies. "But anyway, after that it started getting

weird. She pulled out a little red pouch, a little bigger than a coin purse. She then produced this stringy-looking mushroom."

I cock my head. "What?"

THE SOUND of the front door of our room opening knocks me out of my thoughts.

My pulse quickens, but it ebbs as I realize it's Harrison, back from getting breakfast.

He's been gone a while.

I started rousing right as he left. I found the note he left for me. It's been nearly a half hour since then. Did he go halfway across town to get breakfast?

But no. He's holding bags from Jubb & Jubb Bagels, which is just around the corner.

Maybe they were slow this morning.

I wrap my arms around his neck and give him a kiss. "Morning, handsome."

"Morning, beautiful." He sets the bag on the table. "This place claims to be the best New-York-style bagel in Chicago."

"They're pretty good," I say. "I've gone there before."

He pulls out an everything bagel. "They put a *lot* of cream cheese on this one."

"I'll take it." I giggle. "You'll find I'm able to consume an unnatural amount of cream cheese."

He grins. "My kind of woman."

I take a bagel, bite into it. It's not quite the quality of my favorite place in midtown Manhattan, but it's pretty damned close.

Maybe it's just the company.

I like Harrison. I *love* Harrison.

And even though we have plans to accomplish the unthinkable this evening, I'm not going to let that ruin the entire day I have with him.

I chew through my bite and swallow. "So, *Doctor*. We have the whole day to ourselves. What would you like to do?"

18

HARRISON

You, IS MY FIRST THOUGHT.

Even with sesame seeds on her lips from the everything bagel, even with the onion breath she's going to have after eating the whole thing, even with the adorable smudge of cream cheese in the corner of her mouth...

Bianca is the most beautiful woman on this planet.

The woman I love more than anything, despite having known her for barely a week.

Funny. That's how Maddox told me he felt about Alissa, and I held back laughter then.

Now I get it.

When you meet the right person, it's instantaneous. I fell in love with Bianca practically the moment I met her.

More importantly, I now know she loves me back.

I scoot my chair in the hotel room's breakfast nook next to hers. "I'd like to keep a low profile today, obviously. Definitely want to check in with Alissa and Maddox."

"Of course. That's a given." She takes another bite of her bagel and swallows. "Anything else? I grew up in Chicago, and I've been back for five years, but I've never done the tourist traps."

I flash her a smile. "Neither have I, if I'm honest." I lean back in my chair. "We could take a walk through Millennium Park, maybe to Navy Pier, see what's going on there. Stop in Lou Malnati's or Pequod's and grab some deep dish. As long as we keep to ourselves, we won't have to worry about your sister finding out what we're up to."

She wipes some cream cheese off her chin. "How about the botanical gardens? I've heard they're lovely."

"I've heard the same." I lean in and brush my lips against hers. "Though no flower can match your beauty."

She smirks. "Why do I feel like you've used that line on a woman before?"

"Maybe I have." I shrug. "But I mean it when I say it to you."

She blushes at my words. "Honestly, I don't care what we do. As long as we're together. Hell, as far as I'm concerned, we could just hang out in the hotel room naked all day."

I immediately start getting hard. I was already halfway there just from her presence, but now I'm at full mast. I give her a grin. "There are worse ways to spend a day."

She slowly unties the belt of the terrycloth robe she's wearing, lets it fall around her shoulders. "Oh?"

"Fuck, Bianca." I sweep an arm under her and take her into my arms, carrying her like a damned baby. "Do you realize how much you drive me crazy?"

"About the same amount you drive *me* crazy."

I start to carry her to the hotel bedroom, eyeing the extra cream cheese that came with the bagels—I bet we can put that to some good use—when there's a rap at the door.

"Ignore it," she says.

"Yes, my queen."

But then the knocking again, this time more insistent.

Her eyes widen. "It can't be…*her*, can it?"

"God damn it." I lower her to the floor. "He said he wouldn't say a word."

"He?"

"Just get in the bedroom. Lock the door. Open it for no one except for me."

"Harrison—"

"*Now,*" I growl.

She blinks a few times but then scampers into the bedroom, closing the door behind her.

I turn toward to the knocking and open the door.

A bellhop stands there. Freckled face, wiry red hair. Can't be older than twenty-one.

Maybe I freaked out for nothing.

"Yes?" I ask.

"Hi, sir. My name is Blake." He gestures to his nametag. "Mr. Rose himself sent me up here."

My heart starts thrumming. "Why?"

"He… He wanted to thank you for your patronage, sir." He blinks several times. "It sounds like you're an old friend of his."

I exhale sharply. "Something like that."

"He wants to upgrade you to the executive suite, effective immediately. No additional charge."

I furrow my brow. Rose really doesn't want me spilling the beans about his extramarital affairs. I guess this is his way of sweetening the pot.

Blake peers inside. "If you'd like, sir, I can take your suitcases now as a courtesy. Then you and your companion can make your way up to the suite on the twelfth floor at your leisure."

"Of course." I gesture to Bianca's and my suitcases still sitting by the couch. "They're right there."

"Excellent, sir." He reaches into his jacket pocket and pulls out two keycards. "These will get you into the room. Your items will be waiting for you there." He grabs the suitcases and places them on a luggage cart out in the hallway. "Take your time, sir. But if I may, the executive suite is truly remarkable. You'll want to maximize your time there."

"Will do." I wave the bellhop off and then knock on the bedroom door. "It's me. Everything's okay."

She opens the door. "I heard someone come into the living room."

"Just the bellhop." I shrug. "Apparently we've been upgraded to the executive suite."

She cocks her head. "We have?"

"Yeah. I may have run into some higher-ups in the lobby while grabbing our breakfast."

Her posture softens. "Oh. So *that's* why you took so long getting us breakfast."

I chuckle. "Networking, I suppose."

Really more blackmail than networking, but Bianca doesn't need to know the details. I've already riled her up thinking the bellhop was some disguised assassin, so I'll fill her in on my encounter with Mr. Rose later.

In the meantime, I want to fuck the living daylights out of her in our new and improved suite. "Come on. The bellhop already grabbed our suitcases. Let's head up." I hand her one of the keycards.

She places it in a large pocket in her bathrobe and then nods, eyeing my bulge. "Let's do it."

We whisk out of the room and take the elevator up to the twelfth floor, following the signs to the executive suite.

It puts our last suite to shame.

Elegant velvet couches in the corner surrounding a marble coffee table and a wood-burning fireplace. A kitchenette stacked to the brim with gleaming stainless-steel appliances. Glossy eggshell tiles on the floor, and an elegant chandelier glowing in the center. In an opposite corner stands a black baby grand piano, and abstract art lines the walls.

Bianca frowns. “Our suitcases aren’t in here.”

“They’re probably in the bedroom,” I growl. “Care to join them in there?”

She grins, fire in her eyes. “I’d love to.” She crosses the room and opens the door to the bedroom. “Harrison, take a look at this!”

I walk in behind her. A majestic four-poster bed in a dark oak frame centers the room. Elegant velvet curtains resembling the ones at Aces surround it. An antique dresser and armoire stand at its side across from a vintage vanity.

But I’m mostly interested in the bed. Especially since Bianca has just lain down on it and spread her legs.

I suck in a breath. “God, you’re gorgeous.”

“You, too.” She glances around the grandiose bedroom. “And well connected, it would seem. How did you manage to talk your way into the upgrade?”

“I’ll tell you later.”

“No. Tell me now. I want to know my man’s secrets, how he moves about the world with such an air of confidence.” Her eyes smolder. “It’s hot.”

I chuckle. “It’s not actually that impressive. I ran into the man who owns the hotel downstairs, and he recognized me.”

"A patient of yours from St. Charles?" she asks.

I shake my head. "He didn't recognize me from the hospital. He recognized me from Aces."

Her eyebrows shoot up. "What?"

"It's okay, babe. He recognized me as the Ace of Clubs from Tuesday evening."

"But—"

I press a finger against her pretty lips. "I took care of it. He was… He was trying to take me behind the curtains at Aces. But obviously I refused his advances."

She strokes her chin. "Really?"

I shrug. "I guess both sexes find me attractive."

"I certainly do." She tousles my hair.

"But anyway, turns out he has a wife and family. So when I figured that out, I told him if he didn't want them finding out about his little extramarital exploration, he'd keep silent about seeing me at the hotel."

"Good thinking."

"I thought so. It led me to you nearly naked in this magnificent suite."

She giggles. "Who was it? I always enjoy hearing the tea about the Aces patrons. So many of them act so high and mighty. I love hearing about the sticky situations they land themselves in."

"Of course you do." I brush a lock of hair off her forehead. "It was Mr. Rose."

She sits up with a start, knocking me to the side of the bed. "Mr. Rose? As in *Florian* Rose?"

I frown. "I don't know his first name."

She looks around the room uneasily. "And he *owns* this hotel?"

"Yeah, he does. But babe, it's okay. I fixed it—"

She raises a finger, the color completely drained from her face. “Harrison. We have to get out of here right *now.*”

19

BIANCA

"SHE OFFERED YOU A SHROOM?" I ASK.

Jack cocks his head. "Shroom?"

"It's slang. For magic mushrooms. Psychedelics."

"Oh, yes." Jack scratches the side of his head. "She said that if I were going to be brought on as a King, I had to—how did she put it?—go on a trip with her. Take the mushroom and continue discussing the position."

I narrow my eyes. "How exactly would taking a mind-altering substance help her determine whether you were the right fit for the position?"

"That's what I asked her. She told me it was a test of my merit as a physical specimen, as well as my loyalty to Aces. She did say I could turn it down, but then I would not be looking at a promotion anymore. It seemed like a weird requirement, but it's not like Rouge does things by the book anyway. I figured there was no harm, that if I could stop providing my physical services to the bloated male patrons of the club and make twice as much money, it would be a good trade-off."

"So you took the shroom?"

He nods. "I started seeing these vivid images almost immediately. Rouge told me it was normal, that I would have visions. She apparently had genetically modified them, enhanced their effects."

"What did you see?"

His eyelids tremble. "Lots of things. I was on a beach, but the ocean was made of a sticky red syrup. And then I was in a library, but the books kept turning into bats and flying around my head. The visions weren't pleasant at all. Like the stuff you see when you have a bad dream. And I kept shifting between those visions and what I think was real."

"You think?"

"It was hard to tell. Even when I was clearly back in Rouge's office—or, rather, in the bedroom attached to her office—the things I saw, they weren't quite real." He swallows. "At least, I think they weren't..."

I lean in. "How do you mean?"

"Well... When I first came back to reality, I realized I was in this big bed, the kind with curtains around it. And my shorts had been taken off."

I drop my jaw. "You were naked?"

"Yes. And then..." His face twists. "Someone was fucking me."

"Rouge?"

"No. She made it very clear we would never do anything physical. But someone else was...inside me."

"Who?"

He bites his lip. "Mr. Rose."

"The patron? Florian Rose?"

He nods slowly.

Mr. Rose normally sticks to the Clubs section, but I've seen him come to Hearts, usually to talk to Jack. He's taken a special liking to him and has taken him behind the velvet curtains often.

He's always seemed like a creep, but apparently Jack has made top dollar servicing him. He's grinned and borne it because of the carrots Mr. Rose has dangled in front of his nose.

"But Rouge didn't clarify that someone would be fucking you during your trip. And you couldn't have possibly consented once you were under the influence." I take his face in his hands. "That's rape, Jack."

Again he nods, his eyes wide. "Yes, it was. But that's nothing compared to what I saw next."

I blink. "How could anything possibly be worse than that?"

He draws in a slow breath. "The second time I came to, a second person lay in the bed next to me. A woman."

"Rouge?"

"No. The Two of Hearts. The girl who was supposed to cover me on my shift."

"Was Mr. Rose fucking her as well?"

"No. She was just lying there...and then the visions took over again."

"What do you remember after that?"

"Next thing I remember, I was in this embrace with Rouge."

"She was hugging you?"

*"No. More like she was holding me down." He frowns. "But there was a...*tenderness *to it. It's hard to explain."*

No. I get it. I've been in that exact same position. The position where you're being forced into a false kind of intimacy. The men who take me behind the curtains at the club do it all the time. And I remember Rouge doing it at least once as well...

Story for a different time.

Right now I'm focusing on Jack.

"Anything else?"

"Yes." The color drains from his face. "It was... I mean... Rouge was holding me down, and eventually she turned my head to the side of the bed. And... It was Two again."

"What about her?"

"She was on the floor at this point. And Mr. Rose was over her, pressing a finger to her neck. He said something to Rouge, but I couldn't understand it. And then...he took out a saw."

"A saw?"

"Like the tool. And he placed it against Two's neck. Rouge made me watch as he... As he..." He starts breathing heavily, his eyes wide.

I run into my kitchen and grab a paper bag. I hand it to him. "Here. Breathe into this."

He does, and eventually his breathing slows.

"What did Mr. Rose do to Two?"

Jack steels himself, slowly delivers his answer. "He... He sawed her head off. Removed it from her body."

I gasp. "He didn't!"

"He did. Rouge made me watch the whole thing. He did the same with her hands, sawed them off, too."

My stomach is churning. This can't be true... My sister is a little cuckoo, but she's not this.

"And then...he took a silver chalice, and he... He held her wrist over it, filled it with her blood."

I can't speak. There are no words.

"He took a drink of her blood. Then he gave it to Rouge. Then she gave it to me."

"Did you drink it?"

"No. I couldn't. I couldn't really do anything except just lie there. I was terrified they were going to do the same thing to me. And then...I started sinking into the bed, into the fiery depths of hell itself."

"The shrooms..." I say.

"Exactly. Next thing I know, I'm back in Rouge's office. She tells

me that, regrettably, I failed the test, but that I'm welcome to stay on as the Jack of Hearts."

I scratch the side of my head. "Just like that?"

He nods. "Just like that. I got up and tried to leave the office, but I was locked in. Rouge told me to sit down. Feeling like I had no other choice, I did. She told me that sometimes people have adverse reactions to using the mushrooms. She's still tinkering with their genetic makeup and hasn't quite figured out the right potency yet. She told me I had a bad trip, that if I saw anything frightening or traumatic while under the influence, that it was the mushrooms. My brain playing tricks on me."

I bite my lip. "So... Is that what you think happened?"

He raises an eyebrow. "Bianca?"

I clasp my hands together. "I just mean... It sounds like you had a bad trip."

"I know *what I saw, Bianca."*

"I believe that you believe *that, Jack. But what you're talking about is stuff out of some true-crime podcast. This is Rouge I'm talking about. She's a lot, to be sure—I could tell you stories from our childhood that would shock the color from your hair—but she's not the kind of person who hacks people's heads off, drinks their blood."*

He looks at me, really looks at me, not even blinking. "My God. You're one of them."

I scrunch my eyebrows. "What do you mean?"

"The Montroses. All of you. You're rotten to the core."

"You don't mean that, Jack."

He gathers his things, hustles to the door of my apartment. "Yeah, I fucking do."

I cross the room, grab his arm. "You're not going to quit, are you?"

He whips his arm out of my grasp. "Can't very well do that, can I? Rouge sponsored my green card. Without her, I'll be sent back to the little hovel I grew up in. I thought if I told you what I saw, you'd help me."

"Jack, you have to calm down."

"Besides. If I tried to leave Aces, Rouge would think I didn't dismiss the whole thing as a trip. She'd have my *head next."*

"Rouge would never do anything like that—"

"Of course that's what you'd think. You're her sister. You share the exact DNA that makes her an evil bitch." He opens the door, looks over his shoulder. "Guess that makes you an evil bitch, too."

"Jack, please—"

But he's slammed the door behind him, rattling my entire apartment. The glass of water he was drinking from falls off the coffee table, shattering on the hardwood floor of my living room.

Fragmented into pieces, just like my heart.

I GRAB HARRISON'S HANDS. "Mr. Rose is one of Rouge's closest confidantes. Besides her Kings, he's the one she trusts the most."

"But babe, I told you—"

"You don't understand. When I say he's a confidante, I mean... I think he's part of the organ harvesting process. I think he might have been the person who cut off May's head!"

Harrison drops his jaw. "No. It can't be."

"Jack told me years ago he saw Mr. Rose doing it to another person. But he was high off his mind on shrooms at the time, so I dismissed it. That's why we had that big falling out. But now, knowing what we know now, I don't think it *was* a bad trip."

He rubs at the back of his neck. "Fuck."

"You're telling me. We have to get the hell out of this hotel. Right now." I get off the bed and pad into the living room of the executive suite. I make a beeline for the door and turn the handle.

And my heart sinks.

Because it's locked from the outside.

20

HARRISON

"Please tell me you're joking," I say.

She shakes her head, her lips trembling. "No. It's locked. We're trapped in here, Harrison."

I charge ahead, grip the doorknob with all my strength, and pull.

It won't budge.

I yank on the door, kick at it, pound at it until my knuckles are bleeding.

Fuck!

Rose upgraded our suite not to ensure my silence, but to lock us away. Probably until he can get in contact with Rouge and have one of her Kings come up and take care of us. And then, best case scenario, we'll end up imprisoned like Maddox and Alissa. Worst case, we'll be ripped open with our organs sold on the black market.

I reach into my pocket for my phone. Shit! I took it out of my pocket earlier and the bellhop must have scooped it up when he grabbed our bags. I run to the bedroom to see if he left our suitcases in there, but I already know they're not here.

We have no way of getting out of this room. And none of our personal effects—no phones, wallets, keys…

I sit down on the velvet couch in the living area, pinching the bridge of my nose. "I think I royally fucked things up, Bianca."

She sits beside me. "There's no way you could have known this was a trap. You didn't know what Mr. Rose was capable of."

I shake my head. "I knew he was a fucking asshole. I should have known he couldn't be trusted. I thought I had him cornered, but I was just playing right into his damned hand."

She pats my hand. "He can't keep us in here forever."

"No. Just long enough for him to walk over to Aces, collect Rouge, and tell her he has her star singer and a man who's been disguising himself as one of her employees on his security footage."

"Rouge doesn't know that we know about the organs."

"It doesn't matter." I slide my fingers through my hair. "She'll be able to easily figure out it was me disguised as the Ace on Tuesday night. And she'll know you're involved. It won't be that hard for her to deduce what we discovered from there."

She pops to her feet. "Then we'd better think fast."

"It won't make any difference. He's probably on the phone with Rouge right now."

Bianca's eyes gleam. "One other thing about my sister. She doesn't have a cell phone."

My eyebrow shoot up. "She doesn't?"

"She has a secure landline at her home, and she uses a walkie-talkie when she's on the Aces grounds. But she likes to keep people at a distance, and not having a cell phone is how she accomplishes that."

I jump off the couch. "Then...shit. We might be able to beat him to the punch."

She paces around the room. "The fastest Mr. Rose could get the information to her would be if he drove to her home. And that's if he knows where she lives. Rouge is notoriously tightlipped about her private life. Even I don't know her address."

"So depending on where she lives, we probably have a half hour or so."

"And that's *if* he knows. Otherwise, he won't be able to get in contact with her until tonight, when Aces opens."

"Okay." I scan the suite. God, it's the nicest prison I've ever seen. The front door isn't an option, but there is a sliding glass door that leads to a sizeable balcony.

We're on the twelfth floor, though. Even if we made a rope out of bedsheets and somehow *didn't* slip to our deaths, it wouldn't be long enough to make it to the ground.

But maybe...

Maybe we don't *have* to get to the ground.

Just to the balcony of a room that isn't locked.

I grip the handle of the sliding glass door, but it's sealed shut.

No matter.

I take a heavy-looking modern sculpture off one of the side tables by the couch and ram it against the glass. It takes a few tries, but I eventually shatter it.

Bianca gasps.

I glance over my shoulder. "Guess they'll have to take that out of our incidentals charge." I gesture to the bedroom. "Come on. We can make a rope out of the bedsheets and swing down to the balcony below. That room hopefully won't be locked from the outside, so we'll be able to break in and get free."

"What if there's someone in the room already?" Bianca looks down at the plush bathrobe she's wearing. "Need I remind you this is all I have to wear?"

Shit. I changed before I went to get breakfast, but Bianca has only the robe. And the bellhop never dropped off our bags.

"We'll figure it out," I say. "Worst case, we'll pop into a thrift shop and buy you some clothes."

"With what money? I'm assuming you don't have your wallet on you, either."

Fuck. She's right.

"Again, we'll figure it out. Right now our only priority is to get the fuck out of here before Rose can get in contact with your sister. After that, we'll take it one step at a time."

She draws in a slow breath. "Okay." She heads toward the bedroom, returns with all the sheets in a bundle, and throws them down on a Turkish rug near the sliding glass doors. "Do you know how to make a rope?"

"I think so. We'll have to cut the sheet into strips." I look around. "Anything around here that we could use?"

"Maybe there are some knives in the kitchenette." Bianca crosses the room and opens a few small drawers. She pulls out a chef knife. "Bingo!"

I scoff. "As if anyone who ever rents this room would cook for themselves. But I'll take a win where I can." I hand her the sheet. "You hold it taut while I cut it into strips."

Soon we have a dozen strips of cloth at our feet.

"The next thing we do is braid the sheets into makeshift

ropes. That way they'll be stronger and we won't have to worry about them breaking under our weight."

She nods. "I can do that. I'm sure a flat braid will work just fine. I have lots of practice from braiding my dolls' hair when I was growing up. Never thought I'd use those skills to save my own hide, but here we are."

She lays the strips parallel to one another and slowly weaves them around each other. It takes a while, but within the next forty-five minutes, we have a few yards' worth of material to work with.

"This should be enough for us to swing down to the next balcony," I say.

"But will it be strong enough?" Bianca asks.

"Only one way to find out." I secure the rope to the edge of the balcony, give it a few strong pulls, and then sweep my right leg over the side of the balcony.

"Harrison, no!" Bianca cries out. "We need to test it first."

"We don't have time, babe. It's been nearly an hour since we were locked in this room. We need to neutralize Rose quickly." I wave her over.

"There must be some other—"

"There isn't." I reel her in for a quick kiss. "If anything happens to me, know that I love you more than anything in the world."

"I love you, too." She wipes a tear from her cheek.

I grin. "See you on the other side."

I bring my other leg to the exterior of the balcony and then, before I can think better of it, I take a leap of faith.

The rope holds, and I swing down onto the balcony of the room below us.

"Harrison?" Bianca calls from above.

"It's okay. The rope held."

"All right. I'm coming after you."

I'm not as worried now. If the rope held me, it'll certainly be able to bear Bianca's weight.

She swings down into my open arms and I help her down to her feet.

Her eyes are wide. "I would like to never do that again."

"Deal." I give her another kiss and then gaze into the hotel room.

Damn. It looks lived-in. A few pieces of clothing strewn about the floor, an open suitcase on a luggage rack, and a few faint curls of steam coming from the bathroom door.

"They're in the shower," I say. "We have to get in quickly."

I slide the door open, looking around. No one else in the room. It's a straight line to the front door. Good.

We'll have to act quickly.

I steal into the room and make a beeline to the front. I'm just about to make it when I find an answer to our next problem—getting Bianca some clothes—lying on top of the room's minifridge.

A man's wallet, stuffed to the brim with bills.

Finally, a fucking break for the two of us.

I reach in and grab a few hundred-dollar bills.

"Harrison!" Bianca hisses.

"I'll gladly come back and give this guy twice as much as we've taken once we've gotten the hell out of here." I stuff the bills into my pants pocket. "For now, we need a little cash if we're going to get around. We—"

The shower turns off.

Fuck.

I gesture to the door. "Now!" I whip it open and the two of us clear the room before its occupant can discover us. We run down the hall and I pound the elevator button so hard that its tiny plastic casing cracks.

I'm not sure what our next move is, but we have about thirty seconds before we hit the lobby.

Operating solely on instinct, I head to the front desk. It's manned by someone different from when we checked in, a young man with medium-length dark hair.

He smiles as we approach him, but there's a tenseness to his face. Probably caused by the fact that Bianca is still in a bathrobe.

One crisis at a time.

"Hello, sir. Ma'am. Are you locked out of your room?"

"No. Nothing like that. Actually, we're the couple Mr. Rose just gave a complimentary upgrade to. We wanted to see him and thank him in person for his generosity."

"Of course." The young man rakes his gaze over me, his eyes narrowed. "I understand perfectly."

I hold back an eye roll. Mr. Rose probably brings call boys to this hotel all the time, gives them nice rooms. Of course, I have Bianca with me. I doubt said male escorts have a woman with them. I guess he could be bisexual. He is married with kids, after all.

A three-way with him and Bianca is the last thing on my mind.

"Mr. Rose is in his office." The receptionist picks up a phone. "I'll give him a ring and let him know to expect you."

I hold up a hand. "Please don't. We're hoping to surprise him." I add a wink to seal the meaning of my words.

He swallows. "Oh. Of course. Go right ahead then, sir."

I'll have to take a long shower after all this.

We walk over to the mahogany door. I take a deep breath to center myself and then open it.

Rose is at his desk on the phone. He drops his jaw as we walk in, and Bianca quickly runs to the other side of the office and whips the phone cord out of the wall.

"What... What are you doing here?" he gasps out.

I don't answer him. I leap across the room, soar over his desk with my hands outstretched, and wrap them around his neck. He coughs, sputters, and his eyes start to bulge out of their sockets.

But before I can get him unconscious, he kicks me in the balls.

Oh fuck!

Pain. Such fucking pain! It shoots through my whole body.

I hunch over on the ground in agony.

He scrambles to his feet. But before he can hurt me again, Bianca smacks him across the face with the marble bust of his father.

I get up in time to see blood gushing out of his nose as he turns on Bianca. No way in hell is he going to lay a finger on her. Despite the pains still hurdling through my lower body, I get to my feet, throw myself between the two of them, and land a right hook to Rose's left cheek. Then an uppercut for good measure.

He stumbles back but quickly returns with a punch to my gut. I double over and he lands a kick to the back of my knees, bringing me down again.

The floor is strewn with pens and pieces of stationery. I grab the nearest item to me—a navy-blue fountain pen—and get back to my feet.

Rose is advancing again, but this time I have a weapon.

Before Rose can land another hit, I raise the pen and ram it right into his left eye.

21

BIANCA

I HATE THE SIGHT OF BLOOD.

And this office is now flooded with it.

First from Mr. Rose's nose, and now from his eye. A blue fountain pen sticks out of it. Rose instinctively grabs at it, but before he can pull it out—and likely his eye along with it—he trips on a three-hole punch on the ground, falls backward, and hits the base of his skull on the side of his desk.

He's on the ground now. And he's not moving.

"My God, Harrison." I walk slowly toward his body. "Is he… Is he dead?"

Harrison kneels and takes his pulse. "No. Just unconscious. The blow to his skull plus the loss of blood. But he needs immediate medical attention if he's going to live or have any chance of regaining sight in his left eye."

I swallow. "Should we take him to the hospital?"

"Someone should, but it's not going to be us." He gets to his feet and offers me his hand. "The two of us need to get the hell out of here before the cops show up. We'll let someone at the front desk know Rose had an accident or something, and then we'll get the hell out of here."

I look around, my heart pounding into my throat. "Does Mr. Rose have any cameras in here? The footage of you jamming a pen into his eye will look pretty damning."

He crosses his arms. "It was in self-defense."

"But you attacked first. It's not going to look good. I know what this man is capable of, but the rest of the world doesn't." I continue to scan the area. "It doesn't look like there are any cameras, though."

He chuckles darkly. "Of course not. He probably takes young male callers in here often. The guy at the front desk didn't seem surprised to see me. Rose wouldn't want any video evidence of his affairs to exist."

I bite my lip. "I guess not."

"That said, there is certainly footage of the two of us *entering* his office right before all of this, so we still need to move quickly." He grabs my hand. "Come on."

We open the door to the office and leave, closing it behind us.

Harrison runs up the front desk, a veil of concern atop his face. "Sir," he says to the receptionist. "Mr. Rose got a little... spirited in our meeting. He ended up with a bad injury to his eye. You'll want to call 911 and make sure he's taken care of."

The young man widens his eyes. "Oh, God. What happened?"

"I'm not at liberty to say. Client confidentiality and all that. But I'd call now if I were you. He needs immediate medical attention."

"Right." The receptionist pulls out a pad of paper. "And what was your name again, sir?"

I step forward. "His name is Ace."

He scrunches his eyebrows. "Like the card?"

"Exactly. And my name is Whitney Royale. We're guests of Mr. Rose's. Seriously, call 911 right now. It doesn't look pretty in there."

"Right. Will do." He pounds the three numbers into his phone.

Before he looks back up, Harrison and I have slipped out the revolving door onto Michigan Avenue, with nothing but the clothes—or lack thereof—on our backs.

22

HARRISON

Bianca and I made it out of the hotel safely. I wasn't sure what our move would be from there, but she suggested we hunker down at the Harold Washington Library for a few hours. It's huge, with several hidden corners. We slipped into a thrift store on the way and bought a sweater, skirt, and a pair of tennis shoes for Bianca.

Luckily, there's no charge to go inside the library. We found a table behind a large display of dystopian fiction—something I feel like I've been living through myself—and began to collect ourselves.

I was hoping we could stop by the hospital to check on Alissa and Maddox, but if the cops figure out who I am from the security footage at the Gilded Rose, the hospital will be the first place they'll go. Maybe I'll get on one of the computers available here at the library, log on to Facebook, and try to message Dinah. We're not Facebook friends, so she might not see my message immediately. She probably doesn't have her phone on her anyway. The nurses typically keep their phones in their lockers to make sure they stay focused on the patients' needs.

"They might think it was an accident," Bianca says. "That's what we told them."

I exhale sharply. "How exactly does a man *accidentally* shove a fountain pen into his eye?"

"A very poorly timed fall?"

"Sure." I rub at my forehead. "Let's assume that could happen. Even then, we were the last two people who went into Rose's office before it happened. The cops would want to hear our side of the story."

"Fair enough. So it's a race against time then."

I nod. "We need to implicate your sister as soon as possible. Then we'll be able to connect her to what happened in Rose's office, and the cops will understand we were acting in self-defense."

"Which is perfectly legal."

"Exactly." I sigh. "And here I thought staying in a hotel would make our day *less* complicated."

She pats my hand. "We had no way of knowing."

I shake my head. "I should have looked up who was in charge. I didn't know Rose was Rouge's confidante, but I *did* know he was a handsy little fucker. That he had some connection to Aces."

"You'd be hard-pressed to find a place in this city with*out* a connection to Aces," Bianca says. "Rouge has her fingers in everything. Any hotel in town—certainly the nice ones—could harbor someone who's in her pocket."

"Then we should have stayed in some skeezy motel."

She laughs. "That's almost worse than what we went through at the Gilded Rose."

I look at her, really look at her. After all we've been

through, she's still able to make a little joke. Neither of us is exactly rolling in the aisles at it, but she's found a touch of levity in this gravely dangerous moment.

God, I love her so much.

I grab her hand. Squeeze it. "I wouldn't take it back, you know."

She raises an eyebrow. "Changing the hotel?"

"No. Meeting you. It's been fucking crazy from the get-go, but even if I had to go through all of it again, I'd do it all over if it meant meeting you."

She blushes. "You're just saying that."

"No. I'm really not. I can't believe I went to the club with Maddox all those years and never turned my attention to Hearts. I'd have fallen head over heels for you then and there."

She looks down. "You'd have fallen for a woman who sells herself to the highest bidder?"

A tiny pinch of jealousy tweaks my heart at her words, but I swallow it down. I don't care about her history as long as she's mine now. I tip her chin up, bring her gaze to mine. "I wouldn't have cared. Just as long as you felt for me what I felt for you."

She swallows. "I'm not going to do it anymore, you know. I mean, if things ever go back to normal, I'm done. I want you to be the last person I ever sleep with, Harrison."

I lean across the table and press a chaste kiss to her lips. "You're my once and forever."

She smiles. "I love you."

"I love you, too."

The words fall out of me so easily. Like we've been married half our lives and I've been saying them for years.

We stare into each other's eyes for a few fleeting moments

before Bianca looks at her watch. "It's about time to make our way to Aces."

"Great." Then I realize something. "Wait. You can't go on wearing a sweater and a skirt. You look lovely, but you'll need a gown."

"No problem there," she says. "I keep a spare gown in my dressing room for emergencies. You'd be shocked how many times men spill drinks on me or tear my dress when they're" —a flush crosses her face—"disrobing me."

Another spear of jealousy lances through my heart at the thought, but again she just told me she's done with that for good, so I let it evaporate.

"And there's a spare pair of shorts for me?"

She nods. "Easily. And you obviously won't need anything else for the uniform beyond that."

Right. I'm not looking forward to being next to naked again in the club. Makes you wonder how the rest of the wait-staff feel. I guess they learn to grin and bear it.

At least Rose won't be there. He was trying to get into my tiny shorts the last time I disguised myself as the Ace of Clubs. That won't be the case tonight. The pen protruding from his eye is a good reason to take the night off.

"I also keep a spare car key there," Bianca continues. "And my car is still parked in the Gilded Rose garage, so I'll steal over there once things finish, and I'll be able to follow you on the bus back to the Caterpillar."

"Good thinking," I say.

"Never thought *this* would be the reason I'd use it, but I've learned to roll with the punches the last few days." Her lip twitches.

I sigh. "Understatement of the fucking *century*."

We make our way to Aces, sneak through the back entrance that leads to the ladies' restroom, and slip into Bianca's dressing room unnoticed. We quickly clamber into our outfits for the night, and I can't help sneaking a glance when Bianca's tits spill out of the sweater we bought at the thrift shop. She's perfection. But we don't have time for a quick roll in the hay right now, as much as the blood currently rushing to my cock would like that.

She slinks into her spare gown. It's a tight little black dress, which makes me even crazier.

"That's different from the dresses you normally wear."

She grins. "Yeah, Rouge likely wouldn't approve. The spare dress is black, in case I get a drink spilled on me a second time in a night. That way it doesn't show up as much."

"Will Rouge wonder why you're starting the night in your spare dress?"

She shrugs. "I'll tell her the rest of my gowns are at the cleaners."

"If you're going to play the opposite tonight, you should accessorize." I walk across the room to the pile of stuff from Rouge's office scattered in the corner of Bianca's dressing room. I pick up a dark-gray fedora, the kind Maddox often wears.

Shit, this might actually *be* Maddox's hat. He probably wore it the last night he came to the club with Alissa. Rouge probably threw it in this corner.

All the more reason for Bianca to don it tonight.

She looks at herself in the mirror. "I look like I'm about to play Sally Bowls in *Cabaret*."

"And maybe this time, you'll get lucky." I plant a kiss on her, grind my crotch into hers.

Her face flushes. "I'd love to, Harrison. But we both know we don't have time."

"Right." Blue balls for me then. But I'll deal. My boner will go down once I'm focused on playing the role of the Ace. Especially if another older guy comes on to me. "How much time *do* we have?"

She checks her watch. "None. The doors should be opening as we speak."

Damn. Time really does fly when you're in the company of a beautiful woman.

It's been a full fucking day. Only a few hours ago I was swinging down a hotel balcony on a rope of bedsheets. Then I stabbed a guy in the eye with a fountain pen.

But like I told Bianca at the library, I wouldn't change a thing if it meant meeting her. Caring for her. Loving her. *Making* love with her.

She gives me one more smooch on the cheek, her eyes fiery. "You're on, Ace."

I kiss her hand. "Yes, my Queen."

She grins and then pushes me out of her dressing room. I quickly—but not too quickly—make a beeline to the Clubs section. Mr. Night catches me and his eyes widen temporarily, but then he simply bows his head.

I have a feeling he's playing a part, too. A part I don't quite understand, but I'm ninety percent sure he's on my side. He'll have to be if we're going to pull this off.

I glance around the club. Rouge isn't here, at least as far as I can tell. Maybe she's at one of her other clubs tonight. I hope so. The night will be a lot less complicated if I don't have to dodge her the whole time I'm here.

"Ace, over here!" A man calls out.

I look up and meet the gaze of a middle-aged man sitting in one of the green leather chairs in Clubs smoking a cigarette.

It's showtime.

23

BIANCA

IT'S SHOWTIME.

I open my dressing room door and march over to the stage in Hearts. My band—minus Pierce still—is waiting. They greet me not with smiles but with stony stares.

They know I'm to blame, at least in part, for Pierce's disappearance. Best case scenario, he was fired. Worst case, he's pushing up daisies in some field by the airport.

Just before I ascend the steps to the stage, Jack waylays me, his eyes wide.

He can't speak, of course. We're on Aces property.

But I place a gentle hand on his shoulder. "It's going to be okay. We're going to make sure you're safe when you get back to the hotel tonight."

He presses his lips together.

"Hey, Jack!" a patron shouts.

He glances her way, nodding, and then turns back to me.

"I promise. I won't let anything happen to you."

He nods slowly and then attends to the patron.

Jack doesn't know the whole truth, and I don't intend to

tell him. He knows he might be in danger tonight, but he doesn't know about the organ harvesting plot.

I take a deep breath, paste a smile on my face, and walk up to the stage.

First set went well. Not my best, but my mind is otherwise occupied tonight.

Jack is milling about nearby. I grab his hand and drag him into my dressing room. Once the door is closed, I grab his shoulders. "So tell me. What have you been told to do once you finish up with your shift tonight?"

Jack swallows, scanning the room.

"Don't worry, there aren't any hidden cameras or mics. You can speak freely."

Though now I'm wondering if that's actually the case. Rouge told me there were no security cameras in my dressing room, just as there are none in the private suite. But Chet knew Harrison and I had slept together in the private suite the night we met. So I'm taking a big fucking grain of salt with everything she tells me.

But for right now, I need Jack to at least *think* he can speak freely.

"I was told they'd give me a one-week grace period at the Caterpillar Hotel. By that point I'd have to secure lodging elsewhere and start my new life."

"So they're expecting you to stay there tonight."

"Right. I figured I'd have at least the night after my final shift, since the club stays open so late. The whole week is generous, if I'm being honest."

"And they told you to stay there tonight?"

"Yeah. I was told the earliest I should check out is tomorrow morning, but that I had a whole week to get my affairs in order." He crosses his arms. "Most of the waitstaff I've seen go have left pretty quickly. I don't think anyone has ever stayed the whole week."

I nod, calculating in my head. If they told Jack he could check out tomorrow, then they're likely planning to do away with him tonight.

At this point, we can assume that every server here in Aces—or any of Rouge's other clubs—faces the same fate. The same for any patron who crosses my sister. It's not as if the demand for organs will go down. Every day, people get older and need more complex medical care. Rouge isn't going to stop unless it stops being profitable for her. She has an unlimited quantity of young, healthy organs at her polished fingertips.

I check my watch. My second set of the night is about to start.

"I'll keep an eye on you," I tell Jack. "Stay close."

He nods and we leave the dressing room together. Soon the patrons are descending on Jack with more drink orders and suggestive comments. I head to the stage. The rest of the musicians are in their places—they've taken to staying out of my dressing room ever since Pierce stopped showing up—and I offer them each a weak smile.

Poor Pierce.

Poor everyone.

I'm going to stop Rouge. Even if I get myself killed in the process, I'll do it. One death to stop a hundred more. If I had listened to Jack that night all those years ago, I could have prevented the loss of countless lives.

I squint. A crossed set of drumsticks rests atop Pierce's set.

That's odd. He couldn't have taken the drums home with him, but he would have taken his drumsticks, right?

I hold up a finger to the other members of the band, indicating we'll get started in just a second. I pick up the drumsticks. Maybe they're evidence. They're milky white, and Pierce's name is engraved in the sides.

But as I handle them, I realize something.

These drumsticks aren't made of plastic, or wood, or metal.

They're made of animal—or possibly human—bones.

And as I run my fingers over the engraving, a dark thought spears into my brain.

What if these drumsticks aren't Pierce's?

What if they *are* Pierce?

24

HARRISON

A SMALL CLATTER RESOUNDS FROM THE HEARTS SECTION. I look up. Bianca is standing among the musicians in her band. Her face is sheet white. She quickly bends over and picks something up, placing it on top of the drums, before she crosses over to her mic and begins her set.

"Ladies and gentlemen, my apologies for the noise. I guess there's a reason I'm not in the band!"

Light laughter from the Hearts patrons.

Whatever happened, I'll get the story later. Bianca is safe, and that's all that matters.

I continue serving drinks through the rest of her set. Bianca sings beautifully, though her voice is a little shaken. Something must have really spooked her. I look up as she wraps up her set, and she's staring directly at me.

She darts her gaze toward her dressing room door.

Right. She wants to talk.

I nod before returning my focus to the Clubs patrons. I fill a few more drink orders before I'm able to steal away into Bianca's dressing room.

She jumps off her pink chaise and wraps her arms around me the moment I walk inside.

"Oh, Harrison!" she lets out with a sob.

"What's the matter, babe?" I slide my hands over her arms.

She wipes her eyes, steadies herself. "It's Pierce. My drummer."

"What about him?"

"I told you he stopped showing up the night after I sang the unauthorized song."

"Right."

"I saw a pair of drumsticks he left on his set. Or at least, I *thought* he left them."

"What do you mean?"

She takes a deep breath, lets it out on a shaky exhale. "He... I mean, the drumsticks... The ones I found... I think they were made of *bone*, Harrison. Pierce's bones!"

My stomach sinks. "Fuck. It's a message."

"Yeah, and it's pretty damned clear. Fuck around and find out." She lays her head against my shoulder. "Maybe we should just make a run for it. Run away, get on a plane to some exotic place. Somewhere Rouge will never find us. Live out our days in peace."

I sigh. I'd like nothing more.

Spending my days in some tropical locale with Bianca, sipping mai tais on a white-sand beach, letting the world and all its cruelties roll over us like water off a duck's back.

But...we can't.

"We're the only ones who know what your sister is up to," I say. "We have a moral obligation to confront her about it, do everything in our power to make her stop. So many lives hang in the balance."

She sniffs a few times. "You're right, of course. I just wish we'd met under different circumstances."

"You and me both." I tip her chin up and kiss her on the lips. "But we'll make it out of this. Both of us. We'll live a long and happy life, have lots of kids. And we'll bring them up in a world that's a little bit safer than the one we're currently in."

She blinks away the last of her tears. "Kids?"

I wrap my arms around her waist. "You do want them, right?"

"I've always thought about it. But I never thought it would be possible given my job. Given the way I… At least, the way I *used* to…"

I place a finger to her lips. "All in the past, babe. If you want kids, I want to be their father. It's a big conversation, one we can save for later."

"If there *is* a later," she mutters.

"There will be, damn it." I squeeze her body to mine. After a few moments, her breathing has eased, and her heart beats in tandem with my own. I finally release her. "Besides, those bones might be a good thing."

"How on earth—" She claps a hand over her mouth. "Oh, my God. Do bones have DNA?"

"They do." I grin. "Rouge might have been trying to freak you out, but she might have implicated herself in the process."

"We'd have to get some other sample of Pierce's DNA to prove it's a match." She paces the room. "Maybe he was a blood donor or something."

"We'll figure it out, babe. But grab those drumsticks and lock them away somewhere in your dressing room. Somewhere Rouge would never think to look for them."

"I got it." She flies out the door.

I'm glad Bianca is feeling better. I'm good at soothing her, turns out.

I just wish I was as good at soothing myself.

Because I'm fucking haunted right now.

Bones. A man's bones were removed from his body and carved into a set of drumsticks.

At this point, I shouldn't be shocked. At least with the organ harvesting, another life is being saved. It might be the life of one of Rouge's degenerate friends, but still, the organ serves a greater purpose. With these bones, though… A man's corpse was defiled just to send a fucking message.

But with a little luck, it may be Rouge's undoing.

I hope that's the case.

Or else Bianca's and my bones will end up on that stage right next to Pierce's.

THINGS ARE WRAPPING up at Aces. The bulk of the patrons left around midnight, and now just a few stragglers sit at the bar in Spades, with a couple more sitting in Clubs, high off their minds, I'm sure. Bianca's finished up her final set and her band is packing away their instruments.

Rouge didn't show up the whole night.

I can't believe our luck.

She almost always makes an appearance at Aces every night it's open, at least as far as I can remember. Even if she had an engagement at another club, she always pops in, usually at the least opportune moment.

Maybe she was here, and I didn't notice.

But I would have felt her presence. Her aura of menace. It clings to her like stink to a wet dog.

Of course, the night ending at Aces is just the beginning for us.

My spending the night serving patrons as the Ace of Clubs is just a pretext to get me back on the bus to the Caterpillar Hotel. Keep an eye on Jack from now until the end of the night.

Then my heart sinks.

There's a very good reason Rouge wouldn't be here tonight.

Rose's injury.

Her main confidante—the man who carries out some of her dirty work in secret—currently has a pen sticking out of his eye. By now, it's probably been removed by a doctor. He might make a full recovery, but he'll likely lose sight in his eye.

One fewer eye to look at me lecherously, I guess.

Rouge would certainly fly to his side, and it won't take a deductive mastermind to figure out that Bianca and I were the last ones in the room before the paramedics were called. She'll be able to connect the dots. She already knows I've been poking around about Maddox, but now her sister will be implicated as well.

Fuck!

The whole time this was going on, the one thing that kept me calm was that if I went down trying to make Rouge face justice, at least Bianca would be okay.

That's no longer the case.

I should have just killed him. Left his body in his office and locked the door on the way out. That would have at least bought us a few extra hours.

I take a deep breath, try to ease my pounding heartbeat.

Right now I have to focus exclusively on the task at

hand. If we can save Jack, we can find a way to pin this all on Rouge. Then everything else will fade into the background.

But one thing is clear.

We've got one shot to make this work. No mistakes, no fuckups.

So I'm locking in.

Not concerning myself with what Rouge may or may not be figuring out on her own.

I spend a few minutes helping the other cards with cleanup. Some of them have already changed into T-shirts and athletic shorts, but I have no idea where they got them. I'll stick out on the bus if I'm still in these booty shorts.

"Ace," a soft voice whistles into my ear.

Mr. Night. I turn to him, bow my head.

"I assume you'll be taking the bus back tonight?"

I nod slowly.

"Excellent. You'll want to grab a spare T-shirt and shorts from the supply closet then." He points a bony finger toward a gray door between Clubs and Diamonds.

I mouth the words, "thank you," and then move to the closet. I grab a white T-shirt. It's a little tight, but it'll do. I find a boxy pair of shorts and slip them on, pulling the drawstring to keep them on my slim waistline.

While I'm in there, I grab a vacuum cleaner. I'll plug it in and look busy until the rest of the cards begin piling onto the bus.

It works. Mr. Night gives the Clubs section a final onceover and nods. "Clubs is dismissed."

"As is Diamonds," one of the Blackjack dealers calls.

"Spades." The guttural voice of Dudley—the first words I've ever heard him speak.

"Hearts is set as well," Bianca's soft voice calls from the stage.

"Excellent." Mr. Night turns to me and the other Clubs waitstaff. "Off you go, then."

I get a few looks from the other cards as I line up with them. They don't recognize me. But I could easily be a new hire. I've been here one night before as well, so I have some legitimacy.

A large bus idles in the alleyway outside the staircase of shattered mirror that leads out the red door in the ladies' restroom. The cards and I pile in. Not a word is spoken. I'm guessing none of them are allowed to speak until they are in their rooms at the Caterpillar. One of Rouge's Kings, his face shrouded in darkness, sits at the front of the bus.

I wish I had my phone on me. I could keep in contact with Bianca, make sure she's okay. But she has her spare key, and she'll be following right behind us. I trust her.

Even if the bus loses her, she knows its destination. We've been there before and she can plug the address into her GPS. Everything will be fine.

Unless it isn't.

I wish she were on the bus with me. Then I could make sure she was protected. I could place my body between hers and the King's. Do everything in my power—up to my dying breath—to guarantee her safety.

But that's not the hand we were dealt.

She'll be fine.

She has to be.

I love her so much.

I glance out the bus's back window. The car behind us isn't Bianca's.

But then again, it wouldn't be, would it? She had to sneak over to the hotel and get her car from there.

But... fuck! If Rouge is attending to Rose, she might still be there.

She would have gone straight to the hospital if that were the case.

We should have never left our cars there. We had no way of knowing Rose ran the hotel. It's named after him, but I thought it was just named after the flower.

Damn it all.

It's out of my hands.

Bianca is smart. She'll keep herself out of trouble.

At least I hope she will.

25

BIANCA

It took everything in me not to follow Harrison onto that damned bus after I dismissed the Hearts staff.

The highest-ranking employee in each section dismisses the staff each night. That was me, since Rouge never showed up tonight. Technically, the Kings outrank all of us, but they can't be bothered with something as trivial as dismissing the staff. Most of them took off once the last patrons left, except for the King of Hearts, who's on bus duty tonight.

The King of Hearts is Rouge's favorite. It was the position Jack was auditioning for the night he took shrooms with Rouge. I imagine he's the one who carries out some of her messier tasks. The guy Rouge ended up hiring when Jack failed to impress her is the same one I just saw lead Harrison out the Red Door. I know very little about him, as is the case with the other three Kings. He always wears a fitted wool hat decorated with crowns and hearts and is usually wearing a thick layer of liner under each eye. That's all I know about him.

That and the fact that he's trouble. Anyone close to my sister is.

The Gilded Rose is a quick jaunt from Aces, and I'm walking at a brisk pace. I get there in a little under fifteen minutes and am about to round the corner to the garage where my car is when a thought occurs.

I still have the key to our room at the hotel. I placed it in the bathrobe I was wearing when Harrison gave it to me. I'm not going back to our room, of course. But maybe I'll be able to retrieve our suitcases, along with our phones and wallets.

I walk to the front desk with a smile on my face.

"Hello, ma'am," a blond clerk says. "How can I help you?"

"My husband and I were moved to a new room, but our bags never made it. I was wondering if they got brought down here by mistake."

She raises her eyebrows. "Goodness. I'm so sorry about that. Do you have your room key?"

"Of course." I place it on the table.

"And ID?"

"I'm afraid that was in my bag," I say. "But the reservation is under Whitney Royale."

"Of course, Ms. Royale, and my apologies again. Can you describe the bags?"

"Happy to. Mine is white with pink trim, and my husband's is dark blue. They're both carry-ons."

"I'll go check our storage. And please accept my sincerest apologies again, Ms. Royale."

"No worries. I know things sometimes fall through the cracks."

She goes back into a room behind the front desk. She didn't seem alarmed when I told her my fake name, so she might not be aware of what went down with Mr. Rose this morning. She seems a little vapid, so I might get away with this.

She comes back a few moments later, wheeling two suitcases behind her. "Are these them?"

My heart leaps. "They are. Thank you so much!" I take mine, open it, and grab my wallet and phone. I don't need the keys since I have my spare on me, but I pocket those as well just to be safe. I open Harrison's bag, grab his essentials, and put them in my purse. Once I get to the Caterpillar Hotel, I'll make sure he gets them in case we get separated.

I also grab a scarf and a large pair of sunglasses from the bag.

"Enjoy the rest of your stay," the clerk says.

I nod. I'll never set foot in the Gilded Rose again, but I can be polite. I wrap the scarf around my hair and put on the sunglasses. It's the dead of night, but if this look kept Jackie Kennedy from the press, it'll keep me incognito as well. I head toward the elevator that leads to the parking garage when I stop in my tracks.

Three police officers stand in the elevator lobby.

They're not the reason I stop. I'm in disguise. They won't recognize me from the security tapes.

The reason I stop is the woman they're talking to.

It's Rouge.

26

HARRISON

When we bring Rouge to justice, we'll get immunity for everything else.

That's what I keep telling myself as the bus pulls off the highway.

It's not as if Mr. Rose is innocent, anyway. We have a first-hand witness in Jack. He watched as he sawed the head off the Two of Hearts. One of countless victims who suffered the same fate, probably after being strangled to death.

Of course, he was under the influence of mind-altering drugs at the time, but we'll find other people with similar stories to corroborate. We have the drumsticks made out of Pierce's bones. We'll get a warrant to have the police search Aces, especially Rouge's office...and the little safe where she keeps her red diamonds received in payment for the organs. Maddox mentioned a little ledger in there with all the names of Rouge's victims. That alone might be enough to put her behind bars for life.

That's too good a fate for her, but it's better than her roaming free.

What an evil bitch.

We're going to see that she, Mr. Rose, and anyone else who had a hand in this gets put away for good.

The bus jerks to a stop at the Caterpillar Hotel. My heart starts pounding in my ears.

Time to face the music.

The Aces servers stand and file out of the bus in an orderly fashion. The King sits in the corner, his face still completely obscured by shadow. I keep my head low as I pass him. He's probably been working at the club for years and might recognize me from the times I came there as Maddox's guest. He doesn't react as I pass him, thank God. In fact, he barely seems to be paying attention at all.

Good. I need him off guard.

Since we lined up for the bus as we were dismissed, Jack ended up in the front while the Clubs servers and I were in the back. Once I'm off, I speedwalk up to him and pat him gently on the shoulder.

He presses forward, and I follow him to his room on the seventh floor of the hotel, room 7B.

I make sure no one has eyes on me before I slip into Jack's room behind him.

I close the door behind us and turn to Jack. The color has drained from his face.

"What is it?"

He raises a trembling finger and points. A delicious-looking cherry tart sits on an elegant china plate on his bed, along with a handwritten note.

I pick up the note. It's written in calligraphy—because of course it is—in blood-red ink.

My Dearest Jack,

Congratulations on completing your five-year journey with us here at Aces. From the bottom of my heart, I thank you for your service and wish you the best of luck as you move on and pursue the "American Dream!" Please enjoy this token of my affection—my specialty, cherry tart!—to commemorate your final evening under our employ. It is a recipe that has been handed down from Montrose to Montrose for generations, and I hope you'll enjoy a sweet treat on your final night.

With utmost cordiality,

Rouge

I read it twice, turn it over to see if anything is on the back. I face Jack. "I think it's clear that under no circumstances should you consume that cherry tart. It's probably poisoned." I point to the note. "See. It says this is your 'final night.' She doesn't mean your final night in this hotel."

"Agreed." Jack sits on the edge of his bed. "I was told I had a one-week grace period to move out, so the only way Rouge would know this is my final night is if she guaranteed it herself. And if that's the case, I imagine one of the Kings will be by to check in on me pretty quickly." He runs his hands through his messy blond hair. "What's our move now?"

"We wait." I sit on the bed next to him.

Jack turns to me. "What are they planning to do to me?"

I take a deep breath in. "If I tell you, you can't panic."

"I already know they're trying to kill me. How much more could I panic after that?"

"Fair." I take another breath in. "Bianca and I think Rouge is killing her employees and harvesting their organs, selling them on the black market."

He jumps up from the bed. "What?"

"We discovered a cooler full of human hearts at Aces the last time we were there, on St. Patrick's Day. I think Rouge also has all her servers—and sometimes even her patrons—killed."

Jack paces the room. "But that night—the night I took mushrooms with Rouge—I didn't see Mr. Rose taking the organs out. Just sawing Two's head off, removing it from her body."

"They do that to make the body harder to identify," I explain. "When Alissa and Maddox found the head of May, the Seven of Spades, they found her hands as well. Fingerprints, facial identification, and dental records are the easiest way to identify a body, so remove them and all you have is DNA."

"And if there isn't a match in the police's system..."

"Exactly. They can't prove the person was an employee of Rouge's. No way to concretely tie the body to her, and that's if it's found. The only reason Maddox and Alissa found the head in the first place was because Chet slipped them a riddle that led them to it."

"Chet?" Jack raises an eyebrow. "I don't trust that fucker as far as I can throw him."

"Good instinct. He turned right around and betrayed them when they came to the club next. He's the reason they ended up here at the Caterpillar Hotel, nearly starved."

Jack widens his eyes. "There's so much I still don't know."

"I wish I had time to explain the whole story to you," I say. "It's a doozy, that's for freaking sure."

"A doozy?" Jack asks.

"Like...it's crazy. Unbelievable."

"Doozy. You Americans have a word for everything." He sits back down on the bed, rubbing at the back of his neck. "So what I saw in Rouge's office that night—it was real?"

"As far as I can tell, I think it was," I say. "My friend

Maddox saw something similar. He doesn't remember anything about someone's head getting chopped off, but he remembers being offered a goblet of blood to drink. He freaked out, and my guess is Mr. Rose ended up getting the job Maddox was being tested for."

All color remaining in Jack's pale face drains away. "My God."

"Yeah." I clap a hand to his shoulder. "But we're going to see to it that the same thing doesn't happen to you. Or to anyone else. And we'll start by making sure you don't eat that damned tart."

"Done," Jack says. "But when will—?"

A knock at the door sends a jolt through me.

I'd look through the peephole, but there isn't one.

But I can tell by the chills snaking up and down my spine that it isn't Bianca. She hasn't gotten here yet.

It's the King of Hearts.

Here to collect.

27

BIANCA

I DON'T THINK ROUGE HAS SEEN ME.

Of course, if she has, she wouldn't make it known.

It's like her brain is made of ice. She always keeps things cool, even in the most stressful situations.

She isn't wearing her club attire—the Elizabethan gown dripping in her red diamonds—but her street attire. A smart pants suit with her flaming red hair tied up into a neat bun. I almost wouldn't recognize her but for her long, crimson nails that extend from her fingers like demonic claws.

A small half-wall separates the check-in area from a lounge with cushy red couches, so I duck behind it and listen in.

Rouge's voice is layered with faux sympathy as she speaks with the cops.

"Yes, I'm a dear friend of Florian's. He's in the hospital now, and the doctors have promised he'll make a full recovery. They may even be able to save his eye, though he may require a corneal transplant."

Damn. She's already lining up Jack's organs. If his eye isn't a match, I'm sure Rouge has an arsenal of them at her disposal. Mr. Rose can just pop a new one in, one that was plucked from the unwitting corpse of one of her workers.

"Excellent news, ma'am," the cop next to her mumbles.

Rouge crosses her arms over her large bosom. "And please correct me if I'm wrong, but you say there were two people with him in the office when the accident occurred?"

The cop nods.

"Are you able to provide a description?"

"That information is strictly for the investigation, ma'am."

She fakes a laugh. "Of course. Don't worry. I'm not going to go all vigilante on you. I'm just wondering, as a concerned citizen, if there are any troublesome people I should be on the lookout for."

The cop nods again, and Rouge reaches into her cleavage, pulls out a small baggie. Even from here, I can tell it holds a few of her red diamonds.

"Are you married, Officer?"

"Fifteen years in October," the cop says.

"Congratulations." Rouge reaches into the bag and pulls out one of the diamonds. "Perhaps your wife will be expecting something a little extra this year for such a milestone."

The cop widens his eyes as he scans the contents of Rouge's palm. "Is that a ruby?"

"A diamond, Officer. A red diamond. One of the rarest types. Worth well over the two months' salary that young men are encouraged to put toward engagement rings for their beloved."

The cop laughs nervously. "My wife's ring is cubic zirconium, I'm afraid."

Rouge lays a hand against her breast. “Goodness. Perhaps she’s due for an upgrade then.”

“Ma’am?”

Rouge leans into the officer’s ear and whispers something, depositing the diamond discreetly in his right pants pocket. The cops face reddens, but then he steadies his face as Rouge steps back.

“Do we have a deal, then?”

The cop looks from side to side and then nods.

“The descriptions of the perpetrators?”

“We don’t know if they *are* perpetrators, ma’am. All we know is they’re witnesses who stepped out after the incident.”

“People who have nothing to hide don’t leave the scene. Tell me who they were.”

“A man and a woman.”

“Go on.”

“The man? Tall, broad shouldered. Dark hair, medium complexion. Stubble and a solid jaw. The woman, petite and slender. Pale, blond hair.”

“What were they wearing?”

“The lady was in a bathrobe. The man was in leisurewear.”

Rouge nods slowly. “Do you have a picture?”

The cop pulls a piece of paper out of his pocket and hands it to Rouge.

Her eyebrows twitch ever so slightly.

“Do you recognize them?”

“I’m afraid not.” Rouge folds the printout and tucks it in her purse. “Do you have names?”

“Nothing for the man. The room was booked under the woman’s name, but we’re pretty sure it’s a pseudonym. Whitney Royale.”

Rouge clasps her hands. "Fascinating."

She's figured it out. My name comes from the Italian word for "white." My father named me that because I was born with a full head of hair so light blond that it was almost white. The name Whitney shares a similar root. I always thought it was a clever little puzzle, but now I'm realizing I should have chosen a name completely at random. Rouge would have recognized my face from the picture anyway.

No matter how she found out, though, my stomach is doing somersaults.

Because Rouge now knows.

She doesn't know everything. She has no way of knowing we're aware of the organ harvesting.

But she knows that Harrison and I are working together. And that we know Mr. Rose is a dangerous man. She'll probably go straight to Aces and review the security footage, where she'll connect the dots between Harrison and the Ace of Clubs.

She already knows I was hanging out in the ladies' restroom for a long time the night of the seventeenth.

And there it is.

As soon as she puts it all together, we're fucked.

The clock is ticking.

Without drawing attention to myself, I slink over to the elevator leading to the parking garage, Harrison's and my suitcases in tow, and get in. I throw the luggage in the trunk and then careen out of the garage—breaking through the barrier bar at the exit—and make my way as quickly as possible to the Caterpillar Hotel.

I pray I make it there in time.

28

HARRISON

I draw a finger to my lips, indicating to Jack not to say a word. I inch over to a small inset closet next to where the door to Jack's room opens, a tiny cubby I can spring out of once the King makes his entrance.

Another knock. "Hello?" a dull voice from the other side of the door calls out.

I pause. There's something about the lilt of his voice that's oddly familiar...

I point to the bed. "Lie down," I mouth.

Jack raises an eyebrow, but then he seems to get it. He'll play dead. He even tears a bit of the tart off so it looks like he took a bite out of it and lies back on the bed at a grotesque, unnatural angle.

A third knock, and then the jingling of keys.

He's letting himself in.

My heart pounds, but I force myself to keep my breathing steady, my eyes trained on Jack, my legs ready to pounce once the opportune moment presents itself.

The lock disengages, and the door opens toward the

closet I'm sitting in. The King enters. It's the same man from the bus, still wearing the gray knitted cap over his head, along with dark-wash jeans and a tight-fitting black V-neck patterned with silver hearts. He walks toward the bed and then scoops Jack into his arms.

This is it.

I jump out of the closet, pounce onto the King's back, and wrap my arm around his neck. He lets out a stifled grunt and drops Jack back onto the bed. Jack springs back to life and kicks the King in the gut, forcing him to bend forward.

The King shakes me off and lands a hook to my right cheek. I barely feel it, and I block a second punch before landing an uppercut under his chin. The King snarls and turns on me, his face red as he wraps his fingers around my throat, cutting off my air supply. I struggle to get out of his grasp, but I can't.

Jack, however, sweeps his leg under the King's feet, bringing his knees to the unforgiving tile floor of the hotel room. He loosens his grip on my neck just enough for me to shake loose and force his hands away from me. I pin them to the ground.

And—

What the fuck?

A scar.

A fucking scar on the palm of the King's left hand.

A scar in the shape of an X.

I have one just like it on my own left hand.

It... It can't be.

The King's head bangs against the floor and he loses the gray knitted cap, revealing his medium-length dark hair.

The same way he wore it when we were kids.

There are a few slivers of gray tracing through it now, but

there's no mistaking his signature aesthetic—the half-dozen or so tufts of electric-green highlights popping out of his dark curls.

The King of Hearts is an old friend of mine. A friend who once forced me to torture and emasculate an innocent man in the name of exacting revenge on my middle-school bully.

Ray Sinclair.

29

BIANCA

I'M BLAZING DOWN THE HIGHWAY, GOING NEARLY NINETY MILES an hour, weaving in and out of traffic like a madwoman.

Thank God no cops are out tonight.

I can't afford to be stopped right now.

The sooner I get to the Caterpillar, the better.

Rouge knows. Rouge *knows*.

She doesn't know everything, but she knows enough.

And sister or no sister, she won't let me live with the knowledge of her dark deeds.

She certainly won't let Harrison off the hook.

I shouldn't have stayed at the Gilded Rose so long. I should have said "to hell" with the suitcases and just retrieved my car. I wasted fifteen precious minutes grabbing them and then listening in to Rouge's conversation with the cop.

I got some important intel, I suppose.

Had I not listened in, I wouldn't be aware of how urgent everything is. I certainly wouldn't be going as fast as I am down the highway.

I slam on the brakes and lay on the horn as I nearly hit some old man going ten under. I quickly move around him, catching his middle finger in my rearview as he disappears into the distance.

I can't blame him. I'm driving erratically.

Harrison is probably wondering where the hell I am. I should have gotten to the hotel ten minutes or so after he did. By the time I get there, he'll have likely been there a half hour.

Has someone tried to kill Jack by now? Have they tried to do away with him, dismember him right then and there? Have—my heart clenches—they done something similar to Harrison when he came to Jack's defense?

Jack is an average height, but he's got a terrific build. He's in the gym five times a week, has been since I met him. He's got a fantastic chest and arms, nearly as impressive as Harrison's.

The two of them can hold their own against a King. They're built like linebackers, but they're not completely invulnerable. But if all four Kings are there? Hardly a fair fight.

I wish I could call him. Make sure he's okay, tell him to get the hell out of there. But his phone is in his suitcase, which is in my trunk.

I slam my foot against the gas. I'm nearly going a hundred now. I finally see the Forest Park exit. I take it and swing around the bend—nearly rolling the vehicle over in the process—and land in the Caterpillar Hotel parking lot. I'm the only car here, but fuck discretion.

We don't have time.

30

HARRISON

I TAKE A STEP BACK. "RAY?"

Ray grimaces, spitting out a wad of mucus and blood. "How dare you call me that, Ace? How dare you even speak to me in the first place?"

"No. I'm not a card. I'm just in disguise. It's me. Harrison O'Rourke." I swallow. "*Harry* O'Rourke."

Ray drops his jaw slowly as it dawns on him. "What the fuck?"

"Yeah, it's me," I say, hoping that "old times' sake" is more than just an expression. "Your old pal."

He narrows his eyes. "Hardly an old pal. You ditched me after that night at the Dimpsey house."

Jack stands over Ray, his eyes widened. "I'm sorry. You two know each other?"

I nod. "We were members of the same gang in middle school. Called it the Club."

"Very original," Jack retorts.

"We were kids."

"Yeah, and we *were* friends," Ray adds. "Until Harry here got all pussy-footed after things got a little too real for him."

"I never agreed to castrate a grown man, Ray. That was an awful thing you did."

Ray chuckles. "I didn't do a thing. You did it."

I blink. "But you made me do it."

"I don't recall holding a gun to your fucking head."

I swallow. He's right. My actions are my own. I was pressured into them, but I could have refused. I didn't feel like I had a choice at the time, but deep down, I've always known that I did. That I actively chose to harm an innocent man to impress my friend.

I never did it again. I devoted my life to healing people from that point on.

But now isn't the time to dwell on the past.

"How'd you get mixed up with Rouge?"

Ray exhales sharply. "The same way anyone does. Right place at the right time. Or, as is the case with some of us, the wrong place at the wrong time."

"What the fuck does that means?"

He shakes his wrists under my grip. "Let me go and maybe I'll tell you."

I roll my eyes. "Tell me, and maybe I'll let you go."

He chuckles. "There's that Brother Harry fire I liked. Where the hell did it go that night? Why'd you have to go all *noble* out of nowhere?"

"What we did that night was wrong, Ray. You know it, and I know it."

"We were correcting an injustice."

"Is that what you're doing now? Correcting injustices by killing these innocent people?"

Ray scoffs. "Who said anything about killing?"

Jack grabs the plate with the cherry tart on it. "You weren't going to kill me? Then prove it. Take a bite of the tart."

"Not hungry."

"I don't give a shit." Jack nudges the plate against Ray's cheek. "Take a bite of the tart or admit you're killing people."

Ray darts his eyes around the room, but a tiny grin soon cracks his face. "Fine. You got me. The tart is drugged. Stuff that'll knock you out like that."

"And then, what?" I demand. "You take the body back to Aces and dismember it?"

"Dismember?"

"Don't play dumb with me. I've seen the cooler of organs, Ray. Behind the hidden passageway out of the ladies' restroom at Aces."

Ray's grin widens. "Wow, you two really are little sleuths, aren't you?"

"Not me," Jack says. "Harrison figured it out."

"My girlfriend and I," I say.

Ray raises an eyebrow. "A girlfriend? Finally got over my sister, did you?"

"I got over her the night we stopped hanging," I say. "Any person who shared their DNA with you was sure to be just as fucked up in the head."

Ray shrugs. "You're not wrong. She ended up offing herself in college. Blew her pretty little brains out right in her dorm room. I heard her roommate got the rest of her tuition comped. Some people have all the luck."

"Fuck. I'm sorry."

"Don't be. She was a stuck-up little bitch."

I blink. How can this man talk about his dead sister—clearly a girl who was going through something awful—in such a callous way?

"And then you met Rouge?"

"At Reg's funeral, yeah." He looks up at me, a trace of pain in his eyes. "Really could have used a friend when that happened."

"You had Corey and Max, didn't you?"

Ray rolls his eyes. "If fucking only. I guess they learned that, after you left, they didn't need me either. Within a year of the Dimpsey house, they ditched me. Left me all alone. The last living member of the Club." He glances toward my left palm, at the pink X scarred into my flesh. "But you still bear our mark. You'll never be able to erase what you did to the Dimpseys. What you did to *me*."

He lurches forward, taking me by surprise, rips his hands out of my grip, and bites down onto my left shoulder, sending white-hot pain through my body.

Blood trickles down my arm. "What the fuck, Ray?"

His eyes have an almost reptilian glow to them. Like he's a rabid dog about to rip me to shreds. He opens his jaw and is about to clamp down on my neck when I roll out of his way and land an elbow to the back of his skull.

Jack lands a roundhouse kick to Ray's gut and then a right hook to his jaw, spinning him around to face me again. Ray lands a few punches to my belly before I grab him by his hair and punch him in the nose. Blood gushes out of his nostrils, but he ignores it, pressing forward with inevitable resolve. He grips the wound in my shoulder, pressing his fingernails into it, forcing a cry of pain out of me as I fall to my knees.

The door to the hotel room bursts open, and I look up just in time to see Bianca gasp. "Harrison!" she calls out. "Are you—?"

But Ray takes advantage of this temporary distraction and slips behind Bianca, wrapping an arm around her throat. He reaches into his pocket with his free hand, produces a knife, and holds it against her neck.

Hot anger laced with blinding fear hurtles through me.

I won't let her die. I'll sacrifice myself before I allow that to happen.

"Don't—" I rasp out.

Ray presses the flat edge of the blade against Bianca's throat. "Not one step closer, *Brother Harry*." He rakes his gaze over Bianca. "You really *did* get over my slutty sister. Moved onto another woman." He sniffs her light-blond hair. "She smells the same, though. Just like Regina did before she woke up in the mornings."

"Ray, please—"

"Shut the fuck up, Harry," Ray says. "Here's what's going to happen now." His cell phone vibrates in his pocket. "Okay, first off, reach into my pocket and grab my cell."

"Why would I—"

"Do it, or your pretty little lady friend's blood will spill all over this tile floor." Ray grins. "Don't worry. It washes right off." His gaze darkens. "I've done it hundreds of times."

"She's Bianca Montrose. Rouge's sister. You can't lay a finger on her. She's off limits."

"Is she?" Ray leans into Bianca's ear. "I'm going to let go of your right hand now so I can see what my phone says. One unplanned move and I'll ram my knife right into your throat. Got it?"

Bianca nods, trembling.

Ray lets go of her wrist, and she doesn't move. I hand him his phone and he unlocks it. "Well, isn't this interesting?"

"What?"

"Rouge has authorized the use of deadly force against anyone who gets in my way tonight, up to and including her own flesh and blood. Any last words from the little sister?"

"Please..." Bianca murmurs.

"Begging with your last breath? No wonder Rouge thinks you're so pathetic." Ray spits on her.

Glaring hot rage fills me, but I can't move. Ray will sink the knife into Bianca's neck if I do something. But if I *don't* do something, he'll slit her throat too.

Fuck!

But... I have one tool left in my arsenal. One I've already had to use before, on Mr. Rose.

That night when Ray inducted me into the Club, he forced a kiss on me.

Technically, it was my first kiss.

I got hard, and for months I wasn't sure if I was bisexual or not.

I wasn't. When a guy's going through puberty, pretty much anything can get him excited.

But Ray clearly had a thing for me. He forced me to strip naked and swim with him in the river that same night, and I could tell he was trying to sneak glances at my junk.

So I might not be bi, but Ray certainly is.

And I might just be able to exploit his attraction to me.

"Ray," I say as I casually remove the T-shirt from my body. "Maybe we can work something out here."

Bianca's eyes widen, as do Ray's.

"What?" he asks.

"I think you know what I'm talking about." In one swift motion, I remove my athletic shorts. Now I'm just wearing the skimpy, tight shorts of my Ace of Clubs uniform. "I know you've wanted me since we were kids, Ray."

"But you never looked at me like—"

I hold up a hand. "What I want is irrelevant. It's about what *you* want." I slowly walk toward him, take the cell phone out of his hand, and place his hand against my bulge. I'm the most flaccid I've ever been in my life, but hopefully this is enough to get Ray to let go of Bianca. "So how about it? You let Bianca go, and I let you do anything you want—and I mean *anything*, Ray—to my body."

Ray licks his lips as he looks me up and down, squeezing my dick through the shorts. Then he furrows his brow. "But what about Rouge?"

"You'll tell her you never ran into us. That Jack must have figured it all out and escaped. We'll be out of your hair forever. Well, all of us, except me." To seal the deal, I rip off the shorts. I now stand naked as the day I was born in front of Ray. "Is it a deal?"

"Fuck, Harry." He runs his hands up my chest. "I always knew you'd have a nice cock."

I paste a grin to my face. "Grew it myself."

He bites his lip, rubs at the back of his neck, and finally relents. "Fine. But I want your girlfriend to watch."

"That wasn't part of my offer."

"I don't give a flying fuck. The guy holding the blade to the girlfriend's throat gets to make the demands. And I want her to watch as I fuck you, come inside you, take you in a way she never can."

"Harrison..." Bianca murmurs. "You don't have to."

I hold up another hand. "Fine. Have it your way."

Ray twirls his finger in the air. "Turn around. Bend over. Spread your cheeks. Let me see that tight hole."

I grit my teeth, but then I do as he says. I squeeze my eyes shut. It'll be over soon, and then I can get Bianca to safety. It's the only way. The only way.

The only—

The door slams open. A gunshot. I stand back up to see Ray crumpled over, holding his stomach as blood pumps out of it. Bianca stands next to him, her face paler than I've ever seen it.

A gun. Someone shot him. But who? Who?

Another gunshot. This time to Ray's head. Fragments of skull and brain strew over the tiles of Jack's floor. He's dead before his body hits the ground.

It came from behind me. But my body isn't moving. And it isn't lost on me that I'm still completely naked.

A cool, serpentine voice slithers into my ear. "Sorry about the mess, Doctor."

It's a voice I know too well.

The last voice I want to hear right now.

The voice of Rouge Montrose's right-hand man, the person she trusts more than her Kings, more than Mr. Rose, the one who determines who does and doesn't enter Aces Underground.

I finally garner the energy to turn around.

My savior is placing a gun back into its holster on his waist, his snow-white eyebrows raised and his omnipresent grin sprawled across his face.

"Chet?" I ask. "What are you doing here?"

He shrugs nonchalantly, as if we're talking about the weather. "I was bored," he says. "So tell me, what's our next move?"

31

CHET

"HAPPY BIRTHDAY!" MOTHER AND FATHER YELL. "BLOW OUT YOUR candles!"

Seven tiny trees of wax spring from the top of my cake that's decorated with frosting roses that Mother herself crafted from a mixture of butter and cream.

"But why blow them out?" I ask. "Aren't candles meant to be lit?"

"Always with the questions," Mother says with a laugh that doesn't quite reach her eyes. "You blow them out so your wish can come true!"

"Do the candles carry a celestial link to the divine?" I ask.

"Come on, son," Father says. "Just blow them out. Your mother worked very hard on the cake, and we want to share it with you."

It is only the three of us. Mother invited all the children in my class, but for some reason or another, none of them could make it today. All morning the calls came in, each excuse more outlandish than the last. Their grandparents must be dropping like flies.

I finally blow out the candles, and tiny deposits of wax make their way onto the virgin blanket of icing on my cake. Mother wipes them off quickly and cuts me a slice. "Once you finish your cake, we'll open your gifts."

The gifts are what I'm most looking forward to, and Mother and Father have gotten me something very special. I know because I opened the gifts ahead of time. In the event they weren't what I wanted, I wanted to be able to rehearse my reaction. I've never been good at displaying emotions in the moment—every feeling seems to bring the same smile to my face, even the bad ones like anger—but when I rehearse them, it's a little easier.

But the gifts this year won't require a rehearsed reaction. Mother and Father hit the jackpot—a book of riddles, and the complete works of Shakespeare on compact disc. An excellent departure from Father's gift last year—a baseball glove. I love riddles—figuring them out is like tickling your brain with a goose feather—and I can't wait to share them with all my friends in school. This will surely win their affections.

Perhaps I'll even convince some of them to come to my next party.

The next day, I wear my favorite outfit—a seersucker suit and pork pie hat—to school. My best friend, Benny, widens his eyes when he sees me.

"Everyone!" He points. "Look what the Jerkster has worn today!"

The children laugh gayly. I'm so glad they enjoy my little outfits.

I pull out my book of riddles. "Benny, I've got a thinker for you today."

Benny rolls his eyes—I think he wears contact lenses, so he must be adjusting them—and leans back in his chair. "Yeah, what is it, Jerkface?"

I open the book of riddles. "The man who sells me doesn't need me, the man who buys me doesn't want me, and the man who uses me doesn't know he's using me. What am I?"

"I don't know. A numbskull?" Benny cracks up.

"Skull is close," I say. "Give up?"

Benny crosses his arms. "Sure. What's the answer, Jerkster?"

I grin. "A coffin!"

"That doesn't make any sense."

"Yes, it does, if you think about it. The man who sells a coffin doesn't need one because he's alive, whereas the man who buys one—"

I can no longer speak because Benny is giving me a hug around my neck using his left arm.

He's squeezing harder than he means to and I can't breathe, but it's worth it to feel the warmth of human touch.

Benny is my best friend.

I love him.

University life wasn't for me.

Mother and Father told me my test scores weren't as high as they'd hoped.

"Christ, with how weird he is, you'd think he'd at least be smart," Father said.

"He is smart," Mother responded. "He just has a very...unique intelligence."

Unique.

That's a word I hear often.

Without a match. A child who marches to the beat of his own drummer.

No longer a child, though. I'm eighteen, marching into a life outside of my parents' loving embrace.

Father took me aside a month before my eighteenth birthday. "Look, Chet," he said. "I'm going to have to be frank with you."

"And I'll be Chet with you," I replied with a smile.

Father's name is Frank. It was a good joke.

"Frank as in honest, Chet." He rubbed at his forehead, the wrinkles deeper than they were when I was a child. "Your mother and I can't afford to take care of you after you've turned eighteen. Since it doesn't look like you'll be going to college, you're going to have to find a job once you graduate and support yourself."

"Of course, Father," I said. "But I just don't know what I want to be."

"You've had eighteen years to figure it out. But right now, any job will do. You've got a month before you're out. Start making arrangements now."

I didn't get a cake for my eighteenth birthday. Just a suitcase in my favorite color, purple.

I pack it to the brim with my suits and a few mementos—and that old book of riddles, of course; I've even started to write some of my own—and I head into town, looking for businesses seeking help.

I talk to a few people, but they are taken aback by the way I speak to them. Mother says I'm eloquent, Father says I need to speak more like a man.

I'm not sure what that means. I am a man, ergo the way I speak is how a man speaks.

But none of them hire me.

Father made it clear I couldn't sleep in his house tonight. Perhaps I can spend the night with a friend.

I know Benny's address by heart. I memorized it years ago. I make my way into his neighborhood on foot, knock at his door.

He opens the door, his eyebrows raised. "Chet?"

"Good day, Benny. I was hoping I could make use of your hospitalities for the evening. Perhaps even two or three. Would you be amenable to serving as my host?"

"What the hell?" Benny cocks his head.

Like Father said. Speak in plainer English.

"Can I...spend the night?"

Benny rubs at the back of his neck. "Jesus, Chet. We haven't spoken in years."

"But you're my best friend."

He laughs at that. "How on earth can you think I'm your best friend? I treated you like shit in elementary and middle school."

"You were teasing. That's what friends do. That's what Mother always told me."

"For Christ's sake, Jer—I mean Chet. Will you ever get a clue?"

He closes the door in my face.

I guess he's busy tonight.

No matter.

I sometimes see people sleeping in the green area by the airport. Some of them even have tents. I've always been fascinated by the notion of camping. The reserve is not far from where Benny lives. I walk over there just as the sun is setting and take a seat on a nearby bench.

This is lovely. Cool night air. A blanket of stars above me, and the roaring thunder of planes taking off nearby.

It doesn't get much better than this.

A man with stringy hair with aluminum cans lining his arms and a crown of tinfoil passes by me, giving me a strange look. "First night here?"

"Indeed, sir," I say. "May I ask why you are bedecked in metal?"

"Why what?" He looks at his arms. "Oh, yeah. The cans. It keeps them out."

"Them?"

"The CIA. NSA. Illuminati. Lizard people. Whatever the hell you want to call them. They're listening, and these"—he bangs on the metal can on his left arm—"are the only way to scramble their signal."

I widen my eyes. "Fascinating."

"Yeah, you wouldn't believe what those bigwigs can get up to." The man scratches at the side of his face, and his eyelids twitch. "It's going to rain, I think."

I look up. "Heavens, I didn't plan for precipitation."

"Here." He gestures me over. "I have a tent. There's room enough for two. Come on, you can crash with me. I'll get you some cans, too. Keep you safe from listening ears."

"I'd certainly like that." I extend my arm. "My name is Chester Tabbitt. Chet for short."

He shakes my hand, not meeting my eyes. "I'm Tim. Timothy Mann."

It has been grand getting to become friends with Tim. He's unlike my other friends. They laughed at me, pointed fingers, said unkind things. Tim doesn't do that. When he laughs, I'm laughing with him. And he's never said anything unkind to me in the months since we met.

I've procured my own tent now, which I've mounted next to Tim's. I've gotten to know him well. He ended up here because he fell desperately in love with a woman who did not return his affections. He spent every last dollar he had on her to appease her, but she spurned every fine piece of jewelry, every lavish fur. He turned to alcoholic beverages and other illicit substances to numb the pain she left in her wake. Eventually he lost his house, his car, all his belongings, and still the woman wanted nothing to do with him.

He tells me she stole his heart, that there now exists only a chasmic void in the space behind his ribs. Of course, I know this to be a biological impossibility, but he insists it is the case.

I have trouble empathizing. I've never loved a woman, not in the way Tim describes. I understand that there exists a physical closeness between man and woman with which they express their love for one another, but I've yet to experience it. Tim says it's like a sneeze, but in the most pleasurable way. I rarely sneeze, so again I have little to draw on.

Tim tells me about hearing voices in his head, which he believes are the government trying to read his mind. The cans and the tinfoil hat help, but even then, they're no match for the machines that the reptilians in Washington have at their disposal. Again, I don't experience what Tim does, but perhaps my thoughts aren't as valuable to the president as Tim's.

One bright Tuesday morning, we are taking our daily walk along the Des Plaines River when a devastatingly beautiful woman with vivid red hair wrapped in a silk scarf approaches us.

She takes off her large sunglasses and grins. "Gentlemen. May I have a quick word?"

Tim frowns. "What do you want?"

"Just a quick conversation. I received intel from a colleague of mine, Austin Waverly, that there was a population of people in need of steady work living in this area."

At the mention of the colleague's name, Tim cocks an eyebrow, but he doesn't say anything in response.

She turns to me, extends her long-fingered hand. "Enchanté. *My name is Rouge Montrose."*

I blink a few times. "Chester Tabbitt. Chet for short."

"Chet. I like the sound of that." She turns to Tim. "And you, my good sir?"

"Timothy Mann," he says coldly. He doesn't shake her hand.

"A pleasure, Mr. Mann." Rouge Montrose says. "As I said, I'm in desperate need of loyal employees for two of my business ventures. I have an opening at my flagship club, Aces Underground, and another at one of my secondaries, the Jade Sanctum."

Again, Tim raises an eyebrow at the name of the second club. "The Jade Sanctum?"

"You're familiar?"

Tim crosses his arms. "I have some friends who are."

"Then you must count among your friends some people with exquisite taste." Rouge offers a dazzling smile, but the crinkles in her cheeks don't match the crinkles in her eyes. "Perhaps you would be interested in that position, Mr. Mann?"

"I'd be willing to discuss it," Tim says flatly.

"Lovely." Rouge turns to me. "And you, Mr. Tabbitt—"

"Chet, please."

"Of course. Chet. *Would you be interested in the position at Aces?"*

I offer her a grin. "What would said position entail?"

She smirks. "You're quite eloquent for a man of your economic status."

"Thank you." I believe that was meant to be a compliment.

Rouge twiddles with a ring on her left index finger. "Both positions are as servers. Waiters in the clubs I run. You would take drink orders from patrons, serve them, collect some handsome tips. Housing would be provided while you get yourselves back on your feet. There is also the potential for making additional money by entertaining club patrons."

"What do you mean by that?" Tim asks.

"We'll iron out the details later," Rouge says quickly. "But for now, can I pen you both down as interested? We can go from there."

I look back at the nature preserve behind me, at the haggard little tent I pilfered from a thrift store to keep me dry in the wet. I suppose I don't want to live like this forever, and every attempt I've made at this point to secure employment has yielded no results. Now, out of the blue, this catastrophically striking woman has come down like an angel from the Beyond to offer me help, a place to sleep.

And I would still be able to see Tim while we're off work. I imagine we'd be put up in the same place.

"I'm interested," I say brightly.

Tim sighs. "I guess I am too."

"Excellent. Mr. Mann, I can put you to work straight away as the Jade Sanctum is open six nights a week." She refixes her attention toward me. "And you, Mr. Tabbitt, can report to Aces Underground at six o'clock sharp this Friday."

Today marks six months at Aces Underground.

The job has been a benison of the greatest favor. Her Majesty put Tim and me up at a hotel not too far from where we were living by the airport, a refurbished property called the Caterpillar Hotel. Tim and I don't see each other as often as I'd like since the schedules of the Jade Sanctum and Aces Underground don't quite mesh, but I have a roof over my head and three hot meals a day, so I really cannot be disagreeable against the standards with which

I've been presented. I've found a few trinkets—most interestingly a small shampoo bottle under my bed which I've determined came from the hotel's heyday. I've kept it in my pocket as a little charm, a reminder to be grateful for the boon which has befallen me.

I work primarily in the Hearts section. I am the Jack. The Jack of Hearts. I have a tattoo of a J on my right shoulder, and a red heart on my left. I've taken to rouging my nipples to match.

The other waitstaff at Aces are approached by the patronage now and then and taken discreetly behind the velvet curtains to be pleasured. So far, I have not been propositioned in such a way. The servers who do *entertain the club's members are quite conventionally attractive—the women toned and the men muscled. I'm the tallest of the waitstaff, and the thinnest. My face is one which my mother once referred to as "not quite comely."*

I have no interest in servicing the patrons, anyway. I still have never experienced the physical act of intimacy, but I've done quite a bit of reading on it. It doesn't seem for me.

I'm not the only server who doesn't get as much attention from the patrons. There are a few of us who have never gone behind the velvet curtains. I'm not sure if the others have maintained their purity as I have. It's not really something we discuss. Her Majesty has been hiring a lot of them from abroad, anyway, so many of them don't speak English. We are allowed to speak to one another when we're off Aces property, but even then communication can be tricky.

Tim is always there for me, though. He's a good man.

I am about to begin my shift on the Aces floor when a long set of perfectly manicured fingers—nails painted blood red—close around my naked left shoulder.

Without even looking, I know it is Her Majesty.

I turn, bow my head.

"Chet." Her eyelids flutter. "Do you have a moment?"

I glance toward a clock on the wall and then back to her.

"You can start your shift a few moments late. Come with me into my office."

I nod, follow her into her chambers. It's my first time seeing it. It's gorgeous, aglow with red gemstones from floor to ceiling. Bright ruby sconces line the crimson wallpaper, and an oversized chandelier saturated with garnets and rubies hangs from the ceiling. I take a seat in an armchair across from Her Majesty's desk, enjoying the plushy feel of the Persian rug underneath it on my bare feet.

Her Majesty takes a seat in her one chair, a throne bedecked with more of the red gemstones. At first I think they're rubies, but as I squint I realize they are red diamonds—one of the most valuable minerals found on the planet. I recognize them from a book on gems and minerals I used to read in the elementary school library during lunch.

"Chet," she says. "As you know, I have been running Aces Underground as regent to my ailing father for the last several years."

I nod. I have not been permitted to speak.

She continues. "He has now reached a point where he has determined his best move is to transfer the remainder of his authority to me. As of this morning, I am the sole owner and proprietor of this club, as well as our satellite locations, like the Jade Sanctum, where your friend Tim works."

I bow my head in a way I hope expresses my congratulations to her. Her Majesty has been our leader here in all but name since I started, and for a decade prior. This doesn't change much. She just finally has the official position her father, Robinson Montrose, clung to for years even as his health and mental being slipped away. She finally has a complete hold over her family's clubs. She's been making changes for some time now with her father's approval, which is now no longer required.

"With this in mind, I will be making some new changes. For example, I just got off the phone with my sister who is an actress in New York City. She will be coming to work as a singer in the Hearts section. The main alteration that will affect you, Chet, is that we are streamlining the process in which we hire our waitstaff."

I nod.

"We are adopting a new set of standards to ensure all our servers are—how can I put this delicately?—conventionally attractive. As you are aware, Chet, that description doesn't quite fit your skillset."

I widen my eyes. Am I being fired? After Her Majesty saved me from the squalor of life in the nature preserve by the airport?

She holds up a hand. The gemstones embedded in her fingernails twinkle. "But you need not worry. You have proven over the last six months your loyalty to Aces Underground, Chet. That is not something I take lightly."

I blink a few times, trying to keep my lips from twitching.

"I want to offer you a position as the Aces bouncer. Do you know what that means?"

I pause a moment and then shake my head.

"You would take the position in our lobby upstairs. I'll be refurbishing it over the next few weeks. I've found some delectable couches lined in white rabbit fur. You will sit at a desk in the lobby, take IDs, and ensure that no one gets into Aces Underground unless they are a member or their guest. Does that sound like something you would be amenable to?"

I press my lips together but then nod again.

"It would be easier than your current job. You wouldn't be on your feet all night. And your salary would be double what it currently is."

I cross my arms and lean back in my chair.

"There is, of course, one caveat." Her Majesty reaches into a desk drawer and takes out a small coin purse made of red leather. She pulls out a small mushroom with a slender stem and a tall cap. "Do you know what this is?"

I shake my head.

"A psilocybin mushroom. A naturally occurring mind-altering substance. You must take this, and then you will be presented with a small examination to ensure you are up to the task."

Done.

I take the mushroom and consume it without a second thought. Tim has talked to me before about going on "trips" with these mushrooms. It's something I've always been curious about but have never experienced firsthand. Not unlike the physical act of intimacy.

Her Majesty widens her long-lashed eyes. "Goodness. Usually I have to talk someone into this."

I shrug.

And I sit.

I wait.

Until invisible strings pull at my lips and twist them into a delighted grin. As I gaze around Her Majesty's chambers, the tiny red diamonds begin to sparkle violently, some of them twitching as though they have their own heartbeat. They then begin to dance in an elegant waltz around one another until all I see is a solid wall of cherry-colored crystal.

It's the most beautiful thing I've ever seen.

At first the wall of diamonds is solid, but then tiny bursts of light peer through it. The pores in the wall enlarge, swell, until they reveal a resplendent scene in front of me. Her Majesty, completely nude, bouncing up and down over my naked chest.

My God. My manhood is within her, the walls of her privates closing in on me like a pillowed mollusk.

It feels magnificent.

Is this what Tim meant when he told me the physical act of intimacy was the greatest gift given to man?

Her Majesty is doing the bulk of the work, but I begin to undulate my hips in tandem with her. She bends her head backward, tweaking her own perky breasts as I secrete my own warm fluid inside her body.

Today, the Jack of Hearts is a man.

My vision blurs, and Her Majesty's womanhood opens wide, swallowing my entire body up into it. Somehow, I am inside her body, privy to its stunning ins and outs. Her glorious stomach, her sumptuous liver, her exquisite intestines—all of them lined with the same red diamonds as her office.

Again, glimmers of light begin to burst through, small at first but then broadening until I'm back in Her Majesty's four-poster bed, still completely nude, but no longer experiencing the physical pleasure of her cantering upon my shaft. Instead, she is at my side, a toothy smile splitting her powdered face.

I cock my head, and she gestures to the floor. Her bedchambers are lined with dark-red cherry hardwood, and splayed across it is the body of a woman I recognize—the Three of Hearts. One of the servers in the club who, like me, never got much attention from the patrons. I never saw Three accompany anyone behind the velvet curtains.

I slowly lift my body up and gaze at her. She's in her Aces uniform—a black bikini speckled with silver hearts, baring the bulk of her porcelain skin that is unmarred except for a few faint bruises on her neck.

"Yes, Chet," the serpentine hiss of Her Majesty's whisper glides into my ear. "She's dead."

I blink. Dead?

I feel nothing for Three. We were never close. But how did she die? I dare not ask. Her Majesty still has not given me permission to speak.

She reaches under the bed and pulls out a long, jagged saw. She leans back into my ear, licking the lobe before she croons gently, "Off with her head."

I point to my own chest, as if to clarify that she expects me to do the honors.

She nods slowly, her grin growing. "Of course, Chet. The head must be removed, and then we begin the harvest."

The harvest? What does she mean? It's early March.

But I dare not ask for further elucidation. Her Majesty bade me to decapitate the girl's body, and I owe her everything in my life.

So I do it. I bring the blade against my former coworker's throat, and I saw. Right. Left. Right. Left.

The throat bursts easily, spilling blood over Her Majesty's immaculate floor. It's fascinating, how easily the knife cuts through. There is a little resistance when I hit her spinal cord, but I make quick work of it. Soon Three's head is removed from the rest of her body.

I'm mystified by the biology. The musculature. The fragility of the human design.

Three is plain, but she is still a beautiful woman.

And her inside is even more beautiful than her outside.

FIVE YEARS I've been the bouncer at Aces. I've met so many interesting people. City and state government officials, socialites, billionaire business owners, the crème de la crème of the Chicago metropolitan area.

I have been most enraptured by a man who's been coming to

the club for quite some time. The son of a legacy patron of Aces, Henry Hathaway, the disgraced former mayor of Chicago.

Maddox is his name. Mr. Maddox Hathaway.

He came alone at first. Then he started bringing a well-respected surgeon with him, his best friend. One Dr. Harrison O'Rourke. They're close, but their friendship is normal.

For the most part, at least. They have some sort of shared fascination with teapots. Around Christmastime last year, Mr. Hathaway gifted Dr. O'Rourke a teapot-shaped ornament. It struck me as odd, but then again, all the Aces patrons have their peculiarities.

Her Majesty has told me to keep an eye on him. Apparently, toward the end of his life, Mr. Hathaway's father was making some trouble for her. I don't know the full details, but she has made it clear that if he puts one toe out of line, his membership—inherited from his father—will be revoked.

Aces has hidden cameras and microphones scattered throughout the premises. I've checked in on Mr. Hathaway quite a bit. He's never once indicated any wariness of Her Majesty's methodology of discontinuing her employees' services. He usually just spends his time at Spades, grabs a few drinks—typically a gin and tonic laced with elderflower liqueur—and occasionally courts a woman, takes her home with him.

Tonight the Black Door opens, and in walks Mr. Hathaway. But on his arm is not the rugged Dr. O'Rourke, but rather a petite woman with long blond hair.

She's angelic. Perhaps the most beautiful woman I've ever seen.

I offer her my signature grin, hoping it will entice her into the fray.

She swallows, her eyes widening. The muscles in her arms and jaw tense, and for a moment it looks like she's going to run the other way. Mr. Hathaway leans into her, murmurs something into her ear.

The woman's body relaxes. She then takes a deep breath in and walks toward me, Mr. Hathaway at her side.

Mr. Hathaway gestures toward me. "This is Chet. He'll be checking us in."

I gaze at the woman. "Is this your first time, young lady?"

She swallows. "Yes, sir."

I widen my eyes. No one has ever called me "sir" in my life. "No need to call me sir. I'm Chester Tabbit, the club bouncer. You can call me Chet. I'm responsible for checking members in."

I reach my hand out, and after hesitating a moment, the woman shakes it.

I turn to Mr. Hathaway. "ID?"

He rolls his eyes, like he does every time he comes into the club. "Come on, Chet. You know who I am. I've been coming here for years now."

"And as I have told you before, Mr. Hathaway, the only person who gets in without ID is Rouge. Club policy. Everyone else, no matter who they are—politicians, businessmen, even the President of the United States himself—has to show ID at the front door and be checked against the list."

Mr. Hathaway nods and grabs his wallet out of the inner pocket of his suit jacket. He pulls out his driver's license and hands it to me.

"You too, miss." I nod toward the woman.

She uneasily reaches into her bag, pulls out her wallet, and hands her license to me.

I scan both of them. I've seen Mr. Hathaway's countless times, but the woman's is new. She truly is beautiful. Angelic in her beauty.

"Maravilla. A beautiful name. Spanish, I assume?"

She nods. "Yes. My father was born in Spain."

"It means wonder, doesn't it?"

Miss Wonder.

I find her most mesmerizing.

A hint of a British accent, and the most beautiful hair and skin I've ever seen on a woman.

I don't want to have her in the physical way. I've only done that with one woman—Her Majesty. And only once. Never again. It was a lovely moment, and I don't want to spoil it with another.

But there is something about Miss Wonder that draws me in, something I've never experienced when meeting a woman. Not even Her Majesty.

I pull out a small electronic tablet and pull up the live feed from the Aces security cameras.

The two of them are in Spades, of course. Sitting at a small table, giving their order to the Seven of Spades. Mr. Hathaway is always in Spades, though he did socialize with some charming young women in Diamonds a few weeks back. His manner with this woman is different. Mr. Hathaway is leaning in, and even through the grain of the camera's picture, it's clear by the sparkle in his eyes that he is as enthralled with this woman as I am.

They're close to one of the hidden microphones. I place a bud in my ear and listen in on their conversation.

"Do you ever go to the symphony?" Miss Wonder asks.

He shakes his head. "I haven't. I've always wanted to. Chicago has a world-class symphony orchestra."

She beams. "I'll have to take you sometime. I have a few friends who work in the box office, colleagues of mine from school. They can get us discounted tickets. I catch a performance now and then, when my schedule allows. I usually drag Dinah along. But it would be much nicer to have a handsome man on my arm."

He leans in. "I'd love to accompany you to a concert of theirs sometime. Who's your favorite composer?"

She pauses before chuckling nervously. "Shostakovich."

Mr. Hathaway widens his eyes. "Never heard of him."

"He's a Russian composer. Soviet, technically. He composed some fantastic music, mostly while living under the rule of Stalin."

My soul leaps with joy. Dmitri Shostakovich is my favorite composer as well. The way he uses musical codes in his symphonies and concerti has always enchanted me. I've never lost my love of riddles, and he's the master of flawlessly integrating them into his works.

Not unlike Mr. Hathaway, I'm leaning in.

MISS WONDER HAS ACCOMPANIED Mr. Hathaway to the club every night this weekend. The second night, she burst out of the club suddenly after she and Mr. Hathaway had a minor spat. When I reviewed the security footage, I learned she was very upset by Her Majesty's policy of having the waitstaff entertain the patrons intimately in exchange for monetary tips.

Mr. Hathaway followed her soon after, and the sounds of a distant scuffle reverberated into the Aces lobby. I'd have gone and investigated myself, but Her Majesty has always insisted I remain chained to this desk during patron hours. I'm not even allowed to leave for the bathroom. I only ever leave my station at her own beckoning.

This position has saved me. I no longer live at the Caterpillar Hotel, but rather in a small hovel of my own on the edge of town. But over the years, Her Majesty's constant presence and meticulous micromanaging style has begun to grate on me.

Sometimes I wonder what it would be like if I *ran Aces Underground.*

Perhaps with Miss Wonder at my side.

I'm deeply engrossed in a delightful article in the Chicago Tribune *about a mass murder that occurred in Elgin—unrelated to our doings here at Aces—when the Black Door bursts open.*

And who should it be but Miss Wonder herself!

But the club doesn't open for several hours. What is she doing here now?

"Miss Wonder, what are you doing here?"

"Hi, Chet." She pastes on a smile. "I left my credit card here last night."

I cock my head. "I noticed you left in a hurry. I hope you didn't run into...trouble."

Those noises in the alley last night. I can't help but wonder what happened. But Miss Wonder is clearly okay, thanks be to Jove. Not a scratch on her.

She dusts off her jacket. "I'm fine now. That's what matters. And I need to go downstairs and get my credit card. I won't be a minute."

I want to let her in because I want to give this woman whatever she wants. But Her Majesty would have my head—and that's not just an expression in this case. "I'm afraid the rules of the club still stand. Because you are not a member, I cannot allow you inside unless you are a guest of someone on the list."

"Yes, but I'm not actually going to go to the club. I'm going to settle my tab, turn right back around, and leave. It'll take thirty seconds."

I grin. "Even thirty-second visits are against club policy, Miss

Wonder." I shrug. "If you want to come back with Mr. Hathaway or another member, I'll gladly let you inside."

"That's ridiculous." She points at the door. "I've already been down there. Twice now. It's not like I don't know what it looks like. Plus, if I never settle my tab, you'll never get the money for my drinks."

"One gin and tonic and one dirty vodka martini are hardly enough to put our ledgers in the red."

"That's hardly any way to run a—" She stops, narrowing her eyes at me. "Wait, how do you know what our drink orders were?"

I raise my eyebrows. I dare not tell her I've been spying on her both nights she's been here. "It's my job to know, Miss Wonder."

"It's hardly the job of a bouncer to memorize the drinks of his club's patrons."

I wrinkle my nose. "I'm sure you understand by this point that Aces Underground is no normal club."

"What if I don't come back with Maddox? You have my credit card—my personal property—and I demand that you allow me to go down and retrieve it."

"If you don't want to call Mr. Hathaway or another member to escort you, you're welcome to call your bank to get a new credit card."

She slams her hands down on my desk. "This is ridiculous. Just let me go down there, Chet."

Great Scott. The woman has fire. I already knew that, but this is the first time it's manifested itself into a violent act. I like it.

This woman is the first person I've allowed into Aces who has the power to take down anyone.

Even Her Majesty.

The credit card is clearly a pretext. She wants to check things out in the daylight.

I noticed the Seven of Spades was hovering over her table a lot more than her other patrons last evening. Her Majesty has told me that she's been exhibiting signs of wavering, that I should keep a special eye on her.

Perhaps there's something there.

Either way, things have been too tedious for too long.

It's time to invoke a touch of chaos.

"Tell you what," I say. "Go on down."

INDEED, Miss Wonder sneaked behind the velvet curtains and confronted the Seven. The Seven spoke—actually spoke*—to her, despite the rules to the contrary.*

Our Queen doesn't believe in second chances.

The Seven will be dead by dinnertime.

But perhaps this is my chance.

Miss Wonder is a curious little kitty-cat. And the kitty will be back tonight, her claws bared.

And she deserves a little nudge in the right direction.

I already know where Her Majesty will place the head of the Seven. She picks her spots out in advance, prepares them in case of an unplanned discontinuation of service. It will be in the little clearing out by Dam Number Four in the nature preserve by the airport—the same one where I met Tim all those years ago. It was I who suggested that the byproducts of her harvest be entombed there.

I sit down and pen a riddle. I'll slip it into Mr. Hathaway's coat this evening whenever the opportunity presents itself.

It's some of my best work. Without thinking, I sign it with my initials. CAT.

But then I erase them. I don't want this coming back to bite me if Miss Wonder cocks this up.

But already I know she won't.

For several reasons. I'll make some insurance. The last server to be discontinued was the Nine of Diamonds. I keep a deck of cards in my desk at all times, and I'll slip a Seven of Spades and a Nine of Diamonds into her bag when she returns tonight.

That will seal the deal.

But even without the insurance, I know she will succeed in whichever task she presents herself with.

Because Miss Wonder... She's my angel.

ALL WENT AS PLANNED. I sneaked the playing cards into Miss Wonder's purse in a small manila envelope when she reached into it for her ID, and I had easy access to Mr. Hathaway's jacket when he pinned me against the wall upon his exit. A little sleight of hand goes a long way.

Again, he left Aces after Miss Wonder, but this time it was not in the wake of a quarrel. He seemed to be on Miss Wonder's tail.

It will only be a matter of time before the pieces start falling into place like a king and queen on a chessboard.

I'M overjoyed when my burner phone rings in the dead of night.

I turn on an app to distort my voice and dictate the second half of the riddle to Miss Wonder. It's well written, some of my best work.

Now to wait.

What has been set into motion now cannot be stopped.

A knock at my door.

No one knocks at my door.

I slowly sit up from my inflatable couch and cross the room, look through the peephole.

My heart palpitates as I realize Her Majesty is at my door.

She's draped in a smart pantsuit, her hair tied back into a ponytail and an enormous pair of stylish sunglasses over her face, but even incognito she's easy to identify. The fire of her hair is unmistakable.

I open the door. "Rouge?"

She waltzes in without invitation. "Chet, darling. Put on a pot of tea."

I bow my head. "Of course, my Queen." I quickly fill a kettle with water and set it on my gas stove. "It will just be a moment."

"Excellent. I won't be long." She sits at my kitchen table and crosses her legs. "I'm afraid I have some troubling news to share."

"Troubling?" The kettle whistles—it always seems to heat up faster in Her Majesty's presence—and I pour it over a few teabags into a plain teapot.

"Yes," she says. "You know Mr. Sinclair, my King of Hearts?"

"Of course."

"He telephoned me late last night saying that he spotted two silhouetted figures leaving Dam Number Four in the Forest Park reserve in the wee hours of the morning."

For once I hold back a smile. Mr. Hathaway and Miss Wonder must have figured it out.

"Really?" I pour the tea into two delicate antique cups—housewarming gifts from Her Majesty herself.

"Indeed. Mr. Sinclair then investigated and discovered some of the soil in our rose garden had been disturbed."

"Could His Majesty be mistaken? After all, Seven's crown was placed there fairly recently, was it not?"

"Seven's appendages were placed there the night before, yes," she continues. "But it doesn't take long for the topsoil to dry after it has been exposed to the air. No more than a few hours. But the soil below Seven's rosebush was still quite dark, quite moist. Earthworms all about. Someone had clearly been digging there."

"Could it have been another King?" I place one of the teacups in front of her.

Her Majesty shakes her head. "It was someone unauthorized." She stands, paces my small kitchen. "Upon further investigation, Mr. Sinclair realized that Seven's head had indeed been exhumed."

I place a hand over my heart. "Great Jupiter."

It is a faux gesture. Inside my head, I am giggling like a rabid hyena. Finally a change of pace. Finally one of Her Majesty's meticulously laid plans has a kink in it.

Something to break up the monotony.

Her Majesty approaches me, traces a finger across my jaw. "Do you know anything about this?"

I swallow. "Of course not, my Queen."

She widens her eyes, looks me up and down. Her lips curl gently. "You know, Chet. Two of Seven's organs have been claimed. An elderly couple over at St. Charles General. They were going to give up completely on their search for new organs, but then her heart and lungs matched their profiles perfectly."

I cock my head.

"One person died so that two people could live," she says. "Two lives are more important than one life, as I'm sure you understand. Justice is mathematic."

"I'm not—"

"Of course you're not, love." She draws her hand down my chest, up my shirt, pinches my right nipple. "But if you do happen to come across any information that might be helpful in determining the identities of the people who took Seven's head, I

assume you'll let me know immediately. And who knows"—she leans her head toward mine, running her tongue along my ear as she whispers—"maybe I'll find myself grateful to you. Maybe I'll let you do that thing you liked so much that evening in my chambers."

That thing I liked?

But then the memory comes searing back.

Before the head of the Three came off, when Her Majesty allowed me to—

All the blood in my body rushes toward my bits, and already I'm engorging.

I haven't enjoyed the physical manifestation of love since that night in Her Majesty's chambers. Not once. After you have a Queen, you can't cavort with the peasantry.

She smirks as she looks down between my legs, and then slinks out of the room, leaving me holding myself in my apartment.

What to do now?

It was not my intention for Her Majesty to be this upset, or even for her darkest secrets to be spilled.

I merely wanted to stir things up a bit, rock the boat. Give Her Majesty a challenge to overcome.

But the ripples have expanded wider than my original intent.

Perhaps the time has come to reel things in, control the damage.

All without upsetting Her Majesty, without letting her realize it was I who set this all in motion to begin with.

But if things backfire, I want to make sure Miss Wonder is safe.

So that night, while she is sleeping, I slip into her apartment—foolish of her to leave a key under her mat; I'll have to have a word with her about her safety—and plant a small trinket. The small shampoo bottle I've kept in my pocket ever since I left the Caterpillar and struck out on my own.

If things go south, this will be the one small piece of evidence that might lead the authorities to Her Majesty.

ONLY A FEW DAYS pass before I get my chance. It's Valentine's Day, one of Aces Underground's biggest nights. Nearly everyone who is a member shows up and brings a guest. Some of the higher-up patrons can bring more than one guest. I've dyed my eyebrows in a vivid shade of pink and am wearing a pinstriped suit in a matching color.

The Black Door opens and in walks my angel along with her gentleman escort.

I raise my eyebrows as they make their entrance. "Ah, Miss Wonder. I was hoping we'd see you again soon."

She smiles a touch too quickly. "Can't get rid of us that easily, Chet."

We talk a few minutes more, I drop a few Shakespeare quotes —completely lost on them, regrettably—and they descend into the club's bowels.

They're acting normal.

Perhaps I have nothing to worry about at all.

MY HACKLES ARE RAISED AGAIN. Mr. Hathaway and Miss Wonder left the club very abruptly. Mr. Hathaway said they were going to get a breath of fresh air, but they haven't returned.

They were preceded in their departure by the King of Diamonds—the real King of Diamonds, not Mr. Hathaway's new title—who also looked to be in a hurry.

So much seems to go on here.

Do I really know it all?

I SLEPT *nary a wink last night. I barely had enough energy before coming to the club tonight to wash the pink dye out of my eyebrows.*

Nothing has happened, at least as far as I know.

Perhaps the King of Diamonds killed them.

That would make things a bit easier.

The Black Door swings open, and—can it be?

My two favorite patrons.

I twist my lips into my trademark grin. "Mr. Hathaway. Miss Wonder. We were wondering where you ended up last night."

Miss Wonder wrinkles her forehead. "What do you mean?"

I tent my fingers. "You left rather early in the evening. You said you'd be right back, that you were just getting a breath of fresh air." I raise an eyebrow, keeping my voice steady. "You never returned."

"Plans change." Mr. Hathaway hands me his driver's license. "Alissa will be my guest tonight."

"Of course. Wouldn't expect anything to the contrary." I leer at my angel. "It would appear you've truly captured Mr. Hathaway's attention, Miss Wonder."

She swallows. "I suppose I have."

As I look over Mr. Hathaway's ID, he rakes his eyes over me, the wrinkles in his forehead deepening. Finally he speaks.

"Chet, what's your middle name?"

Ah, so they have *figured it out! But best to play it coy, lest Her Majesty finds out I'm involved. "That's a bit of a personal question, Mr. Hathaway. Whyever would you be asking?"*

"I think you know why," he says.

Miss Wonder grabs Mr. Hathaway's arm. "What does this have to do with anything?"

"Just answer the damned question, Chet."

I bounce my eyebrows a few times. Time to give them their next piece in the puzzle, but this one will hopefully lead them into a trap. "It's Aristotle, Mr. Hathaway. My middle name is Aristotle."

Mr. Hathaway reaches into his wallet and pulls out the riddle I penned mere days ago, with my initials all but completely erased from the bottom. He deduces quickly that I'm the one who wrote it. I deny having any idea of what they're talking about, but I ensure my tone is laced with just enough playfulness that they stay on the line.

Miss Wonder then realizes that I placed the cards in her purse as an additional hint. She is not correct about when I dropped them, but I don't tell her this. All that matters is she knows the intent behind them.

I need to lead them deeper into the rabbit hole.

If only—

Heavens above! Mr. Hathaway pulls out a key encrusted with red diamonds, one that I recognize immediately.

Oh, things could not have worked out better than this!

This key was lost long ago. Her Majesty has a few copies of the key to her safe, but this one has been missing for ages, before I even began working at the club. Before Mr. Hathaway came to the club. Back when his father was a member before his untimely death.

I did a little digging when I first started looking into Mr. Hathaway at Her Majesty's request. I know the late Mr. Hathaway left the current Mr. Hathaway a riddle, one that I was able to decipher immediately but that I did not believe he had the wit to figure out for himself.

The first part of the riddle leads to this key, and the second part leads to the small compartment over the ladies' room where the server's tissues are stored temporarily before being distributed to local hospitals. They seem to have only figured out the first part of the riddle, meaning that tonight is the night the two of them must be stopped.

But again, this must be handled delicately.

I widen my eyes in mock shock. "Looks like you found your way down the river of tears, Mr. Hathaway."

I eventually lead them to the conclusion that the key opens Her Majesty's safe. They bustle down the mirrored staircase.

And now we wait.

My blood-red radio rings. The grainy voice of Her Majesty. "Chet, there's a disturbance in the Diamonds section. I'm going to need you to come down."

My heart leaps. This must be it. Miss Wonder is creating a distraction so Mr. Hathaway can sneak into Her Majesty's office.

I could simply tell her to go after him now, but—

She needs to find both of them. And it has to occur organically. If I tell her to look now, she will be suspicious of me. And I can't lose my job.

I'll make sure Miss Wonder doesn't die. I will make arrangements for her to be held at the Caterpillar Hotel—perhaps even in my old room—and convince Her Majesty to keep Mr. Hathaway alive for his political influence. Miss Wonder will be kept alive as a bargaining chip.

They'll have to be kept there until they break, of course. Likely a month or longer.

It will be a long time to be away from my angel, but it will be worth it.

I descend the mirrored staircase and clamber toward the

Diamonds section. Indeed, I was right! Miss Wonder has tousled herself with another young woman—Miss Pia Linnet, a perennial guest of various clubgoers.

Mr. Hathaway is, predictably, nowhere to be seen. But Her Majesty hasn't noticed. She's far too entrenched in the scuffle occurring at her feet.

I peel my angel off Miss Linnet's body. "Miss Wonder, perhaps you should take a moment to cool down."

"Get off me, Chet!" she growls, trying to wriggle out of my grasp. But I'm stronger than she is, and I clamp down on her body hard. Finally she relents.

"Thank you, Chet," Her Majesty says. "I was worried that this might get out of hand." She looks around. "Where did Mr. Hathaway go?"

No. Not yet. I need to set the scene perfectly.

I raise an eyebrow. "I believe he was grabbing Miss Wonder's coat. They'll be heading out." I let go of Miss Wonder and turn to Her Majesty. "But I do need to speak to you for a moment, Rouge. Somewhere private."

She nods. "My office."

No. Cannot be there. Not until Miss Wonder is in her position. "I'd rather not meet there. We'll just go into a private area." I offer a smile. "It won't be a moment, I promise you."

She narrows her eyes but then acquiesces—a rare victory for me. "Fine." She turns to Miss Wonder. "Ms. Maravilla, I hope you know that we have a zero-tolerance policy when it comes to physical altercations at Aces Underground."

She brushes herself off. "I didn't see you stopping us."

She chuckles. "In an outfit like mine? I don't think I'd be very successful. That's why I called Chet."

"It took him several minutes to get here." Miss Wonder stares her Queen down. "Admit it. You were enjoying the spectacle."

She widens her eyes, making the wings framing them take flight. "Nonsense. I loathe violence. Nothing upsets my poor heart more."

Miss Wonder smirks, but then she heads off.

She'll thread herself through the eye of the needle, and I'll only need to stall Her Majesty for a few moments.

I take her into the grand suite. "Rouge."

She crosses her arms. "Chet."

"How are you doing? I wanted to ask if there had been any development with regard to the Seven of Spades."

She jerks her gaze toward the curtains' opening. "Careful, Chet. These areas aren't soundproofed, as you are well aware."

"Of course." I bow my head. "Apologies, my Queen."

She curls her lips. "And there is no news. But the Kings are out and about trying to track down information. I have it on good authority that Mr. Hathaway may in fact be aware that his father's death was not entirely natural."

I raise an eyebrow. "Oh?"

Again, so much I don't know.

Her Majesty's lips twist into a grin. "It's a story I'm quite proud of. Henry Hathaway was the last person who tried to expose what we do here at Aces. How we...help others. It started with his HOUSE Act, which was meant to make us more transparent. That of course was a complete flop, so he tried taking matters into his own hands. It was ten years ago, back when my father started getting sick and I began taking over. He was already washed up from his last term as mayor and was looking to discover something about me that might help shine up his tarnished legacy. When I caught whiff of his plans to reveal our inner workings, I had his food poisoned with a concoction that mimicked the effects of a heart attack." She cackles. "It was divine."

I cross my arms. I understood Henry Hathaway knew some-

thing about what was going on, because I'd found out about the riddle he'd left his son upon his death. But no one would have taken his rantings and ravings seriously after what happened to his political career.

I want to find out more, but it's been five minutes or so. It's time to take Rouge to her office.

I bow my head once more. "I suppose I should be returning to my atrium. Do you mind if I use the bathroom in your office before I return?"

Her Majesty raises her eyebrows. "You've never asked to use the bathroom before."

"Yes, but I ate something that doesn't agree with me. And it would be improper for an employee to use the guest restrooms during service hours."

She purses her lips but gestures out the grand suite. "Have at it. I'll be right behind you."

I cross the club and make my way to Her Majesty's red door. I open it slowly and sure enough, Miss Wonder and Mr. Hathaway have opened the secret door behind the armoire in the office. I step through. The two of them are surrounded by a small pond of red diamonds and have their noses pressed into Her Majesty's manifesto.

All the evidence they need to put her away. And this is all the evidence I need to put them *away.*

"Miss Wonder. Mr. Hathaway."

Mr. Hathaway looks up, gives me a look I've never seen from him. As if he's actually glad to see me. "Chet," he says. "We need you to escort us out of here as quickly and discreetly as possible."

I clasp my hands and slowly crane my neck over my left shoulder. I'm positively giddy. All my players have landed exactly into their places. "You might want to see what's going on in here," I call out.

Her Majesty narrows her eyes at me but then glides into the office, her lips pursed. When she sees Miss Wonder and Mr. Hathaway through the secret door in her armoire, she draws a slow hand up to the diamond necklace nestled in her cleavage, her eyes widened. She glares at the two invaders. "It looks like you two have been palming an ace."

They don't move.

Her Majesty raises her scepter. "I'm afraid Aces Underground has a strict policy about cheaters in the Diamonds section. This applies to all patrons, even the King and Queen themselves."

Miss Wonder shrieks.

Mr. Hathaway lunges toward her, placing himself between my angel and my Queen.

But Her Majesty is quick, and she smacks her scepter to the back of Mr. Hathaway's skull.

He crumples to the floor, and in a flash Miss Wonder is lying beside him.

I instinctively kneel at her motionless body, place a finger against her neck. She's okay, thanks be to the heavens. A small welt on her forehead, but that will go down in a few days' time.

Her Majesty lowers her scepter, moves toward her desk, and takes a seat. She reaches into a drawer and pulls out two small needles. She injects a small amount into both of their necks. "This will keep them unconscious until after service. Then you'll have to take care of them. Florian is out of town this week."

"Take care of them?" I ask.

"It is not nearly as often that I find myself dispatching patrons, but it is not unheard of." She scans the two bodies. "But their organs are in perfect shape, I'm sure."

"My Queen"—I bow my head—"if I may, perhaps it would be prudent to keep them alive. Mr. Hathaway still maintains some influence in the city's political sphere, and Miss Won—I mean,

Miss Maravilla—could make an excellent bargaining chip to get him to do what you want."

She scrunches her forehead. "The Hathaway legacy is in tatters. Maddox has no more influence than his father."

"For now. But people's memories fade. It's been well over a decade since Mr. Hathaway's father died. I believe there is potential for us. And either way, his family's reputation notwithstanding, he remains a person in the spotlight. A sudden disappearance would draw suspicion."

She crosses her arms. "Perhaps you're right. Take them to the Caterpillar then. Break into their phones. Concoct some cock-and-bull story to their closest friends about going on a vacation together. Fish their keys out of their pockets, go to their apartments, and make them look as though they've packed a bag for a long trip. We'll starve the two of them out at the Caterpillar Hotel until they're ready to play ball."

"As you wish, my Queen."

"And Chet?"

"Yes?"

Her Majesty looks over the pair of bodies, her lips curling into a shrewd grin. "Once you finish, meet me back here. I believe you are entitled to a reward."

I DID as my Queen commanded. Dropped Miss Wonder and Mr. Hathaway off in separate rooms at the Caterpillar, wrote texts to their loved ones and employers saying they would be out of town for an unspecified amount of time, and then staged their individual apartments to look as if they'd both gone on an extended holiday.

I'm not sure I trust Her Majesty to play nice with them once they agree to do her bidding.

The small shampoo bottle I left at Miss Wonder's apartment, however, will remain untouched.

A small clue—perhaps one of their friends will discover it.

Tiny seeds yield bountiful harvests.

A MONTH HAS PASSED. Her Majesty checks the Caterpillar Hotel weekly. Neither she nor I—and certainly none of the cards—have actually communicated with Mr. Hathaway and my angel. They remain in their hotel, slowly getting thinner. Soon they will be on the brink of demise, and that will be when we strike.

That is, if something else doesn't happen first.

And like a lightning flash, the Black Door opens, revealing none other than Dr. Harrison O'Rourke, Mr. Hathaway's best friend!

It is as if the Celestia are begging me to play with these people more.

And, as their vessel, I will happily oblige.

Dr. O'Rourke demands to be let in.

He's curious about his friend.

I will play coy. Tell him it's against the rules. Only when he thinks he's convinced me will I allow him in.

Always let them think they're in control.

He slams his hands on my desk. "Chet. You're not hearing me. I demand that you let me in."

A knock at the door. I open it to reveal Her Highness, Miss Bianca.

She will just get in the way. Damn! "Miss Bianca, aren't you supposed to start singing soon?"

She nods. "Just have to run to my car real quick, grab my finishing powder. I'll be back before my set begins."

"I see." I gesture her through the door. "Be back quickly or you'll be missed."

"You don't have to tell me twice." She walks through the door and stops in her tracks when she lays eyes on Dr. O'Rourke.

There is an instant attraction. Its aroma swaths the entire room. It's almost sickening.

And I realize.

Her Highness might just be a perfect ally to Dr. O'Rourke.

But I mustn't be too hasty. Let it evolve organically. Let them focus on me as a common enemy, and then Her Majesty. They have been speaking for several moments, completely unaware of my presence.

I cut between the two of them. "Yes, and it is just luscious to see a new friendship blossoming. But you'll have to take it outside. Although, Miss Bianca"—I pretend to check my watch, even though its battery has been dead for years—"you'll have to keep it brief. Your first curtain is in ten minutes."

Dr. O'Rourke cocks his head. "Your first curtain?"

Her Highness gestures to the door that leads to the mirrored staircase. "I'm the singer here."

Dr. O'Rourke shoots his eyebrows up. "I thought you looked familiar. You have a lovely voice."

Her Highness blushes. "Thank you. It's a living, I suppose."

More flirtation. I need to seal this deal quickly.

"If it's a singer you're looking for," I interrupt, "you are welcome to scout Michigan Avenue for one, Dr. O'Rourke. But I really must insist that you leave now."

And that does it. Her Highness slowly draws her finger over her left eyebrow, her lower lip trembling slightly as she looks from me to Dr. O'Rourke and then back to me.

"Chet," she says. "I would like to invite Dr. O'Rourke to the club as my guest."

Bingo.

Her Majesty is displeased.

"What on earth possessed you to allow a non-member in?"

"Miss Bianca made a good argument. She is not a full-time employee here, and the rules do not specify anything regarding independent contractors. By her logic, she must be a member who performs additional actions, not unlike Mr. Rose."

Her Majesty crosses her arms. She isn't buying it. She slowly stands and sits on the edge of her desk, her long legs straddling me as I sit in the wingback across from her. "Chet, my darling," she says. "Are you unhappy here?"

"Of course not, my Queen."

"Then why all this acting up? You used to be so obedient, so loyal. Now you're doing things on your own accord."

"I was the one who found Mr. Hathaway and Miss Maravilla in your office."

"And how, I wonder, did they know how to get into my office in the first place? How on earth did they discover the Seven's head in the nature preserve the weekend before Valentine's Day?"

"My Queen—"

"I have no proof, of course." She examines her nails, picks a bit of fluff off one of them. "But you've changed, Chet. You've begun to labor under the delusion that you are your own person." She lifts her leg and pushes her stilettoed heal into my left thigh. "Allow me to relieve you of that misconception."

I don't respond.

She grinds her heel further, ripping through my dress pants and drawing blood. "You are nothing *without me, Chet! Do you hear me? You and your little friend would still be picking cans out of the garbage if it weren't for me. Do you understand?"*

I look down.

She grabs me by the neck, forces me to look her in the eyes. "This will be your last strike, Chet. You know better than most that I don't believe in second chances. Because of your stellar service record, I have looked the other way for several weeks now. That ends today. Do you understand?"

"Yes."

"Yes, what?"

"Yes, my Queen." I bend down and kiss her hand. She responds by prying my mouth open and sticking three of her fingers in it. I run my tongue up and down her fingers in reverence. She moans.

She removes her fingers from my mouth, wipes them dry on her bodice. "Thank you, Chet." She checks her watch. "I'd love to stay and discuss this further, but I'm due at the Jade Sanctum. That will be all."

~

BUT THAT WASN'T ALL.

Because when I came home that night, a surprise lay in wait for me.

In my bed, lying against the pillow, eyes closed as if in a deep sleep...was the head of my best friend in the world, Timothy Mann.

A drop of liquid forms at the edge of my eye and slips down my cheek.

Is this...sorrow?

I've read about it, but I've never experienced it until now.

My lips twist against my will into a grin. Every emotion evokes the same physical manifestation from my oral cavity.

This is a final warning from Her Majesty. One more toe out of line and it'll be my head next on the docket.

All this time, I thought I was immune.

I was the one who could play with Her Majesty. Push her buttons.

But now she's drawn a line.

Even I *am not allowed to cross her.*

I gave my purity to her.

I gave my life to her.

And it wasn't enough to save Tim.

I cradle the head of my best friend in my hands and then kiss it on the lips.

I will do what I must to bring Her Majesty to her knees.

I will achieve justice for Tim, for all the others. Even if it means taking myself down in the process.

I know now where my allegiances lie.

At least... I know where they lie for the time being.

32

BIANCA

"So let me get this straight," Harrison says, his face completely drained of color. "You've decided you're on our side now that Rouge has decided to fuck you over as well? Only when her bullshit begins to affect *you* do you grow a conscience?"

Chet twists his lips. "All you need to know, Doctor, is that I am on your side now. My motives ought not be a factor in your decision. I remain your best shot at taking Rouge down."

"But how can we be sure we trust you?" I ask. "What if that whole story you just told us is a complete fabrication?"

Chet shrugs. "You *can't* trust me. But that does not change the fact that you need me."

I swallow. It's true. Besides my sister, no one understands the ins and outs of Aces Underground better than Chet. Mr. Rose is probably the third-most helpful, but seeing as he's currently recovering from a fountain pen to his eye, I doubt he'll be eager to help us.

"If you need further proof of where my loyalties lie," Chet

continues, "I must point out the slain King currently bleeding out on the bed."

Harrison swallows. "Right. Him. I'd almost forgotten."

Chet's lips twitch. "I believe the two of you are acquainted."

I widen my eyes. "What?"

Harrison glances toward the body of the man in the bed. "We were friends when we were younger. Got into some bull-shit together. Kid stuff." He scratches at his jaw.

There's more to this story. Maybe it has something to do with the fact that he hates the color green. The man in the head has lime-green highlights in his hair.

But we have bigger fish to fry right now.

"At any rate, Miss Bianca," Chet says, his grin pasted on his face like the freaking Joker, "I do believe you owe me a favor. You declared as much the night I allowed Dr. O'Rourke into the club. I'm here to collect."

I frown. "This is hardly the same thing."

Chet raises his snow-white eyebrows. "You asked me to break your sister's rules. Now I'm asking the same in kind. Seems like a good trade-off to me. It's not as if one can qualify favors. One can only *quantify* them."

I roll my eyes. More of his fortune-cookie mumbo-jumbo.

"May I say something?" Jack asks.

I turn to him. He's been silent since the King went down. "Jack, I'm sorry. We've been ignoring you."

He chuckles. "I'm a server at Aces. A male server at that. I'm used to being ignored. It's when people paid attention to me at the club that I knew I was in trouble."

I cross over to him, squeeze his hand. "You're free of them now. We've killed the man who was sent to kill you."

Jack shakes his head. "No. There are three more Kings.

And Rouge herself. I don't think I'll be safe until all of them are behind bars." His gaze darkens. "Or better yet, in the ground." He paces around the room, looks down at the King of Hearts. "At any rate, I'm no longer an employee of Aces Underground. I want to embrace the name I was born with, the name my parents gave me."

I look over. "What is it?"

He swallows. "It's Vanya. Vanya Dmitriev." He runs his hands through his wavy hair. "My God. It's a name I haven't spoken for five years."

I wrap my arms around him. "Nice to meet you, Vanya."

"We're going to do everything we can to make sure you can live the rest of your life as your authentic self," Harrison says.

"You'll have my help," Jack—Vanya—says. "I want to take Rouge down just as much as any of you." He glances toward Chet. "But can we trust *him?*"

"I have already made my argument that you need not trust me to ally with me," Chet says. "I hate repeating myself, but I am truly your best shot at taking down Rouge. I still have Tim Mann's head in my refrigerator in my home. Perhaps that will serve as evidence enough for you all?"

"Christ, no." Harrison rubs at his forehead. "I don't think that would convince me anyway."

I walk up to Harrison, wrap an arm around his waist. "I'm not either, Harrison. But I think Chet makes a good point. And that story was too complex and specific to be a fabrication."

Harrison darts his gaze over toward Chet. "Not for him it isn't."

I frown. "Perhaps. But"—I drop my jaw—"the teapot. That was you too, Chet. Wasn't it?"

His grin widens. "Indeed it was. I planted it in Dr. O'Rourke's car. It was too easy to disguise myself as the valet at your apartment, Miss Bianca."

"And that led us to Vanya." I turn back to Harrison. "Without Chet's intervention, he'd be dead. That's good enough for me. And there's strength in numbers. Like Vanya said, there are at least three more Kings. We've taken down Hearts and Mr. Rose, but we still have the Kings of Clubs, Diamonds, and Spades. She could have more muscles at her disposal that we don't know about, too. And don't underestimate my sister's own strength, either."

Harrison draws in a deep breath, sighs. "Fuck. Fine." He leers at Chet. "But if you fuck us over once, we'll slit your fucking throat."

"I wouldn't expect anything less," Chet replies.

Harrison looks back to the rest of us. "So what's our move from here? Where do we confront Rouge?"

"The club, perhaps?" Chet asks.

I shake my head. "No. She'd be expecting that. It won't be long before she tries to get into contact with the King of Hearts asking about taking Vanya out, and from there she'll be able to figure out what we're up to. We need to catch her by surprise."

"Where can we do that?"

I draw in a breath. "We need to break into her home and confront her there."

"Great," Vanya says. "Where does she live?"

I bite my lip. "That's the only problem. I have no idea."

33

HARRISON

"You don't know where your own sister lives?" Vanya asks.

Bianca whips her hands to her hips. "It's not as if Rouge is a normal person. If she were, I'm sure she'd let me know her address. But she's extremely private. She's something of a celebrity in the city, so she keeps all her personal information on a need-to-know basis."

"It's true," Chet adds. "Even I am not privy to that information."

"Then why the hell are we bringing you along?" I fire back at him. "Your whole argument for joining us is that you know Rouge in and out."

"Emphasis on *in.*" Chet's lips twitch.

I have to swallow to avoid losing my lunch at the visual Chet just conjured. Once the nausea has waned, I pull out my phone. "Surely we can find her on one of those people-finding websites. In this day and age, no one has true privacy."

"Good luck," Bianca says. "Remember when I told you Rouge had every document listing her actual date of birth scrubbed out of existence? Her birth certificate, her licenses, social security? She's made it as difficult as humanly possible to track her down. When you wield the influence and power she does, you can make pretty much anything happen."

"But she must live somewhere," Vanya says. "And it must be within the Chicago metro area. It's not as if she's taking a private plane in every day."

"I wouldn't put it past her. She has billions of dollars' worth of diamonds in her safe in her office," I say.

Chet raises a hand. "I can say with near-absolute certainty that isn't the case. Her Maj—I mean, *Rouge*—is too involved with the goings-on in the city. The only time she leaves the state of Illinois is typically when she is looking for replacement waitstaff."

"If you happen to be telling the truth," I respond.

Chet shrugs. "Our doubts are traitors, and make us lose the good we oft might win by fearing to attempt."

"What?" Bianca asks.

"It's Shakespeare," Vanya says. "*Cymbeline*, if I'm not mistaken."

"Excellent ear, Mr. Dmitriev," Chet says. "You too are a student of the Bard?"

"I read through his complete works to help me master English," Vanya says. "This was after I spent months watching movies with Bianca to get my first grip on the language."

"Fascinating," Chet says.

"And remarkably far from the subject at hand." I turn to Bianca. "Could we simply follow your sister after the club closes? It's not as if she can disappear into thin air."

She shakes her head. "She might as well. She has a system in place. She has a private driver pick her up from Aces Underground every night. This driver takes her to a garage located in an undisclosed location. Rouge owns several vehicles of varying makes and models that she keeps in the garage. She selects one at random and drives herself home from there."

"So we could follow her to the garage?" I ask.

"That would be futile," Chet says. "The garage in question is a very busy one. The kind that has drivers filtering in and out at all hours, even late at night when Rouge departs Aces. By the time she arrives at the garage, she is in disguise, and the car she selects to drive herself home will have tinted windows."

"There won't be any security cameras in the parking garage either," Bianca says. "And I've already told you my sister doesn't have a driver's license. If she owns a home, it's likely under an assumed name, like the one I used to book the hotel."

Chet begins to hum.

"Will you stop that?" I ask. "If the home is owned under a pseudonym, then the public records would be of no use to us."

"And I doubt she's registered to vote." Bianca paces the room.

Chet hums louder. The tune is familiar, and grating.

"Shut the fuck up!" I yell at him.

Bianca widens her eyes. "Wait. He's humming the birthday song. Rouge's birthday!"

"What about it?" Vanya asks.

"Her birthday. No one knows it except me. That's why she

uses it as the code to the employee entrance. No one would guess it because she's wiped it off all official documentation. It's the tenth of June."

"A Gemini…" Chet mumbles.

I roll my eyes at Chet's utterance. "Like that matters."

Bianca holds up a hand. "You never know. My sister loves a game." She pulls out her phone. "Zero-six-one-zero. What if that's a zip code?"

"Zip codes have five numbers, though."

"Right. But we know that all zip codes in Illinois begin with a six," she continues. "So what if I search six-oh-six-one-oh?"

"Why not?" Vanya says.

She pulls up her map app and punches in the code. "That particular zip code covers most of the Gold Coast Historic District. Definitely a place I could see my sister laying down her roots. Very ritzy, very self-contained. Low crime rate."

"Besides her own," I add.

"Fair point." Bianca scratches her arm. "But I'm not sure where to go from here. A zip code is a pretty broad area."

"Wait!" I grab my own phone out of my pocket. "Rouge *does* have a pseudonym we know of. The fake name she uses as the CEO for Shinzo Life Center, the place that distributes the organs she harvests. Romeo Sturgeon. It's an anagram of her name. What if we search within that zip code for that name?"

Bianca widens her eyes. "You do the honors."

I pull up the White Pages website and search for "Romeo Sturgeon" within the 60610 zip code. "Oh my God. I think we found her."

"Really?" Bianca asks.

"Yeah." I read the text on the phone. "Ten East Burton Place, apartment six hundred ten."

"Her birthday again!" Bianca throws her arms around me. "It has to be her!"

I plug the address into my GPS. "Looks like it's about a half-hour drive from here. Let's fucking roll."

34

CHET

Her Highness and Dr. O'Rourke embrace again, and the four of us leave the room, locking the door upon our departure, leaving His Majesty's body behind. I assume they will come and collect him later.

I don't give a fig either way.

"How did you get here, Chet?" Her Highness asks.

I blink several times. "I got a ride."

"So you'll need to come in my car," she says, her voice quivering slightly.

"I suppose I shall."

"I'll drive," Dr. O'Rourke says. "You can sit in the back with Vanya."

"My legs are quite long, like rivers," I say.

"I don't give a fuck. I'm not putting you in the back with my girlfriend." Dr. O'Rourke glares at me. "Take it or leave it."

I grin. "Take it."

They are always so unpleasant to me, despite the fact that I hold their fates in the palm of my hand.

But I won't provoke them. I will allow them to think they wield their own wheel of fortune.

The three of them go to Her Highness's car, a silver vehicle with headlights resembling cat eyes. They set my soul at ease. It is as if they are the eyes of the Egyptian goddess Bast, beckoning me toward Paradise.

"One moment," I say. "I need to tie my shoe."

They ignore me.

They always ignore me.

I reach into my pocket, remove my cellular telephone. It's a newer model, the main one I use when I'm in contact with Her Majesty.

I don't like text messaging—it is so informal—but this will have to do.

I type in Her Majesty's number, and then a short message.

My Queen—they are on their way.

35

BIANCA

"SHOULD WE CALL ALISSA AND MADDOX?" I ASK ONCE WE'RE all piled up inside my car. "They'll want to be updated. This is their fight as much as it is ours."

I'm in the passenger seat of my Lexus, and Harrison is driving. Poor Jack is in the back with Chet, whose neck is bent at an awkward angle to fit.

I suppose I should have offered him the passenger seat for his long legs, but I still don't trust the guy. The prolonged diatribe he offered us after killing the King of Hearts didn't completely subdue my concerns.

Even if he's truly, one hundred percent on our side, he's still a creep. Nothing will change that. I've known him for five years and he's never failed to put my nerves on edge.

"I'd rather surprise them with good news than keep them on edge," Harrison answers after a pause. "They both need several more days of rest before they can exert themselves—Maddox especially—and I don't want to stress them out."

"That makes sense," I say. "I just feel like this is *their* story, too."

"It is." Harrison reaches over and squeezes my hand. "And we're the ones in charge of getting them—*all* of us—a happy ending."

"Every story is a love story," Chet says.

We ignore him.

No one speaks for the rest of the long drive back into town to Rouge's neighborhood. Her building has a garage, but we're not going to keep my car there. We park on the street a few blocks away and walk over.

Her complex is an imposing building lined with chrome accents in an Art Deco style. It's lit by golden sconces surrounding the building, and a parking attendant cocks his head as we waltz through the glass revolving door. The building's lobby is ornately decorated with angular patterns of gold leaf on the dark walls. The heels of my shoes clack against polished white tile as we approach a mahogany desk where the night attendant sits wearing a dark-green baseball cap.

I approach him with a smile. Time to turn on the same charm that got Harrison into the club last week. "Hello, sir."

"Name?"

I come up with an explanation on the spot. "We're a troupe of performers from"—I utter the first few syllables that pop into my brain—"Snicker-Snack. It's a...private entertainment company. We're here to visit the tenant in apartment six ten."

The night attendant raises an eyebrow. "Private entertainment?"

I wink. "You know... The sort hired for bachelor parties and the like."

He blinks. "You're strippers?"

Vanya approaches the desk. "We prefer the term 'dancers,' sir."

The attendant rolls his eyes. "Sure. Whatever." He turns to his computer. "And you're here for six ten?"

"Yes, sir. Romeo Sturgeon."

The attendant widens his eyes but then nods slowly. "Right. Mr. Sturgeon occasionally does host...entertainers."

"Good."

He holds out his hand. "IDs?"

Time to think fast again. "Um, actually, we don't carry ID when we're on the job. We all operate under pseudonyms, sir."

"Pseudonyms?"

"Fake names," Vanya clarifies.

The attendant frowns. "I know what a pseudonym is." He sighs, takes out a sheet of paper. "I don't get paid enough to do this shit. What are your *pseudonyms?*"

"I'm Whitney Royale." I gesture to Vanya. "This is my partner, Jack Corrington." I point back to Harrison. "This is Harry March, and the tall gentleman is our procurer, Chad Tigre."

"The tall gentleman?" The man asks.

I look over my shoulder. Chet has wandered off.

Damn it.

Problem for later.

The nightman writes down the names, and I can tell from the stiffness in his arm that he thinks they're incredibly stupid. He looks up. "Do you have an employee ID from your organization? I can't just let you up to the apartments on your word alone."

I swallow. "Actually, sir, as I previously mentioned—"

Chet pops up from behind the night attendant's chair. He

grabs a small statuette from behind his desk and smacks it against the back of his skull. His eyes roll back and his head comes down to his desk with a loud whack that reverberates through the lobby.

"Chet!" Harrison hisses. "What the fuck, man?"

Chet dusts off the statuette and replaces it where he found it. "He wasn't going to let us in." He places two fingers against the attendant's neck. "He'll live, have no fear. It takes more than a few blows to the cranium to withdraw the spirit from the body. I could have snapped his neck instead, but I chose to restrain myself." He scans the buttons behind the desk and pushes one. "That should buzz us up to Her Majesty's apartment."

"Her Majesty?"

He blinks. "Rouge. Rouge's apartment."

Sure enough, an elevator dings behind us. We all turn around but don't move.

This elevator is brightly lit with vivid pink lights, similar in color to the Hearts section at Aces.

Normally this would be a welcoming color. The color of gentleness, love, even femininity.

But this elevator? It might as well be taking us into the bottomless bowels of hell.

Harrison takes my hand, squeezes it. "You ready?"

I take a deep breath, squeeze his hand back. "Let's end this."

36

HARRISON

I KEEP BIANCA'S HAND IN A DEATH GRIP AS THE ELEVATOR climbs to the apartment's penthouse. I assumed we would stop on the sixth floor based on Rouge's apartment number, but it feels like we're ascending all the way to the top of the complex.

Perhaps Rouge had the apartment number changed to reflect her birthday. I've given up trying to understand how her mind works. The elevator doors open to a long, narrow hallway lined in pinstriped wallpaper with a glossy red door at the end. From here, the apartment's numbers printed on the door almost glow with their resident's malice.

We approach the door. Rouge has a smart lock on it with a code.

"What do you think the code is?" I whisper to Bianca.

"The only code I can think of is the same one she uses for the back door at Aces. Her birthday. Zero-six-one-zero. But there's no way that's her code for her apartment. Not when it's literally the apartment's number."

"Unless that's exactly what she *wants* you to think," Vanya says.

"Worth a shot." Bianca bends over, enters in the four digits.

The smart lock beeps, a green light flashes, and the whirring of gears sounds from behind the lock.

"No fucking way," I say. "That's too easy." I try the door. It opens. I close it quietly, look back at the rest of the group. "I guess no one knows that Rouge lives here, and no one knows her birthday, so..." I rub my forehead. "I don't know."

"It is difficult to fathom to inner machinations of a Queen's mind," Chet murmurs.

"Thank you for that, Chet." I roll my eyes before redirecting them to the rest of the group. "Anyway, we have no idea what might await us behind this door. You guys have to be ready for anything, okay?"

Bianca nods. "We'll take on anything that confronts us together."

I open the door. The four of us step into Rouge's apartment. It's decorated with the exact amount of immoderation I expected. All reds, everything drenched in her precious red diamonds. We open first to a lavish living room furnished with sleek velvet couches in a deep crimson encircling a plush rug of the same color. A square-shaped antique coffee table in dark cherry and a cast iron fireplace. On the mantle are figurines of a spade, a diamond, a club, and a heart carved out of ruby. The entire space is lit by a chandelier crafted from blood-red stained glass that scatters dark-pink light across the space.

The area is immaculate, as though no one has been in here for days. I can hardly imagine Rouge doing something as common as sitting down in her living room with a good book, so this place is purely for show. Odd, considering Rouge doesn't want anyone to know where she lives.

Maybe the show is just for her.

A small part of me would be fascinated to get inside this woman's head.

But the bulk of me would be terrified.

I lean into Bianca's ear. "I guess we can't have any doubt this is your sister's apartment."

She gives a small smile. "Subtlety was never her strong suit."

I can't help a smile myself. Bianca said the same thing when we entered the ladies' room at Aces before we discovered the cooler of hearts. At least she hasn't lost her sense of humor, even in the face of certain conflict. Perhaps even death.

A chill runs through me.

No. Need to focus.

We move to Rouge's dining room, which is dominated by a huge table covered in red velvet. An ornate candelabra sits in the center, flanked by large salt and pepper grinders in the shapes of chess pieces. A buffet topped by a china cabinet stands at the other end of the room. Inside is a set of china, bright scarlet with gold trim. I open a wide drawer to reveal a gleaming set of silverware, including an impressive set of steak knives. I pocket one.

Still no Rouge.

We move then to her powder room, her private library, and a large balcony overlooking the Chicago skyline. We work our way through her apartment until we have only one room left.

Her bedroom.

My heart drops as we approach the door. Unlike everything else in Rouge's apartment, it is painted in the darkest shade of obsidian. I press an ear against the door.

Stifled sounds of moaning, as if someone is bound and gagged in Rouge's bed.

I look to Bianca. "Someone's in there. And it's not just Rouge."

She swallows but then steadies her beautiful face. "Do you think she has the Kings with her?"

"Possibly. But it sounds like she might also have a hostage or something. Like someone is trying to speak but they have duct tape over their mouths."

She widens her eyes. "You don't think... Alissa and Maddox?"

"Fuck," I whisper. "We should have checked in with Dinah before getting here." I pull out my cell phone. "Rouge must have something that blocks cell signal here. I have no bars."

"Then there's only one thing to do." Bianca places her hand on the doorknob. "Whatever is in here, we'll tackle it together."

I place my hand on top of hers. "That we will, babe." I look back at Chet and Vanya. "You guys ready?"

"Yes."

"Indubitably."

I give Bianca's hand one last squeeze, and we open the door together.

And my heart sinks.

Because not only are we greeted by the grinning mug of Rouge Montrose, who seems completely unsurprised to see the four of us.

But the couple in the bed, tied up and gagged like rodeo steers...

They aren't Maddox and Alissa.

It's two different people.

Two people I recognize instantly.

And I know why they're in this bed. I know exactly fucking why.

Jesus Christ.

We're so fucked.

37

BIANCA

*M*Y EYEBROW KEEPS TWITCHING.

Mommy says I'm not old enough to drink coffee.

She says that's the reason her eyebrow twitches sometimes.

So why is mine *twitching?*

Rougey is leading me down to the basement, her hand gripping mine like her life depends on it.

She's going to show me a new game. One that grown-ups play, I guess.

I don't know much about grown-up games. Mommy and Daddy sometimes play a game called Taboo when they have friends over.

Maybe that's what Rougey is going to show me. Taboo.

Rougey closes the basement door and drags me down the staircase.

Our basement is unfinished. That's what Daddy says. We live in a big house, so we don't need the basement for anything besides storage. The walls are made of the same material as sidewalks, and the floors are wood. Daddy says he's going to pay a man to make it look like the rest of our house eventually, but that he's too focused right now on his clubs downtown to get that done. Mommy could supervise, but he told me in secret he doesn't trust her to get it done without him helping her make decisions.

So we rarely go down here. Daddy has a set of weights and a treadmill in the corner, and there's an old set of couches that used to be in our fancy living room upstairs before we upgraded, but it's mostly empty space with a few spiderwebs in the corners.

I don't like going down here. I like it even less right now.

"Rougey? Why do we have to play this game in the basement? It's all dark and spooky down here."

Rougey smirks. "Because the kind of game we're going to play is a secret one. It's so much fun that we don't want to have to share it with anyone else."

"Really?"

"Really."

"What's the name of the game?" I look around. "I don't see any board game boxes down here. Mommy and Daddy keep them upstairs in the playroom."

"Silly Bianca," Rougey replies. "It's not that kind of game. It's a game like tag, one that doesn't need a board."

"Are we going to play tag?"

"I said it's like *tag, not that it* is *tag, dumb-dumb." Rouge walks around to the other side of Daddy's treadmill. "It's called Doctor."*

"Doctor?"

"Yes. We're going to pretend that I'm the doctor, and I'm giving you a checkup."

My eyebrow twitches again, this time twice as hard as before. What the heck is going on with it?

"What do you mean you're going to give me a checkup?"

"Like, I'll pretend to be the doctor, and you'll pretend to be the

patient. We'll do the thing where I bonk your knee with a mallet, I'll check your eyes. And, you know, other doctor stuff."

I cross my arms. "That doesn't sound very fun to me. I don't like going to the doctor very much."

"Well, this version is a little more fun," Rougey says. "Why don't you lie down on the treadmill?"

My eyebrow is going crazy now, but I ignore it. I sit down on the treadmill, let my little legs dangle off the end.

"Good. First we can test your reflexes." Rouge takes a small hammer out. She must have gotten it out of Daddy's toolbox in the garage. She taps it against my knee.

Nothing happens.

She taps it again. Again, nothing.

She then smashes the hammer against my knee, much harder. It hurts like heck and I cry out in pain.

Rougey immediately covers my mouth with her hand. "Don't cry, Bianca. You can't cry at the doctor's office."

I don't like this game anymore. I try to stand up to leave the basement, but Rougey's grip on me is too strong for me to get up.

"Sit, Bianca. The checkup isn't done."

Fighting back tears, I sit back down on the treadmill. There's a big bump forming on my knee where Rouge hit it with the hammer, but maybe if I play along she won't hit me again.

"Next, stick out your tongue and say 'ahh,'" Rougey commands.

I do so, and Rouge pulls out an old popsicle stick and sticks it down my throat. I gag on it, almost throw up, but I don't want her to hit me again, so I keep my tongue stuck out as long as I can.

Finally, Rougey removes the popsicle stick. "Your adenoids don't look too great. We might have to remove them."

I don't know what she means by that, but I just nod slowly.

"Next, you'll have to take your clothes off."

Warmth rushes to my cheeks. "What?"

"You've been to the doctor, Bianca. You have to take your clothes off so the doctor can make sure all your parts are working correctly."

"But... But..."

Rougey grabs the hammer, stares at me. "Would you rather we test your reflexes again?"

My lip trembles, but I do my best to steady it. "No."

"Then take your fucking clothes off, Bianca."

She swore.

Mommy doesn't like to swear. Daddy does it all the time. But Rougey is too young. If Mommy caught her saying the F word—that's the worst one—she'd wash her mouth out with soap.

I slowly wiggle out of the T-shirt and shorts I'm wearing.

"Underwear, too."

"Rougey..."

"Did I stutter, Bianca? The doctor needs to check out your whole body."

A single tear slips out of my left eye as I slip the undies off.

"Good. Now lie back on the examination table..."

I DON'T EVER LET myself think about it.

I can't.

We were young. Kids have a natural curiosity about sexuality.

But it's one thing for two kids around the same age to play a game of "show me yours and I'll show you mine."

Rouge was thirteen. I was seven.

She knew what she was doing. She poked and prodded my naked body that day, even explored inside me briefly. And it wasn't the last time it happened. Every so often she'd drag me down under duress for a game of Doctor.

Eventually she started putting items inside me. Medicine bottles, a roll of quarters, anything that would fit. I learned to bite my tongue to keep from crying out. I knew if we were caught that the games would get even worse.

It did eventually come to an end, around the time I got my period. After that, Rouge seemed to have lost interest in me.

But it was a rough couple of years.

I never told my parents. Rouge would have had my head.

And now I know she would have had it literally.

I know now that my sister is capable of the most depraved, evil acts imaginable. The stuff she did to me as a kid was awful—truly, it was sexual abuse—but it pales in comparison to the destruction she's left in her wake since she grew up.

And now she's abducted two elderly folks—a man and a woman—whom I don't recognize.

But it's clear from Harrison's wide eyes that *he* does.

"You heinous bitch!" he spits out.

Rouge smirks. "Language, Doctor. You really ought to be acting more professional around two of your patients."

I gasp. These are two of Harrison's patients?

"They've done nothing wrong!" Harrison replies.

"Have they not, Doctor?" Rouge pulls out a diamond-studded knife, slides it over the old man's throat. "Within the breast of Lou Chambers beats the heart of the Seven of Spades." She flicks her gaze toward the woman. "And Carol Lutwidge breathes solely thanks to her lungs."

It hits me. Carol and Lou. The elderly couple Alissa and Harrison were talking about back at the hospital. Rouge has now confirmed their worst fears—that they live today because of the death of an innocent young woman.

"They didn't know that!" Harrison's jaw trembles, but he steadies it. "It's not their fault. It's *you* who are guilty, Rouge. You've killed countless innocents, all in the name of profit."

Rouge narrows her eyes. "In the name of keeping people on the brink of death with us. People you love, Doctor. People that Ms. Maravilla, your beloved nurse, loves."

"But Alissa also cared about May!" I cry out. "She didn't want her to die, either!"

Rouge shoots me a glare. "Stay out of this, Bianca. You're in way over your head."

"No!" I stamp my foot against the ground, making the lighting fixture about Rouge's bed shake. "I'm sick of being treated like the little sister, Rouge. I'm a fully grown woman with plenty of life experience." I take a step forward. "Maybe *you* were Dad's favorite, maybe you were the one he saw controlling the clubs, but he never envisioned you doing this. Hurting people! People with nothing to lose, who put their trust in you."

A smarmy grin crawls across Rouge's face. "Oh, Bianca. Sweet little naïve Bianca. I've only been the official head of Aces for five years now. Sure, I was basically in charge for a decade before that, but do you think all of this"—she brandishes her knife over Lou's heart—"was *my* idea?"

I drop my jaw. "Dad was doing this too?"

"Dad, and our grandfather as well." She chuckles. "Aces has been the front for our black-market dealings ever since Prohibition." She shrugs. "I just added a new coat of paint and brought in a higher-end clientele. Increased our business dealings exponentially."

It can't be. My father, the sweet man who bounced me on

his knee, whose shoulder I would cry into when life got too hard. He always preferred Rouge, but he still gave me lots of affection when I was really young, before Rouge started playing Doctor with me. He was doing the same thing my sister was doing, my whole life? All the nice dresses I wore, all the fancy dinners I attended, all the privileges I had due to the Montroses' wealth and status...

The very job I have now that pays for my lavish apartment in the Loop...

My entire life...

It was built on the deaths of innocent people. Innocent people dragged from the most poverty-stricken corners of the globe with the promise of a better life, all to be mercilessly slaughtered like livestock and dismembered like an old car being stripped for parts.

I think I'm going to be sick.

Rouge clocks this and leans back, the smug smile still on her face. "Like I said, dear. You're in way over your head. There's so much you don't understand about the way this world works. Which reminds me." She glances toward Chet, who's been standing behind us silently. "Thank you, Chet, for letting me know your little posse was on its way here. It gave me plenty of time to set the stage, put all our little cast into their positions."

Harrison, Vanya, and I gasp in unison as we look behind us.

Vanya points a finger at Chet. "You betrayed us?"

Chet's lips twitch, but he doesn't say a word.

Rouge takes a step toward us. "I don't know how many times you have to learn this lesson, but Chet remains loyal to me and me alone. Miss Maravilla and Mr. Hathaway made the mistake of placing their confidence in him, and you saw what happened to them." She pulls a smartphone from her bosom, taps on the screen a few times, and displays a screen.

My heart sinks. It's a video feed of the ICU rooms where Alissa and Maddox are recovering.

"You knew?" I ask, my lip trembling.

Rouge cackles. "Baby sister, nothing goes on in this city that I'm not aware of. Within an hour of your little rescue from the Caterpillar, I knew what had happened." She tents her fingers, stares us all down. "Always let your enemies think they're in control. The more vividly the mirage of power gleams, the tighter your grasp upon their fate."

A chill runs down my spine at Rouge's words. She's right. She's been playing us for fools this whole time.

"At least let Carol and Lou go," Harrison pleads. "You win, Rouge. We'll play along. But they have nothing to do with this."

The meekness of Harrison's voice terrifies me. I've never heard him speak like this before.

Rouge has broken him.

It's all over.

"Why do you care about these people?" Rouge asks, waving her knife over their bound bodies. "They live only because of the sacrifice of the Seven of Spades. Her death gave them life. You care about her, so you should hate them for what they've stolen."

"They didn't know what they were doing," I respond. "All they knew is that organs matching their profile became available."

"At the last minute," Rouge continues. "Inexplicably. The two of them signed a form saying they would refuse treatment if matches were not found within a month. And then, like manna from heaven, a match arrives." She twists her lips.

"I'm not a wicked witch, like you think. I'm a miracle worker. A diviner of life."

I spot Harrison and Vanya slowly slinking along the wall through the corner of my eye. Rouge hasn't noticed. She's keeping her focus on me, her stupid little sister.

Maybe there's a chance we can gain the upper hand, but I have to keep her talking.

I scoff. "You can try to substantiate your actions in whatever way you want. But those diamonds around your neck"—I point—"were earned through blood. Blood and blood alone. No wonder they're red."

"These diamonds have paid for every part of your livelihood. From before you were even a zygote in the womb, they have been keeping you living the best life possible."

"I don't need you. I lived for ten years in New York City without our family's financial assistance."

She lets out a haughty laugh at that. "Oh, yes. My sweet, demure little sister who attempted to sleep her way to the top and still couldn't land her gig."

I widen my eyes. "How do you know about that?"

Rouge rolls her eyes. "You really don't get it. Who do you think called up the man who ran Skylight Productions? Who got you in that room? And who made sure, after you gave your greatest asset—your body—to the man running the audition, that you *didn't* get the role?"

I cock my head. "No… You were too busy running Aces."

"Yes, and I needed a singer. But I needed to ensure she would also be willing to sell herself. So I devised a little social experiment. I wanted to see what you would do if push came to shove. And you performed flawlessly."

I swallow. "You're making this up."

"The mirage of power. I've been controlling every move

you've made, Bianca, ever since"—her gaze darkens—"our days *playing* in our family's basement."

I almost lose my footing at her words.

She's right. She's been playing me like a fucking fiddle from my birth.

And she did it so flawlessly that I never had a damned clue.

I'm devastated. My life has never been my own.

But I'm more than upset. I'm angry as all hell.

"Fuck you, Rouge! Fuck you for everything you've done. To me, to May, to Svetlana… To Alissa and Maddox, to Vanya! To Harrison! And every other anonymous voice you've silenced in your ascent to power. If it's the last thing I do, I'll make sure you see justice for your crimes."

"Oh, Bianca." Rouge taps the dagger against her palm. "So foolish, even now. Tell me. If you were in my position, would you undo everything I've done? Would you reverse the fates of the Seven of Spades, the Nine of Diamonds, the Jack of Hearts?"

"Of course I would."

A grin splits her face. "Well, then, I suppose justice must be served after all. And its first casualty must be the man who stole the heart of an innocent young woman."

My breath catches in my throat, and my feet freeze to the floor. "Wait, that's not what—"

But already Rouge has raised the dagger and is plunging it toward Lou's unprotected chest, right over his heart.

"I can't believe that!" *said Alice.*

"Can't you?" the Queen said in a pitying tone. "Try again: draw a long breath, and shut your eyes."

Alice laughed. "There's no use trying," she said: "one can't *believe impossible things."*

"I daresay you haven't had much practice," said the Queen. *"When I was your age, I always did it for half-an-hour a day. Why, sometimes I've believed as many as six impossible things before breakfast."*

Lewis Carroll, *Through the Looking-Glass*

38

HARRISON

I'M NOT READY TO START MIDDLE SCHOOL.

Mom and Dad have told me horror stories from when they were that age. How mean the kids were, how rough the adjustment is from elementary school, and how you're dealing with the onset of puberty all at the same time.

But their sweet little Leprechaun can handle anything. We're Irish. Our people have been through a lot.

I wish Maddox and I were going to the same school.

He's going to a fancy private school. The Hathaways offered to pay for my tuition to go there as well since I saved Maddox's life in the ravine last summer, but Mom and Dad refused to take their charity. I think Harold got in their heads after Henry Hathaway showed up at their door. He certainly got into mine.

But I've gone on the scheduled playdates—complete with a photographer present—with Maddox. Though the whole thing was clearly staged to make the Hathaways look good for Maddox's dad's bid for mayor, I do like hanging out with him.

And he likes hanging out with me.

His dad won the election in a landslide, and even after that Maddox still wanted to hang out with me.

He legitimately likes me. At least, I think that's the case. We've been inseparable for three years now, probably to his parents' annoyance.

Sometimes he sneaks away and we meet at the ravine—the same one I pulled him out from.

Guess we like danger.

He sits on the bank. He's wearing athletic shorts today, so it doesn't matter if he muddies them up. "I can't believe it's been three years since it happened, Harry."

"Yeah, it's crazy." I shrug. "Time flies, I guess."

"For sure." He stares at the rushing water in front of us. "You excited for middle school?"

I swallow. "Not at all. A skinny kid like me, with my big ears? I'm going to be fresh meat for the bullies."

"I'm not looking forward to it, either," he replies. "Like, I know I'm going to this fancy school in the city, but rich kids can really be merciless. If they do something bad, their parents can make it go away. They don't have to face consequences for their actions. So they let their imaginations go wild."

"Huh. I never thought about it that way." I lean back on the soft grass, watch a few fluffy clouds pass by. "Maddox, can I ask you a question?"

"Shoot."

"Are you... Are you only friends with me because I saved you?"

He chuckles. "Harry. We met because you saved me. Because you acted quickly and pulled me out the ravine. But we're friends *because you're good people. I like you, and I like your family a lot." He gazes toward the clouds. "You guys are real. You do the right thing because it's the right thing. You don't do good things just for the clout, like my dad."*

I smile. "Really?"

He nods. "Really." Then he chuckles. "You're a good person, Harry. Only a truly good person would have thrown himself into the ravine to save a kid he barely knew."

I DON'T THINK.

I just leap. Throw myself over Lou's body.

Rouge's dagger buries itself into my right shoulder. The pain is searing, but I don't care right now.

Rouge gasps. "The good doctor fancies himself a hero, does he?"

She brings the dagger down again, this time into my left shoulder. I cry out in pain, but I'm not going to stop protecting Lou and Carol. They may not have gotten their organs by the book, but they're innocent. I know they would have refused the transplants if they had known where their donations came from.

Twin trickles of blood pour down my back, and the pain melts away temporarily as time seems to freeze for a moment.

It's the adrenaline.

Rouge will surely bring her knife down on me a third time. If she hits my spinal column, I'm toast.

She'll summon her remaining Kings from there, and they'll take the rest of us out. Maybe she'll let Bianca live, but I have my doubts. Vanya will certainly die. His head was on the chopping block already. He's just delayed the inevitable.

It's impossible.

There is no way out of this.

But then I remember Rouge's own words from just a moment ago.

Always let your enemies think they're in control. The more vividly the mirage of power gleams, the tighter your grasp upon their fate.

They echo words that Chet said when he recounted his story to us.

Always let them think they're in control.

Rouge claims Chet is loyal to her and only her.

That isn't true.

Chet is loyal to one entity alone.

Chaos.

Rouge can kill all of us right now, tie her whole mess up with a neat little bow.

And Chet won't like that.

Before Rouge can bring her dagger down again, I glance over toward Chet. "That's it, then. Congratulations, Chet. You and your Queen have won."

Rouge cocks her head. "Dr. O'Rourke?"

I ignore her. "Everything will go back to normal now. You guys can run things the way you want at Aces. You'll return to your job as a bouncer. Checking driver's licenses. Never letting anyone in unless *Her Majesty* commands."

"Silence!" Rouge commands.

"Because it will always be what Rouge wants, won't it?" I continue. "Rouge, who killed your friend in cold blood after you let me into the club."

"I think we've heard enough." Rouge raises the dagger once more and—

Chet soars across the room, knocking the dagger out of Rouge's hands and tackling her to the floor. I stand up and roll Lou and Carol off to the other side of the bed. They grunt as they hit the floor on top of one another—they're old, so they might have fractured a few bones from the short fall—but they're at least out of harm's way for now.

"Kreuzer, now!" Rouge cries out.

The door to the bedchamber's en suite bathroom bursts open, and a man I recognize as the King of Clubs barrels out toward Chet. But I stop him in his tracks, throwing a right hook to his jaw. He responds with an uppercut of his own to my chin, but I'm feeling no pain right now, and I land a side kick to his chest, knocking him back a few feet.

Another man walks into the room—the King of Diamonds—but Vanya leaps onto his back and gets a chokehold around his neck. Meanwhile, the King of Spades tries to sneak up behind Chet, but he quickly rams a knife into his throat, sending his body to the floor.

Chet then turns on the King of Diamonds, grabs him by the shoulders, and shakes him hard to get Vanya off him. Vanya tumbles to the floor and Chet takes the sides of the King's head in his hands before snapping his neck. He crumples to the floor.

Now it's the three of us against the King of Clubs, the burliest in the bunch. As Chet approaches, I sweep my feet under his legs, bringing him down to his knees. Vanya kicks him in the face, breaking his nose. Chet steps in and slits his throat in one fluid motion before leaping across the room and pressing the knife—still dripping with the blood of her fallen Kings—against Rouge's fair-skinned throat.

Her lip quivers. "*Et tu*, Chet?"

"*Et me, regina mea.*" He presses the knife against Rouge's throat. "But perhaps there is an agreement to be made here."

My heart starts beating again. Fuck. Did I misread this?

Three Kings lie dead at our feet. Chet had no problem killing them. Why is he hesitating now?

"What are your terms?" Rouge hisses.

"I take the reins at Aces," Chet returns. "I recreate it in my image, and someone else takes on the monotonous duties I performed."

Rouge rolls her eyes. "No one can run Aces like I do."

"Perhaps that's the problem." His grin widens. "Perhaps that's why you've found yourself in this situation, *Majesty*."

Rouge widens her eyes. For once, she's been silenced.

Her eyes glisten with calculations as she darts her gaze around the room from Chet, to me, to Vanya, to the bodies of the three Kings, to Bianca, and then back to Chet. They almost glow with defiance.

And she pulls the final move in her arsenal.

She snaps Chet's blade from her throat and plucks a second diamond-encrusted dagger from her cleavage. Before Chet can retaliate, she aims it at herself, eyeing Bianca.

"You can take Aces out of my cold, dead fingers, sister."

And she plunges the dagger into her breast.

Blood spurts from her chest, and she slowly sinks into a sitting position on the edge of her bed.

"Rouge!" Bianca runs to her sister's side, taking her hand. "What have you done?"

A final grin inches across her face. "No one will feel the beat of a Queen's heart except for me."

The light leaves her eyes, and she lies back on the bed. Dead.

Bianca throws herself over her sister's body. She's crying.

She hated her, but Rouge was still her sister. Bianca must be feeling a tangled mess of emotions right now. I rush to her side, throw my arm around her shoulders.

"It's going to be okay, babe."

She wipes her eyes. "I know. It's just... I don't know." She extends two of her fingers and closes Rouge's eyelids, sniffling. She then looks around. "Where's Chet?"

I look over my shoulder. "Shit. He's gone."

He must have disappeared into the night, the ghost of his grinning mug still lingering over us.

And already I know I'll never see him again.

EPILOGUE

BIANCA

"Maddox Hathaway, do you take Alissa Maravilla as your lawfully wedded wife?"

We're in the Wrigley Mansion, which has been outfitted with streamers in cobalt blue, mint green, and light pink. A wedding arch laced with white roses stands at the forefront of the room, the Chicago skyline standing steadfastly through a wide window, framing the three people standing at the altar beautifully. In the middle is a minister—Father Liam—wearing a sharp dark Armani suit no doubt chosen by the groom himself.

At his right, dressed in a sleek three-piece number with a red velvet bow tie, stands Maddox Hathaway, fully recovered after being brought to the brink of death in the Caterpillar Hotel. After a year of physical therapy and a high-protein diet, he's recovered all the muscles in his chest and biceps that atrophied, and it's clear he chose the cut of his jacket to highlight them.

And to the minister's left stands the most beautiful woman I've ever seen. Alissa Maravilla, shrouded in a lacy veil that resembles the half-melted snow covering half the Chicago sidewalks. Her dress is sleek and understated, the exact opposite of what my own sister would have worn had she ever consented to marry. Her hair is styled in an elegant updo with an intricate bun in the back, and she's holding a bouquet of white roses that match the ones in the arch.

"I do," Maddox replies with a devilish smile.

The minister turns to Alissa. "And do you, Alissa Maravilla, take Maddox Hathaway as your lawfully wedded husband?"

She breathes in, seemingly taking in the aroma of her bouquet and the contentedness in her life as she does so. "I most certainly do."

"Then by the power invested in me by the state of Illinois, I now pronounce you husband and wife." Father Liam grins. "You may kiss the bride."

Mr. and Mrs. Hathaway embrace and lock lips, and I gaze across the room at Harrison. He's in a suit matching Maddox's, standing right at his side as his best man. Dinah is Alissa's maid of honor, but I'm in her wedding party along with a few of her friends from Northwestern. It didn't really seem fair, since they've all known her for years, but she did say playing a part in saving her life was enough to earn a spot in her party for life.

Maddox has been flying back and forth from New Haven. He's attending school at Yale part time to earn his degree in political science to unlock the funds left behind by his father. He has no desire to do anything with the degree once it's conferred, but he's also been taking some business classes. He plans to expand the haberdashery into a second location in the heart of the Loop soon.

Alissa has manned the haberdashery when Maddox is

out of town with the help of Vanya. It took a lot of coaxing to make Maddox loosen the reins of his shop, but a year of being with Alissa has thawed his rigidity. They needed to bring Vanya on after Alissa got a very exciting call from the Chicago Symphony—she emailed them as soon as she could explaining why she was a no-show to her audition. They were very understanding but had already filled the position by the time she got in contact with them. Alissa got a great consolation prize, though—she's the CSO's first call whenever they need a substitute, or if they're programming a larger work that requires extra flautists. She's already performed Mahler's third and Strauss's Alpine Symphony with them this season. Harrison and I have attended every time she's performed, and she's been absolutely glowing when we meet her in the lobby. It's clear this is the path she was meant to walk, and she wouldn't have ever returned to music had she not met Maddox. When she's not working with the orchestra, she's been taking gigs and working with a smaller local chamber ensemble. Another position will open up at the CSO or some other major orchestra eventually, and she'll get a great letter of recommendation from the conductor when it does. She splits her time between her music and helping with Maddox's shop, and she told me she's never been happier.

Of course, between the haberdashery and performing, she had to leave her job at the hospital. That was a blow to both Dinah and Harrison, but they still see each other on the weekends. The five of us and Vanya are often having dinner at each other's places. And she visits the hospital from time to time to play music for the patients, so St. Charles won't see the last of her anytime soon.

Maddox and Alissa's wedding reception is being held in the same place as their ceremony, and as soon as we all walk back down the aisle, the guests move to the tables in the rear of the room. At Harrison's suggestion, they had the reception catered by Brassica Rex, complete with chilled oysters aplenty and a magnificent seafood tower. Balsamic glazed salmon and blackened sea bass will be served as the dinner. Several varieties of hot and iced tea—emphasis on Earl Grey—are available, as well as specialty crafted cocktails for the bride and the groom. Alissa's is a dirty rosewater martini, and Maddox's is an elderflower-infused gin and tonic, the drinks they shared their first night at Aces.

Harrison looks so handsome as the best man. He's dressed in the same style suit as Maddox, but with a red necktie instead of a bowtie. He still works at the hospital with Dinah and recently led a massive effort to make sure all the organs that St. Charles patients receive are from legitimate, consenting donors. I've noticed him fidgeting with a small object in his pants pocket quite a bit throughout the day, and I'm pretty sure he's going to propose to me at the wedding reception. We already live together—I gave up my apartment in the Loop and moved into his house in Oak Park a few months after the events at Rouge's place—so it won't be a big change, but I can't wait to be Mrs. Bianca O'Rourke. I'll be the last person to bear the Montrose name, and I'll be happy to be rid of it.

Speaking of me, I'm in charge of Aces Underground now. I still sing there every night, but I have a rotating repertoire that keeps things fresh, including lots of my favorites from my musical theater days. I've kept all of Rouge's theming—though I allow the servers to use temporary tattoos on their shoulders and give them the option to wear less revealing uniforms if that's their preference—but all club employees receive a living wage and are not required to offer themselves as sexual playthings to the patrons. Everyone is allowed to speak now, too. The servers who've come from overseas have drastically improved their English since they're practicing it constantly while on the job. They can work as long as they want, but most of them have made it clear they'll move on with their lives after they earn enough money to start a stable life. I also just got an exciting email from a regional theater company called the Windy City Players—I've been cast as Johanna in their production of *Sweeney Todd*. Rehearsals start soon, so I'll be auditioning substitute singers who can cover for me while I'm unavailable.

Some of the club patrons didn't like these changes, and we lost a lot of the old guard in the first few months. They demanded the club remain the same, and I informed them they were free to leave. But for every patron we've lost, we've gained two or three. We've loosened the requirements for membership and are bringing in more money than my sister could have ever dreamed of. Everyone who works at Aces is much happier, and the environment is much improved.

The Jade Sanctum, Second Star, MINOS, and the Noir Parlor have all been sold back to their original owners—Aus Waverly, Scythe, Zebulon Minos, and Lucille Vivienne respectively.

I'm plucking a few shrimp off the seafood tower when Harrison takes my hand. "Do you have a moment?"

I give him a smile, knowing what's coming. "Of course."

He holds my hand and guides me out to a private courtyard behind the ballroom. A light dusting of snow covers everything, and I can't help but think about the time we made love in the courtyard behind Brassica Rex at the beginning of our relationship.

We can't do that right now. We're expected at the reception.

But Harrison leads me to the center of the courtyard and places his hands on my exposed shoulders. "Bianca, to say our relationship got off to a rocky start would be the understatement of the century."

I grin. "Agreed."

He grabs both my hands. "But I've said it before and I'll say it again. I would go through all that bullshit a second time —*all* of it—if it meant meeting you."

"Harrison..." My lip begins to tremble.

He slowly drops down to one knee and reaches into his pocket. He produces a small silver oyster shell—of course!— and pries it open, revealing a sparkling diamond surrounded by small emeralds set on a stunning white-gold band lined with tiny inset pearls.

I knew this moment was coming, but I still drop my jaw. The ring is beautiful. Even more beautiful is the man offering it to me.

"Bianca Lynn Montrose, will you marry me?"

I burst into tears and wrap my arms around Harrison's broad shoulders. "Yes, Harrison! Yes!"

He wraps me into a passionate kiss that sweeps me off my feet. It feels endless and too quick at the same time. When he finally breaks the embrace, he's all smiles. "I love you so much, Bianca."

I wipe a tear from my cheek. "I love you, too."

He gestures back inside. "Maybe we should go in, steal some of Alissa and Maddox's thunder."

I giggle. I know he's kidding. Maddox probably already knows Harrison was going to propose. He wouldn't have done it at the wedding without the groom's blessing. Alissa probably knows too.

But today *is* their day. I'll slip the ring on my left finger, but I won't be waving it in people's faces. I'll save that for tomorrow.

Tomorrow, when I return to the life I built from the ashes of my sister's demise.

Where all is how it should be.

The deck was cut and shuffled, but the Queen of Hearts—the new one—has triumphantly returned face-up to the table, standing steadfastly alongside her new King.

And the two of them shall rule devotedly over their realm for the rest of their days.

EPILOGUE II

BIANCA

What a fun reception! My feet and legs are aching from dancing so much.

Of course, everyone noticed my ring. It's a pretty big rock, and it's not exactly subtle. But Alissa was overjoyed when she saw it as we were sitting enjoying dinner at the long table at the front of the ballroom.

I've had quite a few Maddox and Alissa cocktails, and I'm a little tipsy. Harrison and I knew we'd be drinking a decent amount tonight, so we arranged a ride to take us back to Oak Park at the end of the night.

Most of the guests have gone home, but as best man, Harrison is in charge of making sure everyone else has a safe ride home for the evening. We'll catch an Uber back to pick our car up in the morning.

Right now, the only place I want to be is in my bed, lying in my fiancé's arms.

Almost everyone has gone home, and Maddox has dismissed Harrison for the night. He and his new bride are staying in a honeymoon suite in a nearby hotel they can walk to. Harrison asked me if I wanted to get a room there, but it seemed silly for us to get a hotel when we live only a half hour away. I'm beginning to rethink that right now. An Uber to Oak Park and back might be more expensive than simply getting a room for the night. Maybe I'll check my phone to see if there's a room available.

As I take it out of the small clutch I brought to the wedding, it starts ringing.

Aus Waverly. The owner of the Jade Sanctum.

That's odd. I haven't heard much from Aus since I turned the reins back over to him after Rouge's death. Why would he be calling me, especially so late on a Saturday night?

Probably a butt dial.

But just in case it isn't...

I accept the call and bring the phone to my ear. "Hello?"

"Bianca, thank God you answered." His voice is breathy, like he's just run a marathon.

"Aus, is everything okay?"

A pause. "Not really."

My heart starts thrumming. Even a year after her death, I can't help but wonder if this is another mess of my sister's I have to clean up. Her shadow looms large even from the grave.

I'm not nearly sober enough for this.

"What's going on?"

"I've...stumbled upon something. Something I think is left over from your sister's time running Jade."

Fuck. I knew it. Her long-nailed hands still have a firm grip on my throat.

I swallow. "What is it?"

Another long pause. "Suffice it to say that organ harvesting wasn't the only thing your sister was into. I need you to come over right now."

Follow the road of yellow brick to the Jade Sanctum, coming soon!

Thank you for reading *Hearts*!

Want to stay in the know? Sign up for my newsletter! https://www.helenhardt.com/newsletter-sign-up

I appreciate you helping to spread the word about my books. Reviews help readers find books! Please leave a review on your favorite book site. You can also join my reader group: https://www.facebook.com/groups/hardtandsoul

Visit my website: https://www.helenhardt.com/

If you loved *Hearts*, you'll love *Savage Sin!* Enter the dark and thrilling world of the Bellamy Brothers. One-Click Savage Sin today!

Missing Bridgerton? You'll love the sensual world of the Sex and the Season Series. One-click Lily and the Duke now!

Ready to go even darker? Join my Ream community to read *Summer of Thorns!*

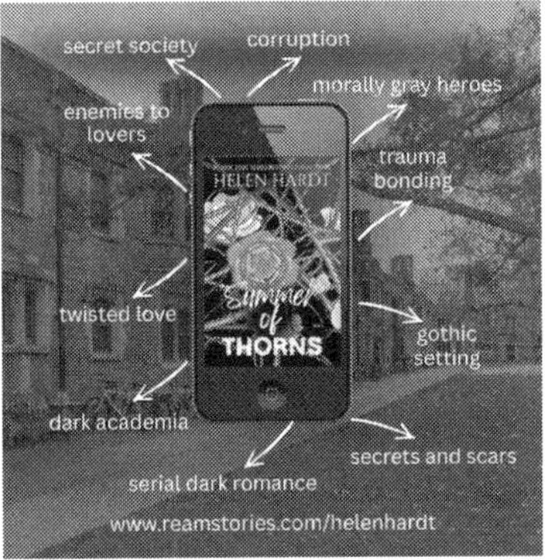

Continue reading for an excerpt...

EXCERPT FROM SUMMER OF THORNS

CONTENT WARNING

THIS STORY CONTAINS MATURE THEMES INTENDED FOR ADULT READERS, INCLUDING DEPICTIONS OF PHYSICAL AND SEXUAL ABUSE, NON-CONSENSUAL AND DUBIOUSLY CONSENSUAL ENCOUNTERS, ABDUCTION, PSYCHOLOGICAL MANIPULATION, BONDAGE, TORTURE, AND OTHER DARK SUBJECT MATTER. READER DISCRETION IS STRONGLY ADVISED.

Episode One

My eyes snap open, but I see nothing.

Panic claws at my chest.

I'm blindfolded. Some kind of thick fabric is pressed tight across my face, cutting out the light.

I try to scream, but the sound is muffled, choked off by something in my mouth. A gag. Rubber? Cloth? I can't tell.

It tastes awful—like dust and salt and fear.

My breath comes too fast, too loud in my ears. I try to sit up, but my arms won't move. They're pinned—tied?—behind me. My legs, too. Ankles bound, knees stiff. I'm on something hard. Cold. A floor? Maybe concrete. The air smells damp, earthy. A basement? A cellar?

I force myself to breathe more slowly. I need to concentrate, gain some kind of control.

Think. Think.

The last thing I remember is...what?

I pull my arms to test the bindings. All that does is chafe my wrists.

Something rustles beneath me. Fabric?

No, it crackles more like a tarp or something.

And it echoes. Only slightly, but still...

Wherever I am, it's vast enough that sound bounces back at me. The rustle of plastic beneath me, the rasp of my breath behind the gag, the frantic thud of my heartbeat. It all boomerangs back.

A warehouse? An underground chamber?

My pulse quickens. Nothing is familiar. No hum of electricity, no light, no sense of time. Just darkness and dread. The air is cool and stale, like it hasn't been disturbed in years.

Until me.

I strain my ears, listening.

And that's when I hear it.

A footstep.

I'm not alone.

My heartbeat drums against the gag. Since when do I have a pulse in my mouth?

My pulse is everywhere now. It's thrumming through my whole body like a medieval chant.

I want to cry out. I want to scream.

But I can't.

So I wait. Trembling. Listening.

Minutes become hours, or maybe it's only seconds ticking by.

This is some cruel game, and I'm an unwilling participant.

Again, I attempt to remember.

Anything.

Any tidbit.

Vague fragments of an evening float around in my mind.

Laughter.

Music.

The fragrance of onions, garlic, tomatoes.

I shift slightly. An icy shiver slithers through me. Was that a breeze? An air current?

Or am I imagining it.

More images emerge.

Dinner. Dishes. The soft clink of silverware. Then...a sharp smell. Something bitter and metallic. My vision blurring. The floor rising too fast. Hands? A voice?

And it slams into me like an Imax movie in vibrant color and surround sound.

I was at the bistro. Waiting tables.

It was busy. After graduation at Elmore, families were in town...

I brought an order to a table, and one of the guys said his pasta was cold.

"I'm so sorry, sir," I said, taking the plate. "I'll get you a fresh order right away."

He smiled at me. He was handsome, I remember. Sandy brown hair that fell across his forehead and dark blue eyes.

I'd see him before, around campus. He's hard to miss.

I walked back to the kitchen with the rejected pasta, and...

That's when I felt it.

Hot breath on my neck.

I turned, nearly dropping the plate of noodles and sauce.

"Shame on you," he whispered. "You should have come on your own."

"What?" I gasped.

Then I remembered.

The invitation to Thorn House that came the previous night. An invitation to a... To a what? A party? A gala? It could have been to a séance for all I knew. All it said was to arrive at eight p.m. tonight and to dress appropriately, whatever the hell that was supposed to mean.

I had to work. So I went to work. Work trumps everything for me.

"I'm afraid you chose the hard way," he said.

I turned to look at him.

It was the man with the sandy brown hair and dark sapphire eyes.

And—

Damn.

That's the last thing I remember—that and the sharp smell, the bitterness, the...

My memory does nothing to alleviate my fear.

It only adds to it.

The man. He's a senior, I think, which means he just graduated earlier today. Or was it yesterday? I have no idea how much time has passed.

My nerves are skittering and I'm still frightened beyond belief.

But I feel something else now.

Anger. A gnawing anger that a fellow student—one with such charisma that I found myself attracted to him in the fleeting moments we crossed paths on campus—would do this to me.

A surge of defiance wells inside me.

I learned how to fight long ago, and I'll fight now. Escape may be impossible when I'm bound and blindfolded, but information is power.

Who is he? Why has he done this?

I take in a deep breath, tasting the stale air of the room. I strain my ears and to pick up any sound that would shed light on my surroundings or hint at my captor's presence.

He's here. I already know I'm not alone.

Then I hear it.

A soft shuffling

Because I hear a soft shuffling.

And then—

A voice.

"Awake already?"

His tone is chillingly calm. As if he's done this type of thing before.

"Yes..." I say, but my voice is muffled and barely audible against the gag. It sounds more like "eff."

He chuckles lightly. "How are you feeling?"

Does he really expect me to answer?

And if I could answer, what does he think I'll say? That I'm absolutely fine, and I love being drugged, bound, gagged, and kidnapped?

Another footstep, and then warm hands on my cheeks as he removes the gag. I wince at his touch.

"Cat got your tongue?" he asks.

I swallow. Or attempt to. My mouth is dry as a desert.

"I asked you a question."

I hate bullies. I fucking hate them. I've been dealing with

bullies since I was twelve. I've beaten some of them black and blue, and some have pummeled me.

But I never backed down.

And I won't start to now.

"Fuck you," I grit out.

He laughs again, the sound grating against my nerves. "Feisty," he says. "I knew you would be. That's why I chose you."

"Chose me?"

"Yeah. It'll make this much more interesting."

A shiver of dread whispers through me, but I power it down and force defiance to take its place. "What do you want from me?"

He doesn't reply. Silence, filled only by his slow and steady breathing.

I wait, expecting the worst. A beating. A rape. Torture. Eventual death. I'll fight with everything I've got. I have people who need me.

After an eternity—

"You'll find out soon enough."

"Wait! Is this Thorn House? Is this about that—"

Something hits my cheek.

A hand?

No. I've been punched enough to know what a hand hitting my flesh feels like.

"You don't get to ask questions," he says. "You should have come on your own. You didn't, and now you'll pay the price."

Episode Two

Nora

Twenty-four hours earlier...

"You know what's bullshit?" Jess groans as she throws

herself across her bed, making the springs creak. "We're stuck with a fucking final exam on a Saturday while the seniors are out getting blackout drunk."

I nod. Or I think I do. I'm not actually paying much attention.

I'm not thrilled about a final on Saturday either, but Professor Leeper, our Freshman Literature Seminar instructor, is leaving tomorrow night for some cruise to Asia so of course the college decided it was okay to make us study on a Friday evening. It's not enough that we have our finals after the seniors leave campus. Graduation is tomorrow, but we underclassmen have one more grueling week.

My laptop is open, and my textbook is highlighted within an inch of its life. Jess, as always, is running at full volume, energy radiating off her like heat.

"Like, seriously," she says. "I want to be partying. I want to be wearing a strapless mini and getting kissed by some dude named Blaine or Preston."

I glance up, rolling my eyes. "You don't know a Preston."

"Details."

I'm not sure how Jess and I were deemed compatible to be roommates. She's my opposite in almost every way. Blond, curvy, loud. She loves glitter, crop tops, and vodka shots. I like cardigans, earbuds, and silence. We're not friends exactly—not in the close, share-your-trauma sort of way. But we've survived a year of sharing a room, and that's something. In fact, we're rooming together again next year. We have nothing in common, but it works.

I shift in my chair and stretch. The words on the screen are blurring. I can't think with her babbling.

"I'm going to the library." I close my laptop.

Jess frowns. "Babe, it's after ten. And it's Friday."

"All the better. It'll be empty. And we *do* have an exam tomorrow, bright and early."

She opens her mouth, but for once, she doesn't say anything.

Instead, she stares at the door. "What is *that*?"

A red envelope lies on the floor. Someone must have slid it underneath.

Jess scrambles off the bed. "Maybe it's a party!"

"Jess—" I start, but I'm too late.

She's already tearing it open.

"It's for me," she says, voice smug. "I can feel it. Probably from Lee Greenstone. He asked for my number yesterday."

I don't have a clue who Lee Greenstone is, and I don't care. Jess is always getting dates, getting laid. She's never serious about anyone.

She furrows her brow as she pulls out a cream-colored card.

"Crap," she mutters. "It's for you."

I freeze. For me?

"What?"

She turns around and hands it to me.

Sure enough, that's my name in elegant script.

Miss Nora Williams.

Miss?

Who uses *that* anymore?

"Who's it from?" Jess badgers.

"I have no idea." I quickly read it.

You are cordially invited to Thorn House tomorrow evening. Eight o'clock sharp. Dress appropriately. That's it. No name. No RSVP.

My mouth goes dry.

Thorn House.

Where the legacy guys live. The rich ones, the ones with names carved on the donor plaques around campus. The ones who drive black sports cars and always seem to get the top grades thought they're rarely seen in class.

Untouchables. Unapproachable.

"What the hell is Thorn House inviting you to?" Jess asks.

"Did you read it?"

She shakes her head. "I recognized the emblem."

Right. The ornate T and H twisted through thorns. It's engraved on the plaque that identifies Thorn House—a large Victorian house that's part of the Elmore campus.

"I don't know."

"Maybe a party?" She tilts her head. "You've been holding out on me, Williams. Who have you been sexting behind my back?"

"No one." My voice is hoarse. I wouldn't have a clue what to say in a "sext."

Jess looks at me like I've grown a second head. "Then why would they invite you?"

"I have no idea."

The invitation feels heavy in my hand. My fingers tremble as I trace the raised edge of the emblem. I read the words again.

You are cordially invited to Thorn House tomorrow evening. Eight o'clock sharp. Dress appropriately.

What the hell does "dress appropriately" mean? Appropriately for *what*?

I grab my cardigan, shove the card and my laptop into my backpack, and head out. The spring night is warm and damp, and a few groups of seniors are laughing and drinking.

The pay me no mind at all, but still...

The back of my neck itches.

I feel like I'm being watched.

I glance over my shoulder. Nothing. No one.

I get to the library and enter. It's dimly lit and nearly deserted. My footsteps echo faintly against the polished wood floors. I decide against the stacks. They're spooky this late at night. I find a good spot in the main room beneath the rows of tall windows. The silence settles over me like a blanket.

I open my laptop. Try to work. But my eyes keep drifting to the envelope.

Eventually, I give in.

I take it out and set it beside me on the table. I run my fingers over the paper again. It doesn't make sense. No one from Thorn House would know who I am.

What is this about?

I rub my arms against a sudden chill and glance toward the main doors of the library.

A figure stands just outside, barely visible through the glass.

I go very still.

He's not moving. Not knocking. Just watching.

I look away, heart thudding.

When I look back, he's gone.

I press my hand to my chest, trying to calm the sudden tightness.

But a sound behind me makes me freeze again.

Footsteps.

Light. Measured. Deliberate.

I rise, walk toward the doors.

No one.

I return to my chair—

And I gasp.

On the floor lies a second envelope.

Black paper this time. Gold ink.

My name again.

I gulp as I open it.

Another cream-colored card. Again, the emblem.

You were chosen. Tomorrow, you belong.

The words blur. I grip the note tightly and look around. Still no one.

I shove it into my bag, my heart hammering. But as I reach to close my laptop, something else catches my eye.

Another note.

This one is smaller, folded once and tucked under the leg of the chair across from me. I didn't see anyone put it there.

Hands trembling, I open it.

You are a token.

I gasp. What could it mean? I pace around the deserted room.

No one.

Until—

A shadow shifts near the stairs to the stacks.

I don't breathe. I don't blink.

When I finally turn back to gather my things, a single red rose lies on top of the desk where I was working.

No note. Just the flower.

I stand slowly, every part of me trembling.

As I back toward the exit, something flickers at the edge of my vision.

A flash of movement. Then a whisper of sound.

When I reach the doorway, I glance back one last time.

Nothing.

Thank God.

But my heart still pounds.

I leave the library and—

Another envelope—this one pinned to the bulletin board just outside the library.

Black paper. Gold ink.

I tear it open.

Tomorrow. Be there. Or we take you.

My heart is pounding out of my chest as fear grips me.

What is this about?

And why, for the love of God, does anyone want *me*?

Continue reading *Summer of Thorns*...

ACKNOWLEDGMENTS

And then there were four!

Hearts completes the Aces Underground series. Some of the comments I've gotten are:

Honest to God, you have effectively blown my mind...again!

Pure genius!

One of the Top three favorite series!

Thank you especially to Eric McConnell, my editor, and Amanda Shepard, my cover artist. Without the two of you, Aces Underground would never have taken shape. Thank you to my beta readers, Karen Aguilera, Corinne Akers, Serena Drummond, and Linda Dunn. You ladies rock! And Thank you to James Sydney and Kaileigh Riess for lending their spectacular voices to Harrison and Bianca (and Chet!)

Thank you to my reader group, Hardt & Soul, and to my Ream community, Black Rose Underground, for your endless support.

Thanks also to my family and friends, and most of all, thank you, my readers. Because of all of you, I get to do what I love most in the world!

Stay tuned for more dark tales...

ALSO BY HELEN HARDT

Bellamy Brothers

Savage Sin

Sweet Sin

Seductive Sin

Vengeful Vice

Volatile Vice

Victorious Vice

Cryptic Curse

Chaotic Curse

Captivating Curse

Aces Underground

Spades

Diamonds

Clubs

Hearts

Vampire Princess Diaries Duet

Princess Fallen

Princess Redeemed

Follow Me Series

Follow Me Darkly

Follow Me Under

Follow Me Always

Darkly

Under

Always

My Heart Still Beats

Black Rose Series

Blush

Bloom

Blossom

Wolfes of Manhattan

Rebel

Recluse

Runaway

Rake

Reckoning

Escape

Moonstone

Raven

Garnet

Buck

Opal

Phoenix

Amethyst

How to Marry a Billionaire

Enticing You

Captivating You

Seducing You

Claiming You

Sex and the Season

Lily and the Duke

Rose in Bloom

Lady Alexandra's Lover

Sophie's Voice

The Perils of Patricia

Steel Legends

I am Sin

I am Salvation

Broken Dream

Healed Heart

Steel Brothers Saga

Craving

Obsession

Possession

Melt

Burn

Surrender

Shattered

Twisted

Unraveled

Breathless

Ravenous

Insatiable

Fate

Legacy

Descent

Awakened

Cherished

Freed

Spark

Flame

Blaze

Smolder

Flare

Scorch

Chance

Fortune

Destiny

Melody

Harmony

Encore

Non-Fiction

got style?

Cooking with Hardt & Soul

ABOUT THE AUTHOR

#1 *New York Times*, #1 *USA Today*, and #1 *Wall Street Journal* bestselling author Helen Hardt's passion for the written word began with the books her mother read to her at bedtime. She wrote her first story at age six and hasn't stopped since. In addition to being an award-winning author of romantic fiction, she's a mother, an attorney, a black belt in Taekwondo, a grammar geek, an appreciator of fine red wine, and a lover of Ben and Jerry's ice cream. She writes from her home in Colorado, where she lives with her family. Helen loves to hear from readers.

Website: https://www.helenhardt.com/

Newsletter: https://www.helenhardt.com/newsletter-sign-up

Made in United States
Orlando, FL
26 February 2026

78773247R00185